Room of Doo

The Chest of Chu Chan

TWO CLASSIC ADVENTURES OF

by Walter B. Gibson
writing as Maxwell Grant

IRON MUNRO, THE ASTOUNDING MAN
illustrated by George Tuska

and **new historical essays**
by Will Murray and Anthony Tollin

SANCTUM BOOKS

This Sanctum Books edition is an unabridged republication of the text and illustrations of three stories from *The Shadow Magazine,* as originally published by Street & Smith Publications, Inc., N.Y.: *Room of Doom* from the April 1, 1942 issue and *The Chest of Chu Chan* from the September 1944 issue, plus "Iron Munro, the Astounding Man" from the July 1941 issue of *Shadow Comics*. These stories are works of their time. Consequently, the text is reprinted intact in its original historical form, including occasional out-of-date ethnic and cultural stereotyping. Typographical errors have been tacitly corrected in this edition.

International Standard Book Number:
978-1-60877-205-6

First printing: April 2016

Series editor/publisher: Anthony Tollin
anthonytollin@shadowsanctum.com

Consulting editor: Will Murray

Copy editor: Joseph Wrzos

Cover restoration: Michael Piper

Shadow circle: Kez Wilson

The editors gratefully acknowledge the assistance of P.C. Hamerlinck, Dewey Casell, Ron Goulart, Bud Plant and Jim Vadeboncoeur, Jr. in the preparation of this volume.

Published by Sanctum Books
P.O. Box 761474, San Antonio, TX 78245-1474

Visit The Shadow at www.shadowsanctum.com.

Volume 106

CONTENTS

Thrilling Tales and Features

Front cover art by George Rozen

Back cover art by George Rozen, Modest Stein and George Tuska

Interior illustrations by Paul Orban

Murder or suicide?—that was the question The Shadow had to answer as he began his investigation of the

ROOM OF DOOM

CHAPTER I
DEATH ENTERS

THE room that Arthur Aldriff termed his "den" was well suited to the description. It was a large room, furnished with a variety of curios and trophies that marked its owner as a man of many pursuits.

Looking in from the door, the square room showed a fireplace on the right; above it, a mantel which bore a very ornamental clock, flanked by a pair of porcelain vases. On one end of the mantel was a model of a trim sloop; on the other, an ancient English drinking horn.

Above the mantel a mounted moose head gazed

with glittering glass eyes; just beneath the stuffed head was the rifle that had killed the moose, set in a horizontal rack. Flanking the stuffed head were two other plaques, mounted with fish that Aldriff had caught.

At the left of the room was Aldriff's desk. Whenever he looked up, he could see the moose-head; but the creature with the glass eyes did not stare back at him. Instead, it admired its own reflection in a large and ornamental mirror that hung behind the desk. Aldriff valued the mirror highly; he considered its gold filigreed frame to be a fine example of Florentine craftsmanship.

On each side of the mirror were bookcases filled with beautifully bound volumes that Aldriff never opened. When he indulged in intellectual pursuits, he preferred chess. The evidence stood in a little nook set in the far wall of the room.

The nook was a solid-walled cubbyhole, not more than six feet in width and depth and only a trifle higher. It contained two light chairs that faced each other; between them, a chess table with inlaid squares of ebony and ivory.

Chessmen of the same materials were standing on the board, set for a game. All that Aldriff needed was a rival player, and he seldom found one. He was too skillful for most players of his acquaintance.

There were other objects in the room: framed paintings, larger vases than those on the mantel, some ornamental lamps, and a silver narghile, or Oriental water pipe. The narghile was a gift from the dealer who had sold Aldriff the magnificent rugs: Samarkands, Kashgars and Baluchistans, which overlapped one another all over the floor of the den.

Of course, the room was also furnished with easy chairs, footstools, ash stands, and such, which made it very comfortable for guests. In a near corner, at the right of the door, was a special case containing cups and medals that Aldriff had won in yacht racing, golf tournaments, and pistol competition.

Aldriff kept his golf clubs in that corner, along with a revolver rack, which contained three pistols and a leather folder holding the permits for them. He would have kept his sailing yacht in the room, too, had there been space for it. Space lacking, the yacht was moored in Long Island Sound, not far from Aldriff's home; but the ship model on the mantel was an exact replica of the craft in question.

One thing in the room annoyed Aldriff. It was a filing cabinet in the corner to the left of the door. A very cumbersome, unsightly thing, that cabinet, but it was necessary in Aldriff's business, so it had to stay.

Nevlin, Aldriff's secretary, had made the bright suggestion of putting it in the corner behind the door, which was something of a help, but it was too big for the door to hide.

So Aldriff had decided to buy a screen to cover the filing cabinet, and Nevlin had located one, a very fine Chinese screen, with gold-leaf decorations that would go well with the Florentine mirror.

Such, then, was Aldriff's den; in the near corners, trophy case and filing cabinet; in the far wall, the nook with the chairs and chess table. On the right, fireplace, mantel with its clock and other ornaments, and the presiding moose. On the left, mirror, bookshelves and desk, with Mr. Aldriff in the chair.

ARTHUR ALDRIFF was a thickset man, with a roundish face that should have been jolly, but wasn't. Instead, his features were deep-lined with worry, which even furrowed the forehead beneath his thin gray hair.

He wasn't even looking at the costly decorations with which he had stocked his den; nor did he seem at all delighted by the fact that he was soon to receive the handsome screen that would make the setting perfect.

There were two windows in the room, one at each side of the chess nook. They were closed and heavily clamped; they had bars on the outside, as a protection for Aldriff's treasures.

Through those windows came dying rays of sunlight, cut off by the high hedge that surrounded the grounds. The fading glow cast long shadows of the bars across Aldriff's desk, and at sight of those parallel streaks, the man winced.

The shadows of other bars were creeping too close for Aldriff's peace of mind. Prison bars, that wouldn't display themselves only at sunset, but would be outside his window, day and night, for years to come.

It wasn't a happy picture—the thought of leaving this fine mansion, with its lavishly furnished den, for a tiny cell in a Federal penitentiary.

Reaching into a desk drawer, Aldriff brought out a metal dispatch box, unlocked it and brought out a batch of papers. He turned on a desk lamp to eradicate the streaks that worried him, and began to look through the papers.

At moments, his worry changed to an expression of sudden shrewdness, only to lapse back again. However, his eyes were taking on a scheming sparkle, when he heard sudden footsteps at the door.

He looked up, somewhat startled, to see a girl standing in the doorway. She was an attractive girl—tall, slender, and with a vigor that spoke of outdoor life. Her face was flushed by the wind; her brown hair had been blown into stray waifs that she was brushing back from her equally brown eyes.

But she wasn't worried about making herself look prettier. Her expression revealed a single emotion: determination.

"I'm Joan Kelburn," the girl announced, in a firm contralto. "I'm sorry to barge in this way, Mr. Aldriff, but I want to talk to you about my uncle. I must see you alone."

Rising, Aldriff waved an invitation for Joan to take a chair. Approaching the door, he motioned at a stodgy butler who had followed the girl from the front door. The gesture meant for the butler to go away, which he did. Aldriff closed the door.

"And now, Miss Kelburn?"

"I'll come right to the point, Mr. Aldriff," stated Joan. "It's about that stock my uncle is selling. You're in back of it."

"If you mean Pharco Stores," acknowledged Aldriff, "I have guaranteed the necessary assets. The Pharco chain will be a group of ultramodern drugstores extending from coast to coast—"

"I've heard Uncle Smead give his sales talk," interrupted Joan. "You don't need to repeat it, Mr. Aldriff. I want to know where the money is coming from to start those stores that people are buying stock in. Will it be Magnax money?"

Aldriff gave a quick negative headshake and waved his hands along with it.

"No, no, Miss Kelburn!" he exclaimed. "The Magnax Corp. manufactures drugs, but does not retail them. True, I am one of the three men controlling Magnax—but the other two, Lloyd Dulther and Hubert Sigby, know nothing about my interest in Pharco. I planned Pharco as my own enterprise."

"And you can make good on your million dollar promises?"

"I *always* make good on my promises, Miss Kelburn." Aldriff's worried expression vanished when he smiled. "Rest assured that everything will turn out precisely as planned."

THERE was a rap at the door. Aldriff opened it, to admit his secretary, Nevlin—a small, officious man who was superintending the moving of a light but very large crate, which contained the Chinese screen.

The crate was very thin, but it was at least six feet long and considerably wider. The servants who carried it had to tilt it cater-cornered to squeeze it through the large door.

"How many sections are there to that screen?" exclaimed Aldriff. "A dozen?"

"Only three, Mr. Aldriff," returned Nevlin briskly. "And now, sir—"

He went to the nook at the end of the room, brought out the chess table and put it down halfway to the fireplace. He was going back to get the chairs, when Aldriff wanted to know what he was about.

"I'm clearing the nook," stated Nevlin. "The servants can move the filing cabinet in there, and I shall set up the screen in front of it."

"And ruin my chess nook?" demanded Aldriff. "Outrageous, Nevlin!"

"But you haven't played chess lately, sir."

"That has nothing to do with it! Leave the cabinet where it is, and put the screen around it."

Nevlin gave a shrug and dismissed the servants. Using a hammer, he began to open the crate and cut the strings around the packing that contained the screen. Since Nevlin required half the floor for the operation, Aldriff ushered Joan out from the den.

They came into a large hall, from which he led her through a lighted reception room to a sun porch on the far side of the house. All during the trip, Aldriff was repeating that there was no need to worry.

"You're sure?" inquired Joan, finally, her brown eyes very quizzical. "Uncle Smead is leaving by plane in an hour, for a long trip. He wouldn't tell me where he was going."

"He is taking a business trip," explained Aldriff. "Nothing more. A business trip to the coast, at my suggestion. Ah!" Looking from the sun porch, Aldriff saw the lights of cars coming in by the dusk-laden driveway. "My dinner guests are arriving. I shall introduce you to them and you will join us, Miss Kelburn."

Outside, the swing of lights produced long, black streaks on the lawn. Streaks cast by trees and shrubs into shapes that seemed alive. One stretch of blackness still moved when the lights had passed it, but by then its motion was invisible, for it had merged with the thickened dusk.

It arrived close to the sun porch and paused there, below the level of the lights. A slight, reflected glow showed the shape in vague outline. It had human form—that of a being cloaked in black, with a slouch hat on its head. A hawkish silhouette was cast upon the shrubbery beneath the windows, as this creature of the night raised his head and shoulders.

He was The Shadow!

Strange master who hunted down schemes of crime, The Shadow did not confine his activities to the lower strata of crookdom. His motto was "Justice for all," and when he detected the beginnings of vast swindles, he ferreted out their perpetrators.

Arthur Aldriff and his chain store scheme constituted a case in point. The Shadow had noted huge sales of Pharco stock, with no signs of any chain stores in operation. Having linked Smead Kelburn, the stock promoter, with Arthur Aldriff, the drug manufacturer, The Shadow was out to learn just how far Aldriff intended to back the stock that Kelburn peddled.

ALDRIFF and Joan were turning back into the house, to meet the arriving guests. Moving from the deserted sun porch, The Shadow heard a stir from the shrubbery at the rear. He caught a short glimpse of a stocky figure moving around the corner of the porch. Immediately, The Shadow took up the trail of the other prowler.

The man was easy to follow because of his stumbles, though the darkness was thick enough to hide him. He went around the rear wing of the mansion, with The Shadow on the trail. There, the fellow must have found familiar ground, for his clumsy methods ended.

Moving along the far side of the house, The Shadow soon recognized that the trail was gone, along with the man who had made it.

The prowler had either ducked into the house itself or had made a quick dash across a short stretch of lawn to the shelter of a high hedge. Choosing the more important of the two possibilities, The Shadow probed along the side wall of the house and came upon a door, which opened when he tried it.

Inside were a few dark steps, a portion of a vestibule. To his left, The Shadow saw the door of Aldriff's den, a stairway just beyond it. To the right was the main reception hall, well lighted, where Aldriff was introducing Joan to several guests. They turned about as the door of the den opened. Nevlin was on the threshold, announcing that the new screen was on display.

The group came toward The Shadow, but he remained right where he was, totally hidden in the darkness. He saw them enter the den and go around the door, to admire the new screen.

Easing out from cover, The Shadow gained a brief glimpse into the room. After nodding his approval of the screen that The Shadow could not see, Aldriff turned to Nevlin.

"You forgot to return the chess table to its nook," said Aldriff. "No, never mind"—he shook his head as Nevlin made a half turn into the room—"I always arrange it myself. Besides"—Aldriff's lips tightened grimly—"I shall stay in the den a while. I have a matter to decide upon, before I rejoin my guests."

It was Aldriff who ushered the guests from the den, while The Shadow was merging back into the darkness of the vestibule. Joan came with the group, and Nevlin followed, closing the door behind him. From the heavy *click*, it sounded as if the door had latched automatically from the other side.

Arthur Aldriff was alone; but a knock on that door would probably summon him. The difficulty was to reach the door, for the guests were remaining in the hall to greet others who arrived. The Shadow was waiting on the chance that they would go into the reception room, on the other side of the hallway, in which case the route would be clear.

All the while, The Shadow was watching the door of Aldriff's den. Others were glancing toward it, too, particularly Joan Kelburn, whose eyes showed increasing anxiety as the minutes passed.

Those minutes were slow but they were few. During that time space, it would have been impossible for anyone to have opened or closed Aldriff's door without the action being noted.

Then, timed by a freak of chance to a lull of conversation, came the sudden sounds that startled the guests in the hallway. The Shadow heard them quite as plainly, for he was close to the den door.

Three sounds, in a slow-motion sequence, each giving the effect that another was to come, until the third struck a final note.

The first sound was the muffled report of a revolver; the second, the crash of a table, accompanied by an odd clatter; the third was the thud of a falling body upon a thick-rugged floor.

Arthur Aldriff was no longer alone in the locked room. Death had entered, to join him.

CHAPTER II
THE SEALED ROOM

IT was Nevlin who called for order among the startled, horrified guests. There were nearly a dozen of them by this time, and men were giving excited exclamations, while women were on the verge of screams—with one exception.

Joan Kelburn was moving toward the den, a fixed expression on her face. She felt that Arthur Aldriff had cheated her of the purpose that had brought her here: the vindication of her uncle. If Aldriff still had life, the girl intended to force a confession of his own guilt from his lips.

It was Joan's move, as much as any other, that prompted Nevlin to efficient action. He sprang past Joan, reached the door and stood with his back against it, calling for others either to join him quietly and promptly or to go to the reception room across the hall and calm themselves there.

Servants were appearing from other parts of the house, and Nevlin snapped orders at them. He told them to go outside and make sure that no one had broken in by one of the den windows; then to stay there and keep watch, until summoned back into the house.

Fortunately, some of the guests were joining Nevlin before the servants had time to start. Since people were blocking the route to the vestibule from which The Shadow watched, the servants chose other ways to go outside, leaving The Shadow in comfortable possession of his convenient lookout post.

Nevlin was rattling at the knob of the den door. Finding it latched, he announced ruefully that Aldriff had the only key. The guests suggested breaking it down, but Nevlin preferred to pound away, shouting through the door in hope of an answer from Aldriff.

None coming, guests hurried away to find implements for breaking down the door.

Two guests met a servant coming in to report that the bars of the windows were still tight in place, the panes of glass unbroken, and the shades drawn. The windows were well up from the ground, but the servant suggested breaking them.

He produced a fire ax from the closet under the stairs, and the guests, considering Nevlin in charge, decided to ask the secretary if he wanted the windows smashed.

At sight of the ax, Nevlin seized it.

"What would be gained by smashing the windows?" he demanded. "You might see Mr. Aldriff, but you couldn't help him. We'd have to tear down the house walls to get those bars out of place!"

Turning to the door, Nevlin poised the ax and took a hard slash at a panel. The wood was stout, but the ax blade cracked it. Another slash, and Nevlin splintered away a chunk of wood. He chopped again, widening the hole.

Motioning the others back, Nevlin tried cautiously to insert his hand through the splintered space. He drew it back as if stung, expressing the fear that gripped him.

"There can't be anyone in there except Mr. Aldriff," began Nevlin. "And yet—"

He shook his head; pushed his hand toward the hole again, and found that it wouldn't go through. He was stepping back for another slice with the ax, when Joan pressed him aside. Unsnapping the sleeve of her dress, the girl bared her slim arm to the shoulder and worked her hand through the narrow space.

Others watched, breathless, admiring her courage, as Joan stretched her arm full length and moved her hand within the door until she found the knob.

Turning the knob, she warded back the others, while she withdrew her arm. Flinging the door inward, Jean was the first to cross the threshold. Her face was grim when she saw exactly what she expected.

Aldriff was lying dead upon the floor. He was across the room, near the nook. The two light chairs were turned askew, facing each other at an angle, to allow room for the chess table.

But Aldriff hadn't put the table where it belonged. He had been beside it when the shot was fired; in falling, he had overturned it, sending the chessmen scattering. Finally, he had struck the floor almost beside the table.

In Aldriff's hand was his favorite revolver, the weapon that had caused his death. The case was obviously suicide, and Joan, wanting no one to doubt the point, turned promptly to Nevlin.

"THOSE chairs are just as you left them," declared Joan. "You moved them around when you took out the chess table. You can see for yourself that Mr. Aldriff was going to put the table back, when he changed his mind and shot himself, instead. This is suicide, and I can tell you why!"

Her eyes were blazing at the rest, along with Nevlin. But the secretary, staring toward Aldriff's body, only shook his head.

"I can't believe it," said Nevlin slowly. "At least, I can't be sure just yet. Please stand back, Miss Kelburn."

As Joan complied, Nevlin began to peer at every section of the room, pointing, so that others would do the same. The nook, of course, was empty, its flimsy chairs offering no place of concealment. The fireplace caught Nevlin's eye, and he urged the servant to look into it.

Crawling into the fireplace, the servant came out again, shaking his head.

"The damper is closed, Mr. Nevlin," he said. "And anyway, the chimney is very narrow.

"I remember," nodded Nevlin. "Take a look behind the desk; but be careful. Someone may be crouching there."

The servant hesitated, so two guests stretched across the desk and made sure that no one was behind it. Nevlin glanced at the near corner on the right, and so did others. That corner was empty. Even a midget could not have hidden behind the small trophy case.

Someone suggested the bookshelves. Nevlin shook his head.

"They're flush against the wall," he said. "No chance of hiding there. We have only one place left. Will you two gentlemen come from the desk and remove the screen from the corner behind the door?"

Glistening with its gilded decorations, the new screen commanded all attention. Shown plainly by the strong light from the desk lamp, the three-fold screen looked flimsy; nevertheless, it could be hiding something more than a filing cabinet.

There might be a murderer behind it!

Two men crept toward the screen, one from each side. As they were reaching for it, there was a quick flash of light from the doorway of the room. One man gave the screen a quick shove and dived away; the other man caught the screen in his arms, flattened the folds together, and landed on it like a boy starting a sled ride.

Each man went in an opposite direction, and

Nevlin, seized by the general hysteria, drove between them, swinging the fire ax.

Nevlin's blow landed with a *clang* that nearly floored him. He had smashed a deep dent in the *only* object that occupied the final corner: the metal filing cabinet. Dropping the ax, Nevlin yanked drawers from the cabinet as though he expected to find a killer hiding in sections. With the ax, he prodded the interior of the cabinet.

No one could have been there, because the drawers had filled the cabinet. Nevlin's gestures with the ax brought *clangs* from the cabinet's thin metal walls. The cabinet, itself, was in the very corner, so no one could be behind it.

Again, a light flashed from the doorway. Turning, Nevlin saw the reason. Among the guests was a society reporter, who was taking flashlight pictures.

No one objecting, the photographer made another shot directly into the room, then walked toward Aldriff's body, turned around and took a flash of the doorway where the witnesses were clustered.

Noting annoyed looks on the faces of the guests, the photographer shouldered through them and waved good-bye. Some persons wanted to call him back, but Nevlin shook his head. Pictures were a good idea; they proved that the room was empty, and that the searchers had probed into every possible hiding place.

Behind the group in the doorway, the hall looked gloomy, as well it might. A shape had emerged from the nearby vestibule, to block off the hallway light.

Peering past heads and shoulders, The Shadow studied the room.

BOTH Nevlin and Joan had been ardent in their search—the secretary anxious to prove there was a hidden murderer; the girl desirous of establishing that there was none.

Near the trophy case, Joan sat in a chair that matched the flimsy ones in the nook, and suggested that Nevlin count noses, to make sure no stranger was among them. Nevlin turned to the doorway and tallied off the witnesses.

Rather than have the secretary count one too many, The Shadow dipped and sidled back to the vestibule. He was turning toward the den again, when Nevlin came out, accompanied by Joan. Others made way for them to pass, then followed them.

The little group was blocking The Shadow's view of the reception hall, when a halt came. Stopping squarely in their tracks, people began to raise their hands. Slowly, fearfully, they were backing away, returning into the room where Aldriff lay dead.

Why?

All were through the doorway, with the exception of Joan and Nevlin, when The Shadow saw the cause of their retreat. A masked man was confronting them with a gun; crouched, his body had a thickset look. His voice was forced and ugly, as he made threatening gestures with his revolver.

Aldriff's death could well be defined as proven suicide, in a room where no murderer could possibly be hidden. But the threat of murder was looming over others, the very witnesses who could swear that Aldriff had died by his own hand.

Why this masked man, entering boldly by the front door, was anxious to enter the sealed room of death, was a strange question in itself. Yet those who were shrinking, fearful for their lives, were not in the serious plight that they supposed.

In the offing was a black-cloaked friend who could save them. No killer ever lived who could commit open murder in the presence of The Shadow!

CHAPTER III
TWISTED FLIGHT

HIS own gun ready, The Shadow held a bead on the masked man, as the latter reached the open door of Aldriff's den. A single spurt from The Shadow's .45 might have sprawled the masked menace on the hallway floor. But the chance was not a certainty.

The masked man was dealing with bolder customers than those who had first cringed from his gun.

Joan and Nevlin were backing through the doorway, side by side, and both showed reluctance. A single misstep on the masked man's part, and one or the other—perhaps both—would be grabbing for the threatening gun. The Shadow could not risk a shot that might be intercepted by a wrong target.

He let the three go through the doorway; as they went, the masked man was between the others, actually using his gun to prod Joan and Nevlin. As soon as they were in the room, The Shadow took swift strides from the vestibule, intending to challenge the masked man from the doorway of the den.

One look into the room in question revealed that such a move would still be dangerous to innocent lives.

The masked man had actually moved into the group itself. He was at the desk, clamping one hand on a box of papers that lay there. He'd overstepped himself, but had corrected the mistake in time. Half turned, he was swinging his gun, motioning persons back. His voice gave an ugly croak.

"So Aldriff got rid of himself." The words came through the draped handkerchief that hid the masked man's lips. "I had a good idea he'd do it. That's why I came for these."

He rattled the papers in the box; narrowed his

In the office was a black-cloaked friend who could save them. No killer ever lived who could commit open murder in the presencc of Thc Shadow!

eyes through the slits in the handkerchief.

"I'm taking this box with me," he announced. "Anybody that wants to keep Aldriff company can try to stop me!"

A threatening sweep of his gun and the masked marauder was turning toward the doorway, where he was certain to be stopped, in a very permanent fashion, the moment he crossed its threshold. The nose of an automatic was like a magnet in The Shadow's fist, actually about to draw its prey.

All the people in the room were dropping back, with hands well raised, Joan and Nevlin included. The girl's eyes were snapping furiously, but there wasn't a thing that she could do.

Nevlin's gaze, though nervous, showed an opposite impression. Half behind Aldriff's desk, Nevlin was in the right place to accomplish something, and he knew it.

Nevlin's foot was out of sight when it hooked the cord of the desk lamp. Faking a cringe away from the masked man's gun, the secretary took a long back step with almost the speed of a kick. It pulled the cord and the lamp came with it, jumping the edge of the desk and crashing to the floor.

The masked man was lunging at Nevlin as the lamp struck, and the secretary was ducking behind the desk. Others were grabbing for the marauder; his gun, when it spouted, sent its shots upward.

It was shooting so fast that its bullets were exhausted in mere seconds, and The Shadow, rather than disturb the wild aim, waited where he was until they finished.

Then, with a laugh that promised a quick capture, The Shadow started a lunge into the fray. The laugh was not heard, nor was the lunge completed.

Hands grabbed The Shadow from the hallway. Wheeling in their clutch, he found himself confronted by servants who had been coming in by the vestibule. They heard the shots; they saw The Shadow. Their conclusion was wrong, but it did not help.

There was only one course for The Shadow: to shake off these misguided opponents and leave the masked man to those in Aldriff's den.

AS for The Shadow's laugh, it was drowned by the sudden smashes within the room itself. The masked man, finding his gun empty, was grabbing up the furniture, and others were returning the favor. The darkness helped the marauder, and he was making the most of it. The excited guests were mistaking one another for the man they wanted to grab.

Chairs were smashed, ash stands flung, bookshelves overturned from the wall. Hands seized the big mirror from in back of Aldriff's desk. As someone cried: "There he goes!" the Florentine piece was hurled toward the chess nook, across the prone body of Aldriff. The crash it made was terrific, glass breaking in a series of smashes.

Joan, for one, dropped into a corner when she saw the mirror go. It missed the masked man, for he suddenly dashed from beside the desk, carrying the box of papers with him.

Nevlin grabbed at him, like a terrier worrying a fox. In his desperate flight, the masked man forgot the importance of the box he carried, for he turned and flung it at Nevlin's head. Another man sprang from the depths of the room and grabbed the marauder near the doorway.

They looked as though they were playing leapfrog when they went out through the hallway,

with Nevlin close behind them, yelling for the rest to come.

Meanwhile, The Shadow had whipped into the vestibule, carrying the attacking servants with him. He wanted darkness, so they wouldn't remember him too well, and he preferred space where he could deal with them lightly. There were only three of them, and they showed no skill at cooperation.

The Shadow tripped one going down the steps to the side door. Clutching another, he slammed him hard against the third, who fell away. The second man managed to preserve his grip and tighten it, but The Shadow settled that matter, a short way from the house.

With a sudden drop, a back flip, and a well-planted foot, he sent the tough servant off on a triple somersault across the lawn.

On his feet again, The Shadow made for the hedge, gave a defiant laugh and crashed into the branches, only to wheel away again. The rallying servants took the bait and went plunging through the hedge themselves, shouting to each other as they reached the next yard.

While the servants were surrounding something imaginary, The Shadow sped back to the house.

HE didn't expect the masked man to be loose, but supposed that if he had managed a lucky escape, he would flee by the front door of the sunporch. For if he knew the vestibule route, the marauder should have used it in the first place. So The Shadow rounded toward the front of the house, where he heard shouts coming from arriving cars.

People were dashing in through the front door; others, seeing where they went, turned and came The Shadow's way. Apparently, the masked man had broken free and fled through the vestibule, after all, having the luck go out just at the time when The Shadow was heading to the front of the house.

Reversing his course, The Shadow saw people flooding the side lawn, spearing in many directions.

There were crashes from the hedge and shouts from the other side. On the chance that they meant something, The Shadow plunged through. He heard yells from his former foemen, the servants. They were running toward a car parked by an old empty house next door.

A man was standing beside the car; he sprang into it, slammed the door, and started the motor, turning on the lights with the same action.

The servants jumped on the running board, and with them sprang a very disheveled girl, whose sleeve was dangling from her arm as she made grabs, not at the driver of the car but at the men who wanted to stop him.

The car was spurting forward. One servant lost his footing; another was dragged from the running board by Joan. The third clung on, blocking any shots The Shadow might have loosed, until the car went out through a driveway in a hedge where the branches brushed the servant off.

It was a deep driveway, ruining The Shadow's chances of shots at the tires of the fleeing ear. Shots, moreover, would have produced trouble for The Shadow himself, considering that he was practically surrounded at the moment. He heard cars starting out in pursuit of the fugitive, so he left the chase to others.

Prepared to make his own departure, The Shadow paused near the hedge, long enough to hear the accusations that the servants threw at Joan when they were bringing her back with them to the house.

They had recognized the man in the car, and they knew that she had, too. The sobs that Joan choked back were just part of her useless denials.

The man last seen in flight from the next door driveway was Aldriff's partner in swindle; otherwise, Joan's uncle, Smead Kelburn.

CHAPTER IV
THE SHADOW'S RETURN

SOON after his departure from the Aldriff

★ ★

As a mongoose whips a cobra—as a cowboy throws a wild steer—as a lion springs on its unwary prey—so, too, does The Shadow attack the hordes of crime and thwart their evil ends! Master of Darkness—Crime-fighter Extraordinary—The Shadow, by wits and thundering automatics, overawes those who seek to break the law and those already beyond its pale!

In his never-ceasing campeign to deal justice to crooks and honest citizens alike, The Shadow at times assumes the role of Lamont Cranston, globe-trotting millionaire. With this disguise, The Shadow makes his ends to meet unbeknownst to denizens of the underworld. There is a real Lamont Cranston; but he is a man of deep understanding, and it is with his tacit permission that The Shadow adopts his identity.

mansion, The Shadow returned. He came back in an entirely different fashion.

No longer was he an invisible figure that traveled on foot, under the cloak of darkness. He was a gentleman in evening clothes, who rode in a chauffeured limousine. The Shadow was his other self, Lamont Cranston.

He had come to Long Island as Cranston, and had later become The Shadow. As Cranston, he happened to be acquainted with Aldriff. Though not invited to the dinner party, there was no reason why he shouldn't claim to be. Aldriff had many friends, and new guests always appeared along with old.

So when the limousine rolled into the driveway, Cranston was immediately greeted as a guest by a self-formed reception committee. Head of the group was a tall, gray-haired man whose square face ended in a blunt chin. He didn't have to introduce himself. He was Lloyd Dulther, like Arthur Aldriff an executive of the Magnax Corp.

"Hello, Cranston," greeted Dulther solemnly. "I didn't know you were coming here tonight. It's too bad. This is a most unfortunate occasion!"

Cranston's usually impassive face showed a slightly curious expression as he noted the crowd around the house.

"What is the trouble, Dulther?" he inquired. "Too many guests?"

"One host too few," Dulther replied. "Aldriff committed suicide, shortly before I arrived."

He conducted Cranston into the house, where they met the other member of the Magnax trio, Hubert Sigby. Like Dulther, Sigby was tall, but he looked younger. His face was pointed of chin, and he had a reddish mustache, though his hair was brown. Sigby, too, had arrived after the tragedy, and he was as solemn as Dulther.

"Bad business, this," said Sigby. "Don't you think we can manage to get rid of all these people?"

"I know we can," returned Dulther, "except the persons who were here at the time of Aldriff's suicide."

With a polite smile, Cranston remarked that he would be glad to leave, considering that he wasn't in the category mentioned. Both Dulther and Sigby pleaded with him to remain.

"The police commissioner is coming," said Dulther, "and you're a friend of his. Belong to the same club and all that. You can help us, Cranston."

"Help you? How?"

"By giving the commissioner sensible advice," put in Sigby. "On business matters, Cranston. There are things we don't want talked about, because they were not our fault. We hope that you can convince the commissioner that we are right."

VERY shortly, Commissioner Weston arrived,

* *

Wherever fliers gather together, whenever the public talks of aviation, the name of Kent Allard is one of the first to be mentioned. World-famous aviator, Allard is a public hero. But what no one knows—save his two Xinca Indian servitors—is that Allard is the real identity of The Shadow!

Assisting The Shadow in his perpetual battle with the underworld is a retinue of aides—men who owe their lives to The Shadow and for whom they gladly do his slightest bidding.

Burbank is the contact man between The Shadow and his aides; through him go all orders and information. Rutledge Mann gives invaluable service to the Master of Darkness through his "front" of investment broker. Harry Vincent is very close to The Shadow, and acts in many cases as his advance man. To Moe Shrevnitz goes the honor of transporting the Crime-fighter to battle—in his taxicab. Clyde Burke, reporter on the Classic, furnishes The Shadow with inside information and advance news.

Cliff Marsland and Hawkeye are purported tough underworld characters; but, in reality, they are aides of The Shadow. When physical strength is needed the Master of Darkness calls on Jericho, giant African, whose muscular power is equaled only by his willingness to fight crime.

These, then, are the aides of The Shadow, characters who are willing to subject themselves to the Master of Darkness because they realize in him a superior force counteractant to crime.

The Shadow knows!

accompanied by his ace inspector, Joe Cardona. They were interested, first, in learning the manner of Aldriff's death; they said discussion of the motive could follow later.

The death room had become a mass of wreckage, with Aldriff's body in its midst, so Inspector Cardona proceeded to reconstruct the scene as it had been when the body was found.

The job was not difficult. Half a dozen witnesses supplied their testimony, and the statements coincided. Nevlin became the final spokesman, while the others listened, and agreed. It was plain that the door could not have been a murderer's exit; nor the windows. Spot by spot, Nevlin pointed out the places where the witnesses had looked.

Examining the fireplace, Cardona decided that it was an impossible outlet. He studied the chess nook at the end of the room and saw that it could be no hiding place. There was only one chair in the nook, but Cardona found the mate to it among the things which had been thrown.

He set the two chairs up in the position described by Nevlin and the others. Two flimsy chairs, with open backs, could not have served for concealment.

The bookcases were impossible to hide behind, and it was evident that the only other place could have been behind the screen in the near corner. Setting up the screen in front of the filing cabinet, Cardona had Nevlin and the others reenact their effort to trap an imaginary killer.

When it was done, Cardona took the folded screen and measured its thickness in folded condition. It came to just three inches, and witnesses remembered that the screen had been picked up when folded.

After tapping the walls thoroughly, Cardona took up the rugs and found that the floor was strictly solid. He merely echoed the unanimous opinion of those who had searched the den, when he disposed of the sealed room mystery with the single word:

"Suicide."

Before the investigation could swing to Aldriff's reason for taking his own life, Inspector Cardona received an important phone call. The chase for a mysterious masked man had failed, even though the man in question was said to be Smead Kelburn.

Other cars had hounded Kelburn's flight, until he abandoned his machine and jumped into a taxicab. Threatening the cabby with a gun, Kelburn had started toward the airport.

Cut off again by other cars, he had reversed his flight and slipped his pursuers. His trip had ended in Manhattan, and the cab driver had called police headquarters. The cabby's name was Tom Demble, and he was being sent back to Aldriff's to tell his story personally.

While Cardona was handling all this, Commissioner Weston was receiving buzzed confidences from Dulther and Sigby. They didn't need Cranston's persuasion to convince Weston that certain matters should be confidential.

Weston asked the witnesses about the masked marauder, and established two points: one, that no one had seen his face while masked; the other, that the raider had tried to take the metal box on Aldriff's desk, only to lose it when he threw it at Nevlin.

With that, Weston sent all witnesses to the sun porch with the exception of Nevlin and Joan. Dulther and Sigby remained, as did Cranston, at their urgent request. Weston gave the nod to Cardona, who promptly addressed Joan:

"Why did you aid your uncle's escape, Miss Kelburn?"

"He didn't escape," defended Joan stoutly. "Why, he wasn't even here! He was parked next door."

"And why would he have been there?"

"Why... why—" Joan hesitated. Then: "He *might* have intended to come here to see Mr. Aldriff. He probably stopped at the wrong house."

"Unfortunately," snapped Cardona, "he knew where this house was. Nevlin and the servants say he came here often, to do business with Mr. Aldriff. You know, of course, what that business was."

Joan finally capitulated, and nodded; but she promptly argued that her uncle wasn't the masked man, that she would certainly have recognized him.

Questioned on that same point, Nevlin felt sure that the marauder was Kelburn, though he finally admitted that his opinion was colored by circumstance.

"You knew your uncle was going to the airport," Cardona told Joan. "If you had impressed people with the matter, he could have been captured there."

"No one asked me," Joan retorted. "And besides, the people who blocked him off from there were started before I could have told them. So it wouldn't have made the slightest difference."

Commissioner Weston caught a slight nod from Cranston, and understood it. Though he regarded Cranston's opinions on crime to be rather weak, Weston felt that his friend gave good advice in handling people. Interrupting Cardona's quiz, Weston turned to Joan.

"We are not holding you as an accomplice," he said indulgently. "Technically, your uncle was not wanted for any crime at the time you aided him. But he is wanted at present, and will be until we locate him. You will do well to remember that, Miss Kelburn."

CARDONA was spreading the papers from

Aldriff's dispatch box. Weston looked them over, gathered them in a batch, and turned to Dulther and Sigby with the question:

"Do you gentlemen know what these documents are?"

Both shook their heads.

"If I told you that they concerned both Aldriff and Kelburn," pursued Weston, "would you be willing to hazard opinions on the question?"

"I would, Commissioner," declared Dulther frankly. "I would say that they had to do with the Pharco Drug chain. Both Sigby and myself had begun to suspect that Aldriff was behind it."

"Some correspondence came to the office by mistake," added Sigby. "Aldriff hadn't been there for weeks—ever since the Pharco outfit started selling stock. We forwarded the letters without opening them, but they bore Kelburn's return address."

"Magnax has nothing whatever to do with Pharco," stated Dulther. "It is our strict policy to stay out of retail trade."

"Nor would we have indorsed Aldriff's connection as an individual," asserted Sigby. "Indeed, we can show contracts signed by all three of us, stating that any individual engaging in any other drug business must first resign from his capacity of an official of the Magnax Corp."

Joan Kelburn sprang defiantly to her feet. Her eyes were like barbs as they darted from Dulther to Sigby.

"My uncle told me that Magnax was behind Pharco!" exclaimed Joan. "He said that he talked with all three of you and promoted Pharco stock on that account. His word is better than yours combined!" Joan swung to the commissioner. "If you want proof, you will find it in those papers!"

Weston motioned Joan back to her chair, then shook his head as he spread the papers on the desk.

"Letters, contracts, memoranda," he declared, "are solely between Smead Kelburn and Arthur Aldriff. In no way is the Magnax Corp. committed, nor are Dulther and Sigby concerned as individuals."

Joan stepped forward to look at the documents. Her eyes became more and more startled as she found out, step by step, that Weston was correct. Joan was returning, quite dazed, to her chair, when the commissioner questioned Nevlin:

"Was the Pharco deal between Aldriff and Kelburn only?"

"It was," replied Nevlin steadily. "Mr. Aldriff told me never to mention that he was backing Pharco. Mr. Kelburn did the same, and actually threatened me, once, in the presence of Mr. Aldriff, if I betrayed them to the Magnax Corp."

It took both Weston and Cardona to quiet Joan after she heard Nevlin's little speech, and the glares the girl gave the secretary actually worried Nevlin. In one breath, he lost the spunk he had displayed earlier.

"You see?" queried Nevlin, turning to Weston. "She knows, Commissioner! My life isn't safe while Kelburn is at large! I'm not a brave man." Nevlin's tone was pitiful. "I wasn't a hero this evening. I knew that Kelburn would kill me, because I knew what was in that box. I had to yank the light cord. It was my only chance!

"I'd like to get away from here, Commissioner"—the pint-sized secretary was darting looks at the door, as though expecting Kelburn to appear—"and be somewhere safer!"

"Go upstairs and pack," ordered Weston. "You can go into town with me, Nevlin. Meanwhile, I shall talk to the servants. I want you to come with me, Miss Kelburn."

Dulther and Sigby decided to go along, too, and took it that Cranston was coming, for he followed them as far as the reception hall. There, Cranston paused.

Alone, he smiled, and a soft laugh came to his lips. It was a weird tone, heard by his own ears alone, and it had a sinister throb. An echo from the recent past, that laugh of The Shadow.

Cranston's eyes gazed upstairs, where Nevlin had gone. They returned to the door of Aldriff's den, that room whose sealed door had been under The Shadow's own surveillance. If anyone should have testified that Aldriff's death was suicide, that witness was The Shadow.

Again, the keen eyes changed direction, as though weighing Nevlin, the living secretary, against Aldriff, the dead employer. Then, gazing afar, as if into the past, Cranston thrust his hands deep in his pockets and strolled toward the room of doom itself.

That distant gaze was another weighing process. The Shadow was balancing the scales double. On one side he was placing Dulther and Sigby, the big men of Magnax; on the other, Smead Kelburn, the missing promoter, and his loyal niece, Joan.

Lamont Cranston could have phrased his opinion, The Shadow's, in a single word, as had Joe Cardona. But a stronger word than suicide was needed to give The Shadow's answer to the death of Arthur Aldriff!

CHAPTER V
THE WRONG GUESS

INSPECTOR JOE CARDONA rubbed the back of his neck, wondering what was wrong with it. He turned around and saw Lamont Cranston standing in the doorway to Aldriff's den. Joe felt his momentary surprise fade. He was used to that tingling sensation when people looked at him behind his back.

"Thought you'd gone along with the others, Mr. Cranston," said Joe. "There's nothing worthwhile looking at around here. This suicide is an open-and-shut case."

"Call it shut and open," suggested Cranston. "I understand that the room was closed when Aldriff died, and that they broke into it later, to find the body."

Cardona nodded.

"It's the same thing either way," he declared. "But the door wasn't all that was broken. Look at this mess!"

It really was a mess. Even the big moosehead was off the wall, lying in a corner where someone had kicked it. Books were everywhere, and Aldriff's cups were scattered, for the trophy case had been overturned in the melee. Vases and the ship model were smashed; they had proven excellent missiles in the wild fray.

Picking his way through the shambles, Joe reached the nook in the far wall of the room and turned around.

"I'd like to have seen this dump before they wrecked it," vouchsafed the inspector. "If Kelburn had only waited a while before pulling that masked gunner act! He was probably sneaking around outside, and decided to come in when he saw the excitement. He couldn't have waited much longer, considering he intended to take a plane."

The quiet Mr. Cranston could have informed Cardona that Kelburn *had* been sneaking around. The stocky man near the sunporch and the fugitive in the car were enough alike to be classed as one and the same. The masked intruder, however, was another question.

The intruder had disguised himself with mask, crouch, and voice. In denying that he could have been her uncle, Joan was merely being loyal. She really didn't know. Nevlin, owing loyalty to Aldriff, had branded the masked man as Kelburn, only to let his claim weaken and admit he wasn't sure.

It was a case wherein The Shadow, himself, would not have cared to give an absolute opinion.

"Some society reporter took photos before the room was wrecked," informed Cardona. "We called his office, and they're sending us the developed plates."

"Clever chaps, those society reporters," observed Cranston. "Perhaps this one doubled back and was the masked man."

"Not a chance," snorted Cardona. "A couple of other reporters met him coming out. They knew he had a story as well as pictures, so they practically ganged him. Hopped in the same cab with him, and would have chucked his camera out the window, if he hadn't made a deal that would give their sheets copies of the pictures. They stayed right with him, from then on."

Knowing the ways of journalists, particularly those who snooped into high society, The Shadow was quite convinced that Cardona would receive copies of the actual photos, free from any fakery. Gazing absently about the room, The Shadow used his calm Cranston tone when he inquired:

"Where are your exhibits, Inspector?"

"Exhibits?" echoed Cardona. Then, with a laugh: "We don't need any in this ease. Aldriff committed suicide because he was in too deep in that Pharco deal. He sold a million dollars' worth of stock, through Kelburn, and probably pocketed the coin."

"Are you quite sure of that, Inspector?" Cranston inquired. "Can you prove that Kelburn turned over the funds to Aldriff?"

"Why, no," Cardona conceded. "There was nothing in the box to show it. Say, this Kelburn is a fox!"

"He might even claim that Aldriff's death was murder, Inspector."

"Hardly, Mr. Cranston. He'd make himself the goat."

Cranston did not agree. He suggested, artfully, that if the police proved Kelburn to be the masked man, they would be laying themselves wide open for Kelburn to insist that Aldriff had been murdered. For the masked man was one person who could not have been in the room of doom when Aldriff died.

IMPRESSED by such logic, Cardona began to gather exhibits. He already had the suicide gun as Exhibit A, while its permit, found in the leather folder, was labeled B. Cardona marked the revolver rack C.

In investigating murder cases, Joe always gathered odd parcels of evidence; this time, he was working in reverse, to conclusively establish death as suicide.

Cardona knew the sharp ways of lawyers and the simple minds of juries. In a courtroom, Joe would have to describe the whole case in detail from the photographs, and he wanted something to show for each step. He picked up two chessmen from the floor to serve as Exhibit D. They would figure in describing the finding of Aldriff's body.

There was nothing to represent properly the search of the room, but the masked man's entry and the confusion that it caused afforded exhibits in plenty.

Cardona took the broken bulb from the desk lamp. He added the smashed ship model from the mantel. He looked longingly at the moosehead, passed it up as too bulky, and began to fish among the books on the floor, looking for those that were most damaged.

"Before you finish the whole alphabet, Inspector," Cranston remarked, "what about the fragments of that big mirror? They are certainly indicative of damage."

Cardona agreed. The big mirror had struck a corner of the nook, bouncing from there to the floor, and the glass had scattered everywhere, even into the nook itself. Picking up the larger pieces, Joe began to lay them on the mirror frame in the manner of pieces of a jigsaw puzzle, and quite as hard to fit.

Large chunks were overlapping when Joe came to a smaller piece, about the size of a shaving glass. He decided that it would make a good exhibit; but Cranston, stooping to pick up another bit of silvered glass, gave the reason for his preference.

"Here's one that's more jagged," he declared. "You'd better take it, too, unless you can find a better one."

Looking, Joe thought he had found a better one, but Cranston, sorting through more pieces and comparing them, produced a better specimen. He even weighed a pair, one in each hand, and also tried to find two pieces that would fit each other.

Rather than dispute Cranston's judgment, Cardona began to take the fragments as they came along, until he had a half dozen of them among his exhibits.

Calling in the servants, Cardona told them he would need them later to put the room in order. Any furniture that was badly broken was to be stored in a closet and kept for future inspection. Cardona intended to have the door repaired and locked.

There were numerous other details, all part of the usual routine. While he was arranging them, Cardona saw Cranston stroll from the den. He supposed that the commissioner's friend was going back to the conference, where Dulther and Sigby were further explaining how Aldriff had betrayed the Magnax Corp.

Though their own hands were clear of blame, Dulther and Sigby had much at stake. Should the Pharco scandal be made public, Aldriff's connection with it would reflect upon Magnax. Huge though the corporation was, it could hardly survive the blow. Mercantile houses would make demands on Magnax, just as depositors would start a run on a bank reputed to be shaky. Unless assets could be rapidly liquidated, the Magnax Corp. would fall.

Instead of remaining as the executives of a great corporation, Dulther and Sigby would be looking for other jobs. The fruits of their long years of service would be gone, nullified by Aldriff's urge to obtain a million dollars all at once.

Cranston could hear such dire predictions floating from the room where Weston had gone with the executives. First Dulther's voice, then Sigby's, with the commissioner inserting an occasional comment.

Joan's voice did not enter the conversation; in fact, the girl could not have found anything to say. Dulther and Sigby were not blaming her uncle, at present; they were bearing down on the Aldriff question.

In fact, when Dulther did mention Kelburn, Cranston heard Sigby promptly say that he hoped Joan's uncle could explain himself when the police located him.

Classing Aldriff as the brain, and Kelburn as the dupe, was quite a logical procedure. A schemer at the end of his rope would have reason to resort to suicide; whereas, a man who found himself betrayed would be the sort to take drastic steps to clear himself. Even such steps as arriving armed and masked, to demand a boxful of incriminating documents.

However, it was the law that would decide the matter, and the law was strict in such cases. Kelburn had sold stock to purchasers who bought it in good faith, and unless funds were forthcoming to pay off the stockholders, Kelburn would pay the penalty.

Aldriff could have saved Kelburn by personally accepting the indictment and declaring that Kelburn was an ignorant party to the fraud. But Aldriff would never testify in anyone's behalf; not even his own. Aldriff was dead, and the question of suicide or murder was immaterial, when considered from the standpoint of the testimony that he might—or might not—have spoken.

CRANSTON did not wait to hear Weston harp on that subject. Leaving the closed door of the conference room, he crossed over to the side door. Guests were gone, and no servants were about to witness Cranston's departure.

Skirting the house, he reached his limousine, which was parked in the wide driveway. There, unnoticed by his chauffeur, Cranston opened the rear door and slid a drawer from beneath the seat.

Taking cloak and hat from the secret drawer, Cranston also outfitted himself with an automatic, and slid the drawer back beneath the rear seat.

Usually, The Shadow carried a brace of those guns. He needed only one .45 for the job ahead. Sliding his arms into his cloak, clamping the slouch hat on his head, The Shadow delivered a whispered laugh as he looked toward a lighted window on the third floor of the Aldriff mansion.

A single gun would be sufficient threat to test the weak link in the human chain. The weak link was Nevlin. Aldriff's secretary could play too smart one moment, too dumb the next, to be a paragon of honesty or innocence.

Entering the mansion, The Shadow found a back stairway and became a gliding shape as he ascended to the third floor.

Nevlin's door was ajar. Inside the room, The Shadow saw the small-sized secretary packing a bag and at the same time taking quick looks across his shoulder. Nevlin was fearful of intruders, but despite his fidgets he didn't sense that The Shadow was in the hall. So far, Nevlin could hardly have realized that The Shadow was in the case, at all.

The servants had spoken of meeting someone outside Aldriff's den, but they had confused The Shadow with the masked man who had been in the room itself. Hence, Nevlin's present mood announced him as a victim of his own qualms. Which was fair enough, considering that Nevlin had played bold or fearful, under circumstances which should have called for consistency, one way or the other.

Almost finished with his packing, Nevlin turned to the window and looked below. He went to a bureau, dug a gun from deep in a drawer, and hesitated, wondering whether to pack it in his pocket or stow it in his suitcase.

He finally tiptoed to the door, and The Shadow eased back into a darkened alcove to let him pass. Nevlin listened at the top of the stairs to find out what was going on below. Hearing nothing, he went back into his room and closed the door.

Moving forward, The Shadow placed his hand upon the knob, intending to inch the door open. The time to confront Nevlin was at hand. The fellow was planning flight, in preference to further bluff. What Nevlin did with the gun would be proof of his final intention. If he put it in his pocket, flight would be his choice.

Before The Shadow could get a look at Nevlin, he heard a light stir on the stairway behind him. Thinking he had moments to spare, The Shadow took time to properly close the door, easing the knob deftly, so that Nevlin could not hear it turn.

But the sound that The Shadow heard was much closer than he thought; in fact, too close.

Swinging to start a sweep to the alcove above the hall, The Shadow stopped short. His hand, traveling to the hem of his cloak, became rigid. Any semblance of a further move might be fatal to The Shadow, considering the determination in the eyes that met his own.

They were brown eyes; they belonged to Joan Kelburn. Eyes that had a hair-trigger expression, for with her cold gaze, Joan displayed a .32 revolver, its muzzle squarely toward The Shadow. Joan's finger had taken up the trigger slack, and was ready to pull farther.

Slowly, The Shadow let his hands come upward and apart, placing himself, quite helpless, against the white background of the door to Nevlin's room.

CHAPTER VI
ONE WITNESS LESS

JOAN KELBURN had made a wrong guess, like the servants who had met The Shadow earlier. She was confusing this invader with the masked man who had made the surprise entry into Aldriff's den. It required some stretch of the imagination, but Joan was capable of it. Actually, the girl's thoughts were confused by recent events.

To begin with, she mistrusted Nevlin for the same reasons that The Shadow did, which was why she, too, had come upstairs.

Finding an invader at Nevlin's very door, Joan's ideas performed a whirl-about, bringing her to the conclusion that Nevlin was really honest, and therefore in danger. Nevlin had struggled with the masked man, so Joan's mind jumped back to that event, and therefore gave her a wrong notion of The Shadow.

As for The Shadow, he was chiding himself for having let a very essential point escape him. He'd taken it for granted that Joan was in conference with Weston and the Magnax executives, though he had not heard her voice. He should have looked in on that conference; if he had, he would have learned that Joan was absent from it, and therefore up to something else.

Regrets were useless. The present task was to nullify Joan's mistaken guess without letting Nevlin learn what was happening; a rather difficult assignment, considering The Shadow's predicament. However, The Shadow remembered something that would help.

He spoke in a whisper that Joan did not recognize. He was picking up a warning that Commissioner Weston had impressed upon the girl.

"Be careful with that gun," suggested The Shadow. "If you fire it, you will have to make more explanations to the police. They have been very tolerant with you so far, but they have their limits. It would be unfortunate if they even knew you owned a gun."

The girl let her hand relax, only to tighten it again. Her grim smile showed that The Shadow's ruse had not quite worked. Joan was thinking that since the police wanted the missing masked man, they would probably thank her for trapping him. Nevertheless, The Shadow's words made Joan consider matters more calmly; which was an important gain.

Over the top of the leveled gun, the girl tried to glimpse the face beneath the hatbrim. The Shadow lifted his head slightly, letting her view his eyes. A good move, since it roused Joan's curiosity the more and enabled The Shadow to shift farther back, giving the impression that Joan held him more helpless than before.

Burning eyes beneath the hatbrim—Joan didn't recall that the masked man had such eyes. She could see the outline of a face, though she could not identify its features. Not for a moment did she class The Shadow as Cranston, for she thought that the commissioner's friend was in the conference downstairs.

"No mask," spoke The Shadow, as if in answer to Joan's thought. "I am not the man who was mistaken for your uncle."

An inspiration, that one. Joan had at last found someone willing to support her belief. She didn't realize, at the moment, that stress of circumstance could have caused The Shadow to pretend agreement with her opinion. Almost ready to accept The Shadow as a friend, Joan lowered gun hand slightly.

The Shadow let his weight relax against the door. He was almost ready for a lunge, and take-off from the door would add impetus to his forward shove. He was gauging the move perfectly.

He needed to grab the gun and suppress Joan's cry, all in one swoop. After that, it would be easy; he'd quickly make her listen to reason. The Shadow didn't want to spoil the business that he planned with Nevlin.

SHOULDERS against the door, one foot slightly raised, The Shadow was motionless one moment; in the next, he became a whirling figure. But he didn't begin a forward surge. Instead, The Shadow surprised himself. He went backward, so suddenly that he didn't realize what had happened.

Nor did Joan. She thought that The Shadow actually vanished. The door, itself, seemed to swallow him—which, in a sense, it did. Only the door was gone, too, like The Shadow. In place of both was vacancy, represented by the open doorway.

Nevlin, ready to leave his room, had yanked the door inward, bringing The Shadow with it. Relieved of his underpinning, The Shadow thought the floor had come up to meet him. He was really in a whirl, but he didn't try to stop it. Instinctively, The Shadow rolled to get clear of the gunshots that he knew would come.

Joan was pulling the trigger of the revolver and it was spurting into the darkened room. The Shadow was rolling one way and Nevlin was dropping back in the other direction.

Nevlin had turned out the lights; hence Joan didn't see him. She was thinking only in terms of a black-cloaked foeman who was gone.

Gone so completely that the girl was actually frightened by the sound of her own shots. She ended with three and made a half turn toward the stairway, gasping with alarm.

Nevlin saw her in the light of the hallway; savagely, he drove out through the doorway, gun in one hand, suitcase in the other. His pale face, coming into the light, was merciless in its expression, and he was shoving his gun toward Joan, intending to deliver shots that wouldn't miss.

Then Nevlin was performing a somersault as surprising as The Shadow's, but his went forward, instead of backward. The Shadow was returning Nevlin's compliment. Nevlin, of course, had not known that The Shadow was against the door; hadn't even seen the black mass that plunged into the room. But The Shadow saw Nevlin going out and deliberately nailed him.

The Shadow did it with a scissors kick, from the side of the door, clipping Nevlin's ankles. The fellow's drive became a long pitch, his hands thrusting ahead of his body. His gun barked and the bullet went wide of Joan, as she darted away from the stairs. Nevlin hit then, instead, and went bouncing downward, his suitcase following after him.

Knowing that Nevlin's shot was meant for her, Joan sprang to the head of the stairs and saw the secretary end his long spill. She thought that he was badly hurt, so she was holding her gun lowered.

Coming slowly from his huddle, Nevlin looked helpless indeed, and Joan was badly deceived. So badly, that she almost spelled her own doom.

She was leaning anxiously over the top step looking at Nevlin, when he flashed his gun upward, gave a gleeful snarl as he tugged the trigger to blast a shot that would bring Joan tumbling down.

Swifter than Nevlin's aim was the living hurricane that swirled from the doorway behind Joan. It took the girl in its twist, carried her sideways from the stairs, and sent her on a dizzy tumble into the safety of the alcove.

Joan actually thought she was somersaulting down the stairs, until her high heels thwacked the alcove wall. She was lying on her shoulders, her head tilted backward, giving her an upside-down impression of a black-blotted shape that was spinning back to the head of the stairway.

The echoes of Nevlin's shot were still ringing in Joan's ears, only to be broken by a weird, defiant laugh that must have been uttered by the singular fighter in black. Below, Nevlin heard the challenging mirth and knew that it was meant for him. A mad clatter told that Nevlin was taking to rapid flight.

Reaching the ground floor, Nevlin saw people coming into the reception hall. Weston was emerging from one room, followed by Dulther and Sigby. Cardona was shouldering forth from the den, followed by a pair of Aldriff's servants.

Suitcase in one hand, Nevlin waved his gun with the other, gesturing back toward the stairs as he cried:

"The Kelburn girl! Stop her! She fired those shots! She wanted to kill me!"

The Shadow heard Nevlin's howls, but didn't think that anyone would be foolish enough to believe the fellow's words, considering that the secretary was carrying a gun, himself.

Figuring that Nevlin would be chased outdoors and forced to dart around the house, The Shadow went down by the backstairs in order to cut him off.

There was no car available except The Shadow's limousine, which was well down the driveway. However, The Shadow started in its direction, to intercept Nevlin should he try to reach the limousine and intimidate the chauffeur.

LIGHTS blazed suddenly from the driveway, right in front of Aldriff's house. They came from the taxicab that was arriving to report on Kelburn's flight. Nevlin jumped right into the glare, waved his gun at the driver and climbed into the cab.

Tom Demble, the taxi driver, wasn't the sort to argue with a gun. He'd let Kelburn have his way, and thus was still alive; so he used the same policy with Nevlin.

Before the cab could pull away, Nevlin heard a laugh from the darkness ahead. Frantic, he thrust his gun from the window just as the cab was starting. Demble gave a quick turn of the wheel as a shape like a mammoth bat wheeled into the glare of the headlights then swooped away again. It was gone, that weird figure, when Demble straightened the cab again.

Nevlin saw the figure in black and began to shoot; his aim wide by dozens of yards. He was shooting at a forward angle, whereas The Shadow had cut to the rear of the cab. Nevlin might have seen him had he turned around; but Nevlin didn't look back.

Just within the glow from the front doorway of the house, The Shadow was taking deliberate aim at the figure shooting from the rear door of the cab.

The noise of Nevlin's shots drowned out crunches on the gravel. Men flung themselves upon The Shadow as he fired, and his bullet merely dug a chunk from the driveway.

Wrestling with these new attackers, The Shadow heard the cab roar rapidly ahead—Nevlin's shots spurring Demble quite as effectively as if the fleeing secretary had kept the gun muzzle against the cabby's neck.

Nevlin was off in the flight he wanted, making one less witness to the things that had happened in the Aldriff mansion. In flight, Nevlin was carrying with him the story that he should have told to—The Shadow!

CHAPTER VII
JOAN FINDS A FRIEND

THE struggle in the driveway was brief; much like one in which The Shadow had earlier engaged. For he was dealing with the same tacklers who had proven themselves quite soft: Aldriff's servants. This time, there were only two of them, and The Shadow spilled them without trouble.

He hooked one with a flying mare and slapped him down in the driveway. Rolling back to his shoulders, The Shadow met the other attacker with a pair of driving feet that tossed the flunky clear across to the lawn. Coming to hands and knees, The Shadow made a racing start to the darkness at the side of the house.

More cars were coming into the driveway—the ones that had pursued Kelburn earlier. Cardona was coming from the front door of the house, and he yelled for the cars to go after the same cab that they had chased before.

Since Cardona was arranging to overtake Nevlin, The Shadow went in through the side door to see what was happening inside the house.

Cardona had used sense in starting the servants after Nevlin; but others weren't exhibiting the same judgment. Weston, accepting Nevlin's accusation of Joan, had started upstairs to find the girl and both Dulther and Sigby were following him.

They spotted her on the second floor, and Joan made a sudden dash for the main stairway. Clattering down as fast as she could come, she stumbled as she reached the reception hall, and The Shadow saw her revolver slide ahead of her. Then, frantically, Joan scooped up the weapon and tried to hide it, as she looked for the best path toward further flight.

The men from the second floor were coming down. Weston was shouting for Dulther and Sigby to look out, that the girl was dangerous and armed. Seeing Cardona turn in from the front door, Joan took the only route left—past the den and toward the darkened vestibule of the side door.

Huddled, Joan was clutching the revolver to her breast and hiding it with her flapping sleeve, as she darted quick looks back at her pursuers. The pack was close, and two things were inevitable. First, that Joan would stumble when she reached the little steps she couldn't see; second, that she would be overtaken and captured before she could regain her feet.

But Joan didn't stumble. Instead, solid blackness met her as she reached the steps, took her in its folds and carried her downward. Joan heard a whispered laugh close to her ear, and recognized it. The subdued tone seemed to tell her that all was well.

Indeed, suddenly sure that The Shadow was a friend, Joan expected him to transport her somehow into the invisible realm which seemed his habitat. But the miracle didn't happen.

Whirled about, Joan felt herself sprawl down the steps, and gave a frightened cry as she flung her hands to stop the fall. It stopped itself, thanks to The Shadow. He caught the girl again, buffered her as she reached the wall, and left her sitting there very much surprised.

Joan was indignant, too, as she heard The Shadow's fleeting laugh whisper back from the doorway. For, by then, her pursuers were almost upon her and she had no chance to get up and run.

The most she could do was huddle her arms and keep the revolver hidden. Hauling her back into the hallway, the men tugged her folded arms apart. Despairingly, Joan relaxed, spreading her hands, expecting to hear the revolver thud the floor. It didn't fall and Joan found herself staring, quite as surprised as the rest.

Commissioner Weston strode to the vestibule. He found a light switch and pressed it. He looked for the gun and could not find it, even when he opened the door and looked outside. By then, Joan was rallying her scattered senses.

Recalling The Shadow's whispered tone, she realized what it meant. By starting her into a fall, then catching her, The Shadow had caused Joan to fling her arms without realizing it. That had been his opportunity to pluck away the incriminating gun.

ACCUSED of harboring a gun, Joan blinked blankly and shrugged. Cardona was on her side, arguing that Nevlin could have done the shooting that Weston blamed on Joan; that the secretary's subsequent gunfire backed the supposition.

Weston finally admitted that he wasn't sure Joan had a gun when she went down the stairs. Both Dulther and Sigby proving doubtful, the commissioner decided that the girl's status was still acceptable.

He only wanted to know why she had gone upstairs, and Joan declared honestly that she had wanted to talk to Nevlin, to assure him that her uncle certainly intended him no harm.

She hadn't managed to convince Nevlin, she declared; in fact, he hadn't given her the chance. He'd sprung from his room like a madman, and had taken shots at her while going down the stairs. In order to be fair to Nevlin, Joan added that he had fired very wide and probably didn't intend to hit her. She felt that he had been excited, nothing more.

Joan rather regretted the statement, when she recalled the way Nevlin had tricked her from the bottom of the stairs; but her partial defense of Nevlin proved wise. Since she showed no animosity toward the fellow, the listeners accepted her story and asked no more questions. Thus Joan was saved from any quiz that might have produced mention of The Shadow.

One man had that subject on his mind: Joe Cardona. He had seen the spills the servants had taken out in the driveway. He remembered Nevlin's frantic shots, and knew that they were the sort that men delivered when The Shadow baited them.

But Cardona did not care to cloud the issue by bringing in The Shadow. Joe was on pins and needles, much like Joan.

It was Cranston who relieved the situation, when he strolled in from the front door. He had joined the pursuit of Nevlin, but his limousine had proven too unwieldy to keep up with the chase. Cranston dropped a few remarks regarding Nevlin.

"The chap was skittish," Cranston claimed. "Do you know, just before he went upstairs I spoke to him while his back was turned, and he jumped as though I'd pressed a gun against him. I believe he'd have drawn his own gun, right then, if he'd had it.

"That's probably why he brought the revolver from his room. His nerves were so on edge that he would have fired at shadows. Why, the servants told me that he was shooting at nothing when the cab drove away! They even caught the fever and went grabbing for someone they thought they saw. Someone who just wasn't there to grab!"

Joan gave a grateful smile. Cranston's opinions helped the statements she had made. Then other men were coming into the house, to report that they hadn't caught Nevlin. His cab had slipped them, as it had when Kelburn was its passenger.

Twenty minutes later the cab, itself, returned. Demble, the driver, came shakily into the house and reported. Nevlin had spotted a local train stopping at a little suburban station and had jumped from the cab to take it. The train had pulled out before Demble could do anything about it.

Cardona put in a call to the Pennsylvania Station, only to learn that the Long Island local had arrived there and discharged its passengers.

While Cardona was grousing, because Demble's information had come too late, the telephone rang. Answering it, Joe listened intently, then turned to the others and exclaimed:

"It's Nevlin!"

IT was Nevlin, all right, but the fellow wouldn't listen to reason, not even when Commissioner Weston got on the wire to cajole him. Weston ended with words that had the tone of threats, whereupon Nevlin must have hung up at the other end, for the commissioner very angrily slammed the telephone on the table.

"From the way the fool talks," asserted Weston, "you would think the devil was after him! He's afraid of Kelburn, afraid of Joan, even afraid of himself, I'd say. He talks of imaginary enemies, and says he can't count on us to protect him. He wants to hide, so I suppose the best plan is to let him. He'll show up later, on his own."

"After we find Kelburn, he will," put in Cardona. "That ought to end his worries."

"He may reappear sooner," observed Dulther. "You know, I think that Nevlin felt that he had spoken out of turn."

"When he admitted knowing of the transactions between Kelburn and Aldriff," agreed Sigby, with a nod. "It might brand him as a party to the swindle they perpetrated."

"If he knows that he is only wanted as a witness, we shall hear from him," added Dulther. "That is why I say that he may reappear before we find Kelburn."

Oddly, Joan did not feel impelled to make another outburst in defense of her uncle. The recent excitement had sobered her, and she realized the mistake of being too impetuous. She knew that The Shadow had befriended her, even though she had fired shots that might have killed him, and such generosity on his part made her quite humble. She hoped that she might sometime meet that unknown friend and thank him for all that he had done.

Meanwhile, she did not feel entirely friendless. Among those present was one who had likewise stood in her behalf. As she watched the group, Joan caught a glance from Cranston.

His eyes did not have the fiery gaze of The Shadow's; instead, they were very calm. They were deep eyes, though, that showed understanding, and Joan not only trusted them, but their owner, too.

She was glad when Cranston offered to take her into town in his limousine. Not only did it offer her a chance to talk to him alone; it suited the police commissioner.

Weston decided that Cranston's surveillance would be sufficient, in Joan's case. Of course, he was counting upon Cranston to press some subtle inquiries during the trip; but that didn't occur to Joan.

When they entered the limousine, Joan saw something on the rear seat. Without a gasp, the girl quickly covered it with her arm. As soon as the car had started, Cranston reached across, lifted Joan's arm and picked up the hidden object.

It was a .32 revolver, which he weighed as he inquired:

"Yours?"

Joan hesitated; then nodded.

"I thought so," said Cranston quietly. "I found it in the car when I went after Nevlin. Who put it here"—he shrugged—"well, that can be left to speculation. The main point was to clear up its ownership, which we have."

He tucked the gun in a side pocket of the car, as though he intended to forget it. Decidedly, Cranston was Joan's friend, and she needed only a slight stimulus to bestow upon him the gratitude that she was reserving for The Shadow. Subtly, Cranston made it a mutual answer.

"You will be hearing from your uncle," Cranston predicted. "When you do, assure him that you can help, if he will tell you how and where to find him. I have a friend who would like to meet him." Cranston paused; with a trace of a significant smile he added: "The friend is not the police commissioner."

Joan's nod proved that she understood. Cranston wanted Smead Kelburn to meet The Shadow, the mysterious personage who, upon this evening, had proven that he held an open mind when it came to judging men upon their innocence or guilt.

Cranston left the girl at her apartment. Alone there, the girl gazed from her window, along the street where the limousine had gone. Joan's happy sigh was sponsored by the thought that she had found two real friends: Lamont Cranston and The Shadow.

Joan was wrong. She had made only one new friend. But that lone friend, personalized both as Cranston and The Shadow, was to prove himself more powerful than a multitude!

CHAPTER VIII
THE NEEDED MESSAGE

THE world called Aldriff's death suicide, as well it might, considering the circumstances. The newspapers printed their pictures of the death-room scene, to prove conditions that could never have permitted murder. Reporters roved in and out of Aldriff's mansion, examining the locked windows of the room of doom, tapping walls, floor, and ceiling, as Cardona had done.

From door to nook, the place was airtight, proving that Aldriff must have died by his own hand alone.

One of those reporters was Clyde Burke, a secret agent of The Shadow. When Clyde came through with a suicide verdict, it was usually a convincer. The Shadow had trained this particular agent to be more than thorough when examining such scenes.

CLYDE BURKE

Nor was Clyde the only one who brought that verdict home.

Inspector Cardona kept pounding it into Cranston's ear every time he met him, until Commissioner Weston finally called a halt.

It happened at the Cobalt Club, where Cranston had dropped in to see Weston and idly inquired if the police had obtained any traces of either Kelburn or Nevlin.

"Of course, Aldriff's death was suicide!" snapped Weston, addressing Cardona. "To hear you harp on it, Inspector, you would think that someone held a doubt!"

Cardona looked at Cranston, whose return gaze showed he understood. Cardona hadn't forgotten Cranston's remarks regarding the neat loophole that Kelburn might choose in order to feign innocence on the business of selling phony stock.

Cardona wanted Cranston to know that Kelburn could never find an out by arguing that Aldriff's death was murder. No one could possibly believe it.

Nor would anyone believe that Aldriff was not party to the Pharco swindle. The newspapers had aired the thing completely, despite the contrary wishes of Dulther and Sigby.

The past few days had been unhappy ones for the big men of Magnax. They hadn't just been bothered by reporters. They'd talked with the Federal district attorney; they had been to Washington to state their case to the heads of various governmental departments.

A congressional investigation of the entire drug business was predicted for the near future, and when it began, Dulther and Sigby would have to repeat the testimony that they had already given.

They welcomed it as an opportunity. They had proven absolutely that the Magnax Corp. had no connection whatever with the Pharco chain, and the more that fact was impressed upon the public, the better.

"Fine men, Dulther and Sigby," Weston told Cranston. "It was a shock to them, the way Aldriff betrayed their trust. All this trouble has been a credit to their integrity. No scandal can wreck such reputations as theirs.

"If Magnax weathers this storm, it will be a stronger corporation than ever before. If it fails, no one will blame Dulther and Sigby. They have both received offers from bigger companies than Magnax, proving that honesty is recognized.

"But they have their shoulders to the wheel, in the effort to carry Magnax through. Win or lose, they will have shown their merit, and their reward will be great. It is an impressive fact, Cranston, that not one scrap of evidence exists to stamp Dulther or Sigby with the brand that Aldriff bore."

The Shadow could picture Dulther and Sigby with their shoulders to the wheel, each pushing in the opposite direction. A wheel that had crushed Aldriff, and would grind Kelburn, as well.

The statement with which Weston had ended his harangue was, indeed, impressive. The fact that no scrap of evidence could link Dulther and Sigby with Aldriff's deals, was something quite too perfect. It was the sort of thing that Dulther and Sigby could have planned to happen.

THAT evening, Cranston dined with Joan. He expressed the opinion that he hadn't given Weston. Joan's eyes lighted when she heard it. Over the table, she responded:

"It fits with what my uncle claims. He talked with all three men, Mr. Cranston. They purposely arranged that Aldriff would take all responsibility in backing Pharco."

"Which rather marks Aldriff as a big fool," commented Cranston calmly.

"Not at all," insisted Joan. "Uncle Smead thought it very fair, and he is no fool. My uncle felt this way: if Magnax refused to support Pharco, he could take it up with Aldriff. To protect himself, Aldriff would force Dulther and Sigby to come clean. It would have put my uncle and Aldriff in one boat, Dulther and Sigby in the other. An even match, Mr. Cranston."

Slowly, Cranston nodded.

"We can assume, then, that Dulther and Sigby double-crossed Aldriff," said Cranston. "He turned the funds over to them, as agreed, thinking they couldn't possibly betray him—"

"And they murdered him!" broke in Joan forcefully. "There is no other answer, Mr. Cranston. Why should Aldriff have committed suicide, when he could have forced the use of Magnax funds to back the Pharco stock?"

Cranston was quite impressed. Without indicating that Joan was merely driving home the issue that he, himself, had pictured, he remarked:

"I suppose those are your uncle's opinions."

"They are," acknowledged Joan. "You see, Mr. Cranston"—her forehead wrinkled as she earnestly tried to make her statement convincing—"my uncle really feared that Aldriff was working with the others. Aldriff kept reassuring him that everything would be all right. Aldriff must have believed that it would be."

Joan felt that she had sold her argument, for Cranston's eyes agreed. His tone was speculative, when he said:

"I hope you hear from your uncle shortly, Joan. My friend still wants to meet him."

"I'm sure I shall," returned Joan sincerely. "If you don't mind, Mr. Cranston, I'd like to get back to my apartment, just in case Uncle Smead should call. Of course"—her tone was hasty—"I'll let you know, if he does."

"Of course," acknowledged Cranston. "I shall stay here a while, Joan. Phone me if you hear from him."

BURBANK

As soon as Joan had left the little cafe, Cranston turned to another table, where a very becoming brunette was dining alone. As he sat down, Cranston smiled.

"Nothing sentimental about that friendship," remarked Cranston. "You heard for yourself, Margo. She called me 'Mr. Cranston' every time. Never once was it 'Lamont.'"

Margo Lane registered mock surprise.

"Why, Lamont!" she exclaimed. "What a fool you are to think I could be jealous!"

"What a fool *you* would be," corrected Cranston, "if you thought I'd think that you were jealous. So let's drop it before we turn the thing into a chain letter proposition. Joan Kelburn has heard from her uncle."

Margo's eyes were quickly alert.

"You're sure?"

"No question about it," returned Cranston. "She told me everything she knew, the other evening, and now she knows a great deal more. In fact, she quoted some points that her uncle could not have thought about until after Aldriff's death."

"Why is she holding out, Lamont?"

"Because her uncle isn't willing to meet me yet." As he spoke, Cranston smiled: "Nor my friend, The Shadow, for that matter. Joan should have told me that much."

"Why didn't she?"

"Only one possible reason, Margo. She knows where to reach her uncle, and she's afraid that if she admitted that much, she'd give the rest away."

"And the next step?"

Cranston answered Margo's question by outlining a simple plan. Joan's return to her apartment indicated that she might be on the verge of convincing her uncle to accept Cranston's advice. Cranston decided to call Joan later; if she still proved silent on the subject, he would introduce her to Margo.

Perhaps meeting with a girl she could trust would stiffen Joan's determination to make Smead Kelburn meet people who struck Joan as real friends.

MARGO'S table was convenient to a telephone booth, where a bell began to ring almost as Cranston finished outlining his coming tactics. Cranston was prompt to answer it, for he knew that the call might be from Joan.

It wasn't, but it proved almost as important. Burbank was on the wire.

Burbank never called unless it was important. For Burbank was The Shadow's contact man, and almost as mysterious a figure as the chief he served. Few people had ever seen Burbank; he lived in a burrow, lost from the world, though it was close to the center of Manhattan.

There at a switchboard, day and night, Burbank kept contact with The Shadow's active agents, men like Clyde Burke. Active they were, at present, for The Shadow had set them to the task of scouring the city for a certain man named Nevlin.

First, The Shadow had analyzed the type of places where Nevlin would be most likely to head after a storm. With the search thus narrowed, finding the missing secretary was simply a matter of time; not more than a week, by The Shadow's calculation.

The Shadow had figured well. Over the telephone, Burbank, speaking in a methodical voice, told the quiet-toned Mr. Cranston that a man of Nevlin's description was living in Room 308 in a very modest hotel called the Montview.

Such news received, Cranston returned to Margo's table and gave her the details.

"I'm going over to the Montview," said Cranston. "Nevlin has probably been finding it lonesome there. Besides, he's been having too easy a time of it. The police haven't started looking for him, because they think he'll soon get over his scare and look them up, instead. They don't know how permanently scared Nevlin is."

In parting, Cranston told Margo to wait around and introduce herself to Joan, in case the other girl called. It would not mean waiting long, because Cranston expected his visit with Nevlin to be brief.

If it brought the results that he expected, he would call Joan himself. From Cranston's tone, Margo knew that he would get these results with Nevlin.

She knew that he would be visiting Nevlin as The Shadow. Watching Cranston enter a cab out front, Margo could picture him sliding into garments of black even as his trip began. For the driver of the cab was Moe Shrevnitz, one of The Shadow's secret agents.

Like the limousine, it was one of the favorite spots wherein Cranston transformed himself into The Shadow while on the rove.

Only five minutes after Cranston's departure, the bell in the booth gave an ominous tingle. Margo answered it, alarmed without understanding why. She heard Joan's voice, inquiring anxiously for Mr. Cranston. In her most friendly tone, Margo responded.

"Mr. Cranston has just left. I'm Miss Lane, a friend of his. He asked me to introduce myself to anyone who called, because—"

There couldn't have been anything indiscreet in what Margo said, but the result certainly indicated that there was. A receiver landed abruptly, cutting off Joan's call. Margo could only suppose that some undue stress had gripped Joan. Something of such serious import that it might predict trouble for The Shadow.

MOE SHREVNITZ

Hurriedly, Margo put in a call to Burbank, hoping she could get word to The Shadow before he reached the Montview. The minutes lost proved just too many. Burbank reported that Moe had just phoned in, saying that The Shadow had dismissed the cab a few blocks from Nevlin's hotel and was covering the last stretch alone.

All Margo could do was wait and worry. Her alarm, for some peculiar reason, would not abate. She felt that danger lurked at the Hotel Montview, even for The Shadow—and she was right.

Danger did lurk; and with it, death!

CHAPTER IX
WHERE DEATH PRESIDED

THE Hotel Montview looked as if it catered to guests who preferred to enter and leave unnoticed. Its lobby was dim, almost deserted; its elevators were unattended except when someone shouted loud enough to bring a sleepy operator from a bench around the corner.

The Shadow did not shout. Instead, he glided through the lobby in a style that would have surprised a ghost. Streaky darkness, nothing more, was the only evidence of his passage. The clerk who drowsed behind the grimy marble desk didn't even miss a snore.

Past the elevator was a stairway as dark as the entrance to a Coney Island fun house. Ascending it, The Shadow was swallowed in gloom after the first four steps. Taking a look behind him, he saw a space as dark as the one that he had chosen.

It was a side passage, leading from the lobby to another street. Probably the route that Nevlin used when going in and out.

For Nevlin didn't want to be found; very specially, he wanted to avoid the police. His own reason—fear of Kelburn—was good enough. If groundless, said reason only pointed to a better one.

The Shadow was thinking in terms that he had considered this evening, when Weston had mentioned that no link existed to incriminate Dulther and Sigby in Aldriff's swindle.

A link did exist, a human one, in the person of Nevlin. The secretary could certainly have supplied, in part, the evidence that death had sealed on Aldriff's lips. Where Aldriff would have had to tell it to save his own hide, the case was just the opposite with Nevlin. If bribed by Dulther and Sigby, Nevlin would regard it profitable to keep silent.

Even more, Nevlin could be regarded as an actual factor in crime. On the night of Aldriff's death, the secretary had acted like a man who was seeing something through. An actor playing a part in the presence of two very important critics: Dulther and Sigby. Such was Nevlin, and he'd been begging for an out, when he had found one.

He'd used Joan and her gun as a pretext to top the build-up he'd begun by expressing fear of Kelburn. To square himself with the police, he had telephoned them later. That call could also have been for the benefit of Dulther and Sigby, letting them know that Nevlin was going to stay away, so he wouldn't have to talk.

But Nevlin, though he didn't know it, was merely postponing talking time.

He was due for an immediate meeting with a personage who dealt in chills that froze crooks entirely, except for their tongues. Nevlin was receiving a visit from The Shadow.

Like filtering smoke, the black-cloaked ghost reached the second floor and checked the numbering of the rooms, to have such information when he reached the third. Continuing another flight, The Shadow stopped halfway along a corridor and merged with a doorway bearing the number 308.

Light showed from the cracks around the door. It increased as The Shadow gave the knob a silent turn, for the door proved to be unlocked. The fact was hardly a surprise, if Nevlin's fears of Kelburn were interpreted as a sham. The open door indicated that Nevlin feared no one; and it might also mean that he was expecting a visitor.

Very well, he would have a visitor.

With a single motion, The Shadow swung the door half open, using his left hand to push it to the right. With a complete twist, he was full about, a gun pointing from his right fist, while he closed the door behind him with his left.

It was the sort of entry that should have left a witness baffled, for it gave the effect that The Shadow had appeared right through the closed door.

The illusion was lost on Nevlin, the only person in the room. Nevlin wasn't looking at the door; he was staring at the ceiling. But if The Shadow had materialized through ceiling, instead of the door, Nevlin wouldn't have appreciated it.

Nevlin was lying dead.

SOMEONE had planted a towel-wrapped gun against Nevlin's chest and let him have a bullet squarely through the heart. The towel was lying beside the body, and it bore the marks of powder burns, along with the name: "Hotel Montview."

Guns didn't make an over amount of noise when wrapped in towels, and considering the rattle-bang of trucks that could be heard from the street below, it was probable that a murderer had timed his shot to a moment when the outside noise was heavy.

Nevlin's shirtfront was splotched with blood, and the way his coat lay open indicated that whoever killed him had gone through his pockets.

Searching through those same pockets, The Shadow found money, keys, and fountain pen, but nothing in the way of papers or similar data, until he thought of something that might well have been overlooked.

In folding back Nevlin's coat, to run through vest pockets and turn them inside out, a previous searcher had laid Nevlin's breast pocket away from sight. On the outside left, such a pocket usually contained nothing more important than a handkerchief; but some people had the habit of tucking odds and ends into it. Nevlin, it seemed, had such a habit.

Probing deep in the one pocket that had been missed, The Shadow's fingers came upon a folded bit of cardboard and fished it out. It was a business card, which read:

WILSTEAD & CO.
WHOLESALE ART DEALERS

Slipping the card beneath his cloak, The Shadow dipped it into Cranston's breast pocket and arose. He had noted that Nevlin's body was still warm; but for the passing trucks, The Shadow might have heard the death-shot. If a murderer happened to be about, The Shadow was quite willing to meet him.

Like the keen eyes beneath the slouch hat, The Shadow's .45 was searching hopefully for some living person who would answer in place of the dead man, Nevlin.

Incriminating circumstances never deterred The Shadow. Many investigators, finding themselves in a room with a murder victim, would have been eager to clear out before considering the next course. The Shadow's policy was precisely the opposite.

If he could coax a murderer back to the scene of crime, so much the better. The thing could be done, if the killer hadn't gotten too far away.

The Shadow let his silhouette pause momentarily upon the lowered window shade. He returned to the door, turned its knob with just the slightest *click*, enough to whet a listener's curiosity.

There were side doors in the room, opening to adjacent bedrooms. The Shadow approached one, then the other, trying each. Both were locked on the other sides, but The Shadow gave the knobs trifling turns.

He was back again to the first connecting door, listening intently. He sensed a slight stir beyond it, but the sound was deceptive and could have come from another source. Having given the second door time to bear fruit, The Shadow returned to it and heard a sound there. This sound was definitely from the next room.

The Shadow made sounds himself as he crossed the room again, to give a listener the impression that he was going away. A pause, on The Shadow's part, as he heard a creeping sound again; for the noise proved that he was right the first time. It was beyond the door where The Shadow had originally heard it!

OUT into the hallway, The Shadow stayed blended with the gloom of the poorly lighted corridor. His ears were detecting very evasive creaks. Someone was sneaking from the room to the right of Nevlin's, toward another corridor.

Moving toward a corner, The Shadow heard what seemed an echo: footsteps past a corner in the opposite direction.

The old hotel was full of creaks, but these were not mere fancy. Keeping midway in his own corridor, The Shadow thought he heard the sounds merge. He was moving after them when he heard the two again, and one set of stealthy footfalls was coming toward Nevlin's room. They ended in the corridor itself, as The Shadow swung back around the corner.

They might have gone into Nevlin's room, those footsteps. If so, their owner would be keeping a sharp eye on the door. So The Shadow chose the room on the near side of Nevlin's. Finding it unlocked, he entered and reached the connecting door.

There wasn't a sound from Nevlin's room, but The Shadow was sure that he was on a proper trail, and intended to stick with it, rather than be misled by imaginary creepings elsewhere.

He turned the bolt lock of the connecting door. It was locked on this side only, giving The Shadow access into Nevlin's room. First, The Shadow worked the door in inching fashion, so slightly that no one could have spotted its motion.

Through the tiniest of cracks, The Shadow viewed Nevlin's room. What he saw of it was empty; but he couldn't spy Nevlin's body. It lay between this door and the one that connected with the room opposite.

A vague *click* sounded. Someone was evidently copying The Shadow's own tactics, the sort he had used earlier, baiting him with the opposite door. The Shadow let the trick continue until he was sure that the other door was open partway.

The idea was plain. The man opposite had opened his door far enough to get a view of The Shadow's. He expected The Shadow to try a cautious peek, that would lay him open to damage. Whoever came out the winner in this grim version of peek-a-boo would hold the advantage, if it came to a gun duel.

The proper system was to change the game. Nevlin's room offered plenty of scope for a fighter who could shift and fade out, as The Shadow did. The thing was to get into Nevlin's room before the other man expected such a thrust—and The Shadow was a swift hand at that practice.

He took his crosswise hold upon the door, gave a lunge and whirled into the room itself.

It was the same trick turnabout that had brought The Shadow upon Nevlin's body; but this time, the cloaked master was working it on a living man. The Shadow did not stop as he swung the door shut behind him.

Instead, he carried his spin between Nevlin's body and the window, as though intending to wind up behind the opposite door when it came wide.

The door shot open in a hurry. The Shadow's adversary wasn't going to be fooled by such a scheme. Instead, he was fooled by another. Reversing in his tracks, The Shadow looked straight across Nevlin's body, toward the other door. The man driving from it had slammed the door so hard that it smacked the wall, proving that The Shadow wasn't there.

With a leap toward the center of the room, he turned, gazing across Nevlin's body, too. He stopped right where he was.

Eye to eye, gun to gun, The Shadow and his opponent stood with death between them. Death in the form of Nevlin's body, which presided over the singular scene.

A casual witness would have supposed that The Shadow and his challenger were about to dispute the past, not the future. Each or either could have been Nevlin's killer, and both looked as though they were here to advance the claim.

In a sense, the past did concern The Shadow, along with the future. From the moment that he began to match wits with a single prowler, he had weighed the chances as to which man would defy him: Dulther or Sigby. He had gone so far as to attribute Nevlin's death to one or the other, on the grounds that they were fellow conspirators.

But The Shadow was not prepared to meet the man who did confront him; at least, he had not calculated on a meeting such as this. In one brief instant, The Shadow found his past conclusions tumbling into dust, along with all the purposes toward which he had been working.

The man whose glare promised death, if he could give it, was the very man whose cause The Shadow had adopted: Smead Kelburn!

CHAPTER X
THE SHADOW'S CHOICE

IF a cameraman had been present to snap Kelburn's portrait, the picture would have been as perfect an exhibit as the photograph of Aldriff's death room. If ever a man wore a vicious gloat, it was Smead Kelburn. His face was an excellent study of satisfied hate.

Kelburn was pleased by the sight of Nevlin's dead form. Whatever Kelburn's motives, Nevlin had injured them, and deserved all that anyone might give him.

Kelburn's broad face wore a turned-down smile that had been intense, at first, but was losing some of its gloat regarding Nevlin. The leer, as Kelburn renewed it, was all meant for The Shadow.

He'd heard from Joan, Kelburn had, and for reasons of his own he had chosen not to trust the friendship offered by The Shadow. Perhaps Joan had asked the reasons for his apprehensions, and he had promised to supply them. Certainly, Kelburn could not have produced anything more satisfying than this scene between himself and The Shadow.

It could be taken or left, as anyone preferred. Kelburn could be Nevlin's murderer, tricked into betraying himself by The Shadow, who had promised to aid him. Or, for those who liked to be different, this scene could represent The Shadow as the killer, trying to pin the blame on Kelburn.

Such niceties made little difference. Kelburn had satisfied himself that his feud lay with The Shadow, and his glare was the signal for duel. Giving his gun a jerk, Kelburn showed himself as quick-triggered as Joan by stabbing the opening shot. His bullet found blackness.

The blackness crashed. It was the pane of Nevlin's window. Kelburn had forgotten that the Shadow was poised at the finish of his lunge, whereas Kelburn had turned and stopped flat-footed. The Shadow had simply wheeled toward Kelburn's doorway, the direction in which Kelburn couldn't swing without tripping over his own crossed ankles.

The stocky man made an awkward shift; as he did, his snarl was drowned by The Shadow's sinister laugh. In his skillful cut-back style, The Shadow was springing upon Kelburn to take his gun away from him.

If Kelburn wouldn't yield it, The Shadow had an implement that would help. His own gun was poised for a blow to Kelburn's head; a light one, of course. The Shadow wanted to make Kelburn talk, since Aldriff and Nevlin could no longer do so.

Kelburn tried to talk with his gun, and managed it, though the revolver barks were no worse than a dog's. The Shadow was gripping Kelburn's wrist as the man's stubby finger worked on the gun trigger. Kelburn planted a bullet into the wall, another into the ceiling. Then, frantically, he swung his hand across his ducking head to ward off The Shadow's swing.

It was The Shadow's effort at restraining that produced a break for Kelburn. The stocky man stumbled as he warded, and The Shadow let him go, but kept right after him. He wanted Kelburn to receive the gun stroke while his head was moving away from it, which was quite as good as a buffer, in easing a strong swing.

But Kelburn ended his stumble by tripping, long and hard, carrying The Shadow with him.

Nevlin's body was in the way. Even in death, the scheming secretary was mixing into matters that didn't properly concern him. His dead form seemed to roll in laughter as it sent two figures plunging toward the window.

However, Nevlin was no longer consistent in his meddling. This time, he favored Kelburn, the man he had hitherto bothered.

In the sprawl, Kelburn managed to wrench free of The Shadow and leap toward an open door. The Shadow was coming up behind him, looming after him, actually picking the spot where he could down his adversary.

For Kelburn, in his clumsy style, showed too apparently that he was intending to swing about and try another stab at the cloaked target that he couldn't hit.

The second break came then.

IT was the tone of a police siren from the street below the hotel. As if actuated by Kelburn's futile shots, the siren screeched an admonition.

The vibration of that wail actually jarred Kelburn onward. Instead of turning, he increased his heavy lunge toward the doorway and was through it, as The Shadow, already on the leap, found space where Kelburn should have been.

Bringing up against the wall, The Shadow wheeled about and took after Kelburn. Always, the stocky man was just barely out of sight. Around a corner of the corridor; down one flight of stairs; then the next.

As Kelburn reached the lobby, the clerk and the elevator man came running up to stop him. Brandishing his gun, Kelburn sent one diving behind the desk, the other into the elevator.

Kelburn didn't fire. He needed what shots he had left. Charging through the side exit, he reached the street, where he was spotted in the lights of a police car.

Banging out wild shots, Kelburn turned and dashed into an alley. While the officers were springing from their car, The Shadow rounded the corner and sped after the stocky fugitive.

Going through the alley, The Shadow did some necessary weaving from one wall to the other. The police were doing all the shooting, and he had to avoid their path of fire.

Up ahead, Kelburn seemed to be outracing bullets, though actually, the officers were simply spoiling their own aim by firing while on the run. The Shadow had to stop at a corner to let them go by; then he took up the chase behind them.

In his skillful style, The Shadow was springing upon Kilburn to take his gun away from him.

A block farther on, Kelburn heard new sirens and the shrill blasts of police whistles. He was running right into a trap. The vicinity was filling with police, who would soon cut off his flight.

Seeing a taxicab, Kelburn sprang into it and tried the tactics that he had worked at Aldriff's. He shoved his gun at the driver and snarled for him to get going.

There wasn't any driver, though Kelburn had seen one when he'd jumped aboard. He'd made a bad mistake in choosing that cab. It was The Shadow's, and its driver, Moe Shrevnitz, was too quick-witted to fall for bandit tactics. He'd gone out the front door while Kelburn was springing in the back.

Nor could Kelburn find Moe when he looked for him. The wiry cabby had rolled right under the running board and was calmly roosting beneath the cab itself. No chance of Kelburn starting it and running over Moe. Moe had the ignition key in his pocket.

Kelburn sprang out through the opposite door and ran around the back of the cab. By then, the police were looking for him the way he had for Moe. They'd gone ahead of the cab, to flay it with bullets when it started. But the lights didn't even come on, and when they reached the cab, they stared blankly, finding it had neither driver nor passenger.

They suddenly spied Kelburn running the other way, and went after him again, only to see him turn a corner with a peculiar, sliding plunge. Kelburn was shying away from something that the officers could not see.

In fact, Kelburn did not see it himself; he heard it, the throb of a mocking laugh from darkness just across the street.

The Shadow was blocking off Kelburn, forcing him to turn a corner, where The Shadow could cut in and overtake him. The duel was about to end in Kelburn's capture.

A strange duel, this. Throughout it, The Shadow had not fired a single shot, while Kelburn had wasted all the slugs in his revolver. It put everything in The Shadow's hands, for he had the loaded gun and Kelburn the empty.

All that The Shadow regretted was the intervention of the police; if he could throw them off the trail, he would shape Kelburn's destiny to his own liking.

There was a short arcade along the side street; The Shadow had noted it while on the way to Nevlin's hotel. He saw that he could overtake Kelburn and veer the stocky man into the arcade before the police reached the corner. It would be difficult to do a disappearing act with Kelburn as a handicap, but that loaded gun would be an argument toward Kelburn's cooperation.

As The Shadow swung across the street to make the interception, headlights bore down upon him. They couldn't mean a police car, for they weren't accompanied by a siren, nor were guns pegging away. But the car's purpose was deadly enough.

A sudden veer of the lights told The Shadow that they were meant for him, and the whole bulk of the car with them. He halted, made a backward leap, throwing himself full around. Even at that, the car would have struck him with its fender, if the driver hadn't shown a final ounce of pity and swayed away from him.

At least, it had cut The Shadow off from Kelburn. But the driver didn't let the stocky man continue his puffing run. Overtaking Kelburn, the car climbed the curb beside him and a girl's voice called for the man to hop in and take the wheel.

Dropping out on her side, the girl waved Kelburn away, calling that she'd be all right.

THE girl was Joan, and Kelburn took her at her word. He sped the car from the curb, and was off for the next corner. He narrowly missed another car that was pulling out from a parking space, and it swung the corner after him.

Sirens were howling from half a dozen directions, but not from the one that Kelburn had taken. Speeding madly away, he wasn't worrying about chance pursuers. He was sure that he could shake off all except those police cars that shrieked the maddening message for others to join in the chase. At least, Kelburn was free of them.

He was free of The Shadow, too. For Joan was making good on her promise. She'd swung about, gun in hand, looking for the black-cloaked avenger. She was the Joan of an earlier evening—a determined girl ready to meet all opposition, even that of The Shadow. Her eyes had a blaze; she seemed anxious to pull the gun trigger.

Her opportunity was at hand.

Almost beside her, Joan saw The Shadow. He had cloaked his gun and was driving in, hands ahead of him, to deprive Joan of her revolver before she could fire it.

Joan's shift was not clumsy, like Kelburn's. It was a quick dancing step, worthy of admiration despite the reason behind it. Joan's lips voiced a warning; when The Shadow did not heed it, she thrust the gun right at him.

Split seconds to go and they were all in Joan's favor. At that late moment, The Shadow might have changed his lunge into a dive and escaped the first shot, though he would have been sure game for the next, had Joan chosen to follow it up.

But The Shadow did not falter. Even when Joan's lips promised death, in a tone of full conviction, The Shadow kept on coming.

HARRY VINCENT

By Joan's own ethics, she had the right to fire. The Shadow had tricked Kelburn, was on the way to capture him, when Joan intervened. But the same strange impulse that had caused Joan to swerve the car from the victim in its path took hold of her again. It was a paralyzing impulse. It wouldn't let her finger budge.

An instant later, Joan was off her feet. Swept by The Shadow's drive, she was half smothered in the folds of his black cloak. She struggled as he swung her across the sidewalk. She still had the gun, but her finger wouldn't act, so she tried to swing the weapon. The Shadow's hand caught it, took the gun as though it were a toy belonging to a naughty child.

Joan's defiance had reduced itself to angry chokes when The Shadow rushed her through the arcade. Arriving police saw them go, a curious medley of blackness.

Reaching the arcade, the patrolmen called for the fugitives to stop, and getting no response, began to shoot. The sounds of gunfire echoed along the narrow rear alley where The Shadow had turned with Joan.

Moe was back in his cab when they reached it. The Shadow rolled Joan into the rear seat and joined her. Police, coming back, saw a supposedly driverless cab off on a mad race.

There weren't any police cars around when Moe cut past the next corner. Those cars had all converged at the Hotel Montview in response to lusty shouts from the hotel personnel, who were screaming murder all along the block.

For the first time in her series of misadventures, Joan Kelburn was sobbing, and she thought that anger was the cause. She had lost her nerve in the pinch. Her pride was hurt because The Shadow had so easily overwhelmed her after she had given him the chance. She hated The Shadow, so she thought, until she heard his whispered laugh beside her.

It carried no taunt. Rather, it was full of understanding that impressed Joan more than words. Very suddenly, she realized the true reason for her sobs. She was actually expressing the gratitude that she had promised to show The Shadow when she met him again. She really trusted him; and that trust was even greater than her loyalty toward her uncle.

Her first meeting with The Shadow had taught Joan things she hadn't fully appreciated until the test came. He hadn't judged her, nor her uncle, by the fact that circumstances were all against them. His was the true fortitude, the ability to keep anger from controlling action whenever occasion called. Joan had captured that attitude, and The Shadow recognized it.

That was why he had rushed the gun, knowing that the girl would never fire it. When The Shadow sealed a friendship, it was permanent. Hence Joan had known, despite the things she saw, that The Shadow was still on her side and on Kelburn's, too, provided that he actually deserved it.

As Joan's eyes met The Shadow's, their burn seemed to melt the mist that dimmed her own. The girl was seeing many things, more clearly than ever before.

Again Joan heard The Shadow's whispered laugh.

CHAPTER XI
THE MANHUNT

COMMISSIONER WESTON was talking in terms of all-out effort. A murderer was at large, a desperate murderer named Smead Kelburn, who was proving himself the swindler that he was, by following up his frauds with larger crime.

Weston was telling all this to his friend Lamont Cranston, at the Cobalt Club.

"From what you say, Commissioner," declared Cranston, "it rather amazes me that Kelburn didn't murder Aldriff."

Inspector Cardona, hearing that comment, started to say something, and stopped. He was remembering that Kelburn had something of an alibi at the time of Aldriff's suicide. It made him wonder just how Kelburn stood in the matter of Nevlin's death.

"No doubt Kelburn wanted to murder Aldriff," snorted Weston. "He was too late, that was all. He came to Aldriff's house masked, and with intent to kill."

"Odd that he didn't manage to kill Nevlin then," observed Cranston. "He had a perfect opportunity. It seems to me you're building something of an alibi for Kelburn, Commissioner."

Cardona considered Cranston's statement a smart one, but Weston didn't. Emphatically, the commissioner tried to show Cranston where he was wrong.

"Nevlin feared Kelburn," Weston said. "So much, that tonight, Nevlin called us again and said that Kelburn was on the way to the Montview Hotel, to kill him. So we started there, but arrived too late to prevent the murder."

"And you found Kelburn's gun?"

"No. We found Nevlin's. Kelburn murdered him with it, which shows how cunning he is."

Slowly, Cranston shook his head.

"Very odd, Commissioner," he said. "Nevlin knew that Kelburn was coming to kill him. Nevlin had a gun to protect himself. So when Kelburn arrived, Nevlin supplied him with the gun and let him go ahead with murder."

Cardona was grinning behind Weston's back, while the commissioner fumed in various ways. Weston resorted to the fact that Kelburn had fled from the hotel shortly after Nevlin's death, which proved that Kelburn had certainly been there. But Cranston remarked that the thing still didn't settle the riddle of the gun.

When Weston declared that the murder had been deliberate, done with a gun wrapped in a towel, Cranston promptly added the point to his own arguments.

"Perhaps Nevlin had the gun all wrapped," remarked Cranston. "If so, his intent was to murder Kelburn. Nevlin's call to you, Commissioner, could really have been a build-up for a claim for self-defense. But the circumstances prove that Kelburn, not Nevlin, was the man who had to save himself."

"Next thing, Cranston, you'll be claiming that Nevlin invited Kelburn over to the hotel!"

"He probably did," asserted Cranston. "It would have been easier for Nevlin to learn where Kelburn was, and contact him, rather than the other way about. Nevlin didn't have to keep hidden continually. You weren't searching for him as thoroughly as you were for Kelburn."

Cranston's final comment reminded Weston of something very important. The commissioner swung glaringly toward Cardona and stormed:

"I'm giving you just twenty-four hours to find Kelburn, Inspector. If your famous hunches don't help you within that time, I'll order a general manhunt, and you won't be in charge of it! I'm tired of your dilly-dally tactics!"

MARGO LANE

Apparently, Cranston's arguments had not convinced Weston on the chief point at issue: that there was no real proof that Kelburn had murdered Nevlin. Even The Shadow's own meeting with Kelburn did not incriminate the hunted man, for the meeting had occurred after Nevlin's death.

In a sense, Weston was challenging The Shadow along with Cardona, for the twenty-four-hour leeway before the manhunt began gave both of them the task of locating Kelburn within a given time limit.

"You won't learn anything from Kelburn's niece," said Weston to Cardona. "I phoned her right after Nevlin's death. She was home and in bed. I had a patrol car stop to make certain. She couldn't have been at Nevlin's and returned to her own apartment so soon."

HOME in her apartment, Joan was seated at the living room window, looking out. She felt breathless when she recalled her quick trip back. Commissioner Weston hadn't allowed for the remarkable speed that Moe, The Shadow's cabby, could show in Manhattan traffic.

When the cab dropped Joan at the apartment house, The Shadow warned the girl to expect an official phone call and a visit from a patrol car.

Joan had just reached her apartment when the phone bell rang. She'd faked a sleepy voice when telling the commissioner that she had been awakened by the call. From her darkened window, she saw the patrol car stop, and she'd made a mad scramble in getting undressed and into bed.

Fortunately, the patrolmen didn't ring; they

came upstairs to hammer on Joan's door, and the few extra minutes had enabled her to win the race.

Rolling in one side of bed and out the other, Joan had put on dressing gown and slippers and answered the door, to say, quite sweetly, that she'd just finished a telephone chat with the police commissioner himself.

The apologetic cops had left, but Joan hadn't returned to bed. She wasn't sleepy, and wouldn't be until she'd unburdened herself of facts that she had not had time to tell The Shadow. In parting, he had said that she could tell them to Cranston later.

At last, the awaited phone call came. Answering it, Joan tried to pour out a dozen statements in one breath. Interrupting, Cranston told her to get dressed; that he would come for her in his car.

Joan was just about ready when she saw the limousine stop out front. She went downstairs to meet it.

Margo Lane was with Cranston, and he introduced her to Joan, who was all apologies because of her hasty action earlier. They rode to a quiet little cafe, where, in an isolated booth, Joan poured out her entire story—which was something of a confession.

She had heard from her uncle the night before, and he had told her where to reach him, but only on condition that she would inform no one. Torn between two promises, she had simply hoped that she could convince him of Cranston's friendship.

"I did come back to the apartment, intending to call my uncle," affirmed Joan. "But before I got around to it, I received a call from someone else. From Nevlin."

The news astonished Margo, but Cranston received it without a change of his expression.

"Nevlin said he had to see Uncle Smead," declared Joan. "He told me where he was stopping, and the room number. I called my uncle, and he was eager to go over. He said that Nevlin must have come to his senses at last.

"So I called Nevlin and told him. And then"—Joan frowned—"well, I realized I'd been very one-sided. Since I hadn't told you that I'd heard from my uncle, I should certainly have let you know first, Mr. Cranston, when I had that call from Nevlin.

"It was worrying me. I was beginning to see that it could be a trap. When I phoned the cafe and Miss Lane answered, I was afraid that something else might have happened. So I hurried straight to the garage where my uncle kept his car, and drove for the Hotel Montview."

Joan's testimony was the very sort that Cranston wanted. It would prove strong stuff in combination with The Shadow's analysis discounting the circumstantial evidence that marked Kelburn as Nevlin's murderer.

"I'm sure my uncle didn't murder Nevlin," added Joan. "If he killed him, it would only have been in self-defense. You must know that, Mr. Cranston."

"At least it proves that Nevlin didn't fear your uncle," acknowledged Cranston, "and that is an important item. Which brings us to another point: who, then, would have murdered Nevlin, since he had no one to fear?"

Names were on Joan's lips, but she withheld them. It was all reverting to the original enigma: the question of Aldriff's death. Suicide which, by the inside facts, should have been murder.

Joan was overwhelmed by the burden of the thing. Men who could so completely cover crime in Aldriff's case would certainly have covered themselves in Nevlin's case, even though they were letting the secretary's death pass as murder.

The Shadow, however, was thinking of a different fundamental, when he said in Cranston's quiet tone:

"We are back to our first question, Joan. Where, and when, can I find your uncle and talk to him personally?"

"I'll tell you where to find him," blurted Joan. "And you can reach him anytime. What's more, I won't let him know that I told you. He wouldn't be where he is, if I hadn't helped him out this evening. From now on, I'm running the affairs of my family!" Joan hesitated, then smiled: "Or rather, you are, Mr. Cranston."

She wrote the address on a slip of paper and handed it to Cranston, who placed it in his breast pocket. As he poked the paper deep, his fingers struck the folded card that he had found in Nevlin's same pocket.

There was a reason for the faint smile that showed on Cranston's lips—a reason that neither Joan nor Margo recognized. It was known only to Lamont Cranston and to his other self:

The Shadow.

CHAPTER XII
MEN IN THE DARK

EARLY the next evening, Cranston's limousine rambled leisurely along a side street of Manhattan, as though it had caught the idling habit from its calm-mannered owner.

Deep in the cushions of the big car, two passengers were noting the scenery that this area offered. They were particularly interested in brownstone houses.

Cranston, of course, was one passenger, and Joan was the other. They checked on the basement of a closed house, noting the very heavy boarding on all the windows, from basement to top floor.

The basement level was only a few feet below the sidewalk; the door into the basement opened at the side of the high steps in front of the house.

The door below the steps was the only way of

getting into the house. Joan knew, because her uncle had told her. Besides, she was acquainted with that house. It actually belonged to her uncle; he had acquired it in a stock deal from a friend who was lately deceased, but he had not yet registered the deed.

"Don't misunderstand me, Mr. Cranston," Joan pleaded, as they rounded the corner past the house. "There was nothing shady in the deal, and my uncle's friend died a natural death."

She couldn't see Cranston's face in the gloom of the car, but Joan was quite sure that he would understand. Only momentarily had she feared that Cranston was catching the common fever of prejudice against Smead Kelburn. Always, common sense restored Joan's confidence.

If Cranston did doubt Kelburn, he had only to inform Commissioner Weston and be thanked for bringing a wanted criminal into the hands of the law. So far, Cranston had not turned Kelburn over.

"The basement is really separate from the house," explained Joan, as they continued around the block. "The man who owned it used to keep his valuables down there, and he made it like a fortress, even walling off the stairway up to the first floor. There is no back way into the basement, Mr. Cranston."

Cranston's own observation confirmed Joan's statement. Through a space between houses in the next street, he could see the rear of Kelburn's hide-out. Unlike a house adjacent to it, the closed brownstone had no door on the basement level; not even a boarded barrier. Joan felt quite pleased to see her statement proven by the visible evidence.

She was a bit perturbed, however, when Cranston put a direct query:

"You are quite sure that your uncle did not leave the house late this afternoon?"

"I'm positive!" voiced Joan. "You see, I phoned him there. I mentioned that fact before, Mr. Cranston."

"But he may have left later."

"I don't think so. Because—"

The tenseness in Joan's voice reached a more than noticeable pitch in the word "because." Recognizing the fact, the girl clipped her sentence short. Cranston picked it up with the very word that Joan had used to drop it.

"Because you came by here this afternoon," declared Cranston, very steadily. "Against my advice."

Guiltily, Joan nodded, but she caught a glimpse of Cranston's face as they were crossing a lighted corner. It didn't seem to carry accusation, so Joan asked rather timidly:

"How did you find out?"

"From The Shadow," Cranston responded. "You used his cab when you toured this neighborhood."

JOAN could hear her own gasp of surprise. She should have remembered about The Shadow's cab. Not having noted its driver's face, she couldn't have identified it by him. But she was sure that she had ridden in a dark blue cab the night before, while the one parked at the hack stand outside her apartment, this afternoon, was painted a deep maroon.

It didn't occur to her that the color, itself, was deceptive. Dark-red cabs were rather conspicuous, and The Shadow wouldn't have chosen such a hue but for its special merit.

Moe's cab was the sort that could be spotted along toward dusk, only to undergo a self-transformation as darkness deepened. Maroon, a combination of red and purple, favored the former shade in sunlight; the latter under artificial illumination.

A useful feature when The Shadow took up a late afternoon trail, the time when crooks were apt to move. Conversely, it helped when The Shadow was shaking off followers, who might have noted a strange disappearance of Lamont Cranston at the all-important hour when daytime merged with nightfall.

In a mere swing past a corner, Moe's cab had been known to disguise itself so completely that the keenest of eyes had supposed it to be a different vehicle.

It wasn't the cab, however, that concerned Joan's present reflections. She was thinking of the driver. If his report had been an accurate one, it must have included the fact that Joan had not betrayed her visit to the block of brownstone houses. Joan spoke frankly, when she said:

"I didn't stop at the house, Mr. Cranston. I just rode by a few times, to make sure my uncle didn't leave. If he had mistrusted my call, he would have packed and left quite promptly. Not seeing him come out, I am quite sure that he is still there."

"And are you sure of something else?"

"I don't know," responded Joan slowly. "Those men across from the house might not have been watching it, even though they did slide from sight very suddenly."

Her statement was finished before Joan realized that she hadn't mentioned the men in the first place. She had simply picked up the reference to "something else." She couldn't have given any better proof of her sincerity than through that statement. Cranston had evidently been informed about the men in question.

"I didn't see them this evening," added Joan. "If I had, I would have mentioned it. Really!"

The limousine was rolling back through the brownstone block, and Joan could see no sign of any lurkers during this final inspection trip.

Cranston's eyes were keener. They sighted hunched shapes in the shelter of steps; sidling figures at a narrow passage between buildings, at an angle across the street from Kelburn's hideout.

Near the extremity of the block, certain of those vague forms seemed to signal. Joan didn't see them; she would have been puzzled if she had. The girl had no idea that The Shadow utilized secret agents other than Moe; men who were apt to be patrolling the fringe of this area. Even had she guessed it, Joan wouldn't have expected to see such agents signaling to Cranston that all was well.

To Joan, Lamont Cranston was simply a man who didn't let one friendship interfere with another. He already knew both The Shadow and Commissioner Weston, and wanted to diversify the list further by adding Smead Kelburn.

But he was evidently leaving the initial introduction to The Shadow, for when the car arrived at Margo's apartment, Cranston ushered Joan inside, then announced that he must keep an appointment with Commissioner Weston.

ACTUALLY, Cranston was leaving the Kelburn business to The Shadow, but in so doing, he was postponing his meeting with Weston.

A few blocks away, the limousine paused beside a cab that could have passed for dark-blue, or near black, but which was actually a self-effaced deep red. Transferring to Moe's cab, Cranston rode back to the brownstone area.

He was The Shadow when he emerged from the cab outside the cordon set by his agents. He tested the cordon by gliding through it unseen; then gave blinks with a flashlight so tiny that it made only a speck of light. The glimmer was green, and it brought the agents trailing along behind The Shadow.

Soon the spot blinked yellow, a signal for them to slacken their approach. When the dot showed red, The Shadow had marked the limit of their advance. They were to stay as they were, unless emergency summoned them. The Shadow depended on their judgment in such cases.

This promised to be one of those cases.

As The Shadow merged with the brownstone steps of the old closed house, he detected motion across the street, much like the sort that he had earlier observed. Motion from huddled shapes that didn't belong to The Shadow's crew. In fact, The Shadow's agents had not spotted the lurkers in question, which indicated that they must be a very crafty crowd.

This unidentified tribe had picked a very close location. Their watch on Kelburn's house might be with the special purpose of spotting The Shadow, should he approach the hideout. Considering Kelburn's mistrust of Joan's new-found friends, the hunted man might have hired these watchers.

The door beneath the brownstone steps was locked, and strongly so. The Shadow probed the dock with a special pick much like a pair of long-tipped tweezers. He paused when he heard sneaky footsteps on the sidewalk.

They didn't come past the brownstone steps, however. The Shadow heard them recede gradually, and doubted that his agents had spotted the furtive visitor from across the street.

One man might have made that trip unnoticed, but The Shadow questioned that the fellow could summon others without the agents spying them. The Shadow had tightened his own cordon just to give the agents such a chance.

Working anew on the lock, The Shadow paused at timely intervals, but it wasn't until the job was done that he heard the footfalls again.

Someone was actually crawling up the brownstone steps to peer down at the space beneath. Instead of waiting where he was, The Shadow opened the door and eased through.

As he squeezed the door shut behind him, he heard something *plop* in the cement space just outside. Hand on the knob, The Shadow held the door pressed shut and listened.

Nothing occurred. Evidently the prowler was satisfied to remain crouched in the snug nest that The Shadow had abandoned. The Shadow left the door unlocked. Rather than reveal himself by slight clicks with the pick, he preferred to keep the door available for a surprise exit.

The door still required careful handling, however. Unlocked, it was looser than before, for the latch was not a heavy one. So The Shadow let the door come back very slowly in its frame, a matter of perhaps a quarter inch.

Flashlight flicking cautiously from his cloak, The Shadow probed the basement, to find it quite the fortress that Joan had mentioned. It even had an inner citadel in the form of a strong-doored storeroom, which The Shadow marked as Kelburn's headquarters for several reasons.

Kelburn was nowhere else about; the storeroom was compact; finally, a telephone cord ran beneath the metal-faced door, proving that the inner stronghold was the place where Kelburn received his calls.

This discovery called for a return trip outdoors. By phoning Margo's apartment, The Shadow could obtain Joan's cooperation. The right kind of a call, from Joan to her uncle, would lure Kelburn into the outer basement, at least.

There, closets, alcoves, old pieces of furniture, afforded the very lurking spots from which The Shadow could so capably emerge and trap Kelburn, to make him listen to the words of someone willing to be his friend.

It was well that The Shadow resolved to communicate with Joan. Moving back through darkness, he was turning a corner toward the outer door when the faint rustle of his own cloak gave him warning. His gloved hands, his face shrouded in the upraised cloak collar, did not sense the breeze that had made the cloak folds *swish*.

The token marked the closing of the very door that The Shadow had entered. It was shutting behind intruders who were hoping to outdo The Shadow with their stealth.

Men who by their very measures identified themselves as foemen seeking a quick, decisive duel with the crimemaster cloaked in black!

CHAPTER XIII
THE SHADOW'S PRISONER

HERE was a real dilemma for The Shadow. To deal with men in the dark was easy, but not under circumstances with the present angles. Whoever these foemen were, they knew that The Shadow was the lurker in the basement, for only he could have done such tricks with the lock on the outer door.

The man who had dropped down beside the steps must have felt the door edge and found it farther depressed than on a previous inspection. Therewith, he had summoned his companions from across the street, that they might trap The Shadow. Forewarned, this crew would be dangerous.

Completing the dilemma was the fact that The Shadow did not seek battle on these premises, because strife would spoil his plans concerning Kelburn. Sometimes, however, a dilemma could prove its own solution, and The Shadow suddenly decided that it might answer the present problem.

He was struck by the thought as he sidled noiselessly across the front portion of the basement, guiding by telltale creeps that had begun to come from the direction of the door.

If these men were watching the house in behalf of Kelburn, they would not want battle, either!

Any strife, other than a silent struggle, would give away the hideout, spoiling it for Kelburn in the future. Indeed, by their creeping tactics the prowlers must be holding Kelburn's welfare in mind, for they were spreading, trying to work farther into the basement, thus blocking The Shadow off.

In his turn, The Shadow was actually weaving in between the gropers, playing the very game that they would not expect. He wasn't going to start the combat; instead, he planned to leave them an empty battleground, where they could worry for themselves. Maybe they would decide that The Shadow had not entered the place at all.

There was only one tough angle to the job. Nearing the door, The Shadow found a guard there. He could have touched the fellow in the darkness; instead, The Shadow gripped the door itself. He performed the very action that he had earlier avoided, when he moved the door sharply, enough to bring a grate from its hinges.

The door reached the guard's shoulder, and he sprang about, alarmed. His hands were busy, both at once, aiming a gun and pressing the switch of a flashlight. He flashed the light behind the door, where he thought The Shadow was, and pushed his gun muzzle in the same direction. But there wasn't any Shadow.

Deftly, the cloaked master had wheeled away as he gave the door its swing. He was around behind the guard's back when the flashlight turned the other way. Out through the doorway itself, The Shadow was sheltered close beneath the brownstone steps, when snarling voices reached him from the doorway.

The leader of the prowling crew was bawling out the guard, telling him he ought to know that doors would move, if jostled. He made the fellow douse the flashlight and keep outside the doorway. The Shadow heard the guard emerge, while the leader stole back into the basement.

All would have been perfect, if the guard hadn't felt a touch of jitters. In the space beside the brownstone steps, he fidgeted; then gave a quick flash with his light. He didn't turn it toward The Shadow, who had cannily picked a spot almost behind the turning man. Instead, the fellow swung it toward the front of the brownstone steps.

Instantly, things happened. Another man, caught in the light, came lunging at the guard, while a second man sprang down from the top of the brownstone steps. Seeing the first attacker, the guard aimed his gun and pulled the trigger before the second man could intervene.

But the gunshot didn't hit. The Shadow was swifter than any. He caught the guard, whirled him about and sent his gun flying high in the air, after its useless bullet.

Those men that the guard had flushed were The Shadow's own agents. They'd seen the mob move from across the way and had closed their cordon tighter, to be ready at The Shadow's call!

FROM the darkness where the guarding crook was spinning, with his flashlight smashing as it hit the stone, the agents heard the laugh they knew: The Shadow's.

To them it was an order to follow their chief's immediate lead. To others who heard it, the mirth was a challenge, gaining power in its strident mockery as it pealed through the confines of the basement.

The Shadow wheeled from the entry when crooks began to shoot. They heard his gun respond, but it was away from the door, out toward the sidewalk. Thinking they had taken The Shadow by surprise, they charged, blasting as they poked their guns ahead of them, out through the door.

Though The Shadow could have clipped the fists that betrayed themselves by the glisten of their revolvers, he didn't. Again, his laugh receded; he was gone from the brownstone steps. His return shots meant that he was actually retreating across the street.

Guns rampant, the whole ugly crew surged out to find him, hoping to down him with massed fire.

They still hadn't guessed that The Shadow's purpose was to draw them from this area. Nor did they realize that he knew the ground from earlier observation. As they reached the sidewalk, mobsters heard The Shadow's laugh from an angle that they did not like. He was finding the passage between the buildings opposite, the very base that they had used earlier!

Therewith, the leader of the thuggish band gave an order that proved their own undoing. He yelled for his men to keep going while they fired.

Their shots were wild, as a result, and The Shadow was already swinging from the passage to greet them with steady shots. His fire seemed too deliberate, however, to halt the human tidal wave. Crooks were almost across the street, when they found how thoroughly they had been lured.

Other marksmen opened from the flanks, joining The Shadow's cause. Every flight of brownstone steps was a pillbox from which The Shadow's sharpshooting agents were getting in their fire. Between them, The Shadow and his aides could have annihilated the tribe they had trapped.

Instead, The Shadow was lenient; remarkably so. Not one of the enemy had hit the paving, though a few were staggering from minor wounds. The Shadow had given quick word to his agents to scatter them; nothing more. The whine of bullets, the ping of ricocheting shots, proved quite enough.

Crooks did scatter, off in every direction, fleeing like madmen, seeking cars in which they could ride away. After them came the hounding bursts of guns, accompanied by a sardonic laugh that rang its triumph wide and far. So far, that every fleeing thug thought The Shadow was after him, in person, whereas The Shadow's agents were doing all the shooting.

One lone foeman reached The Shadow. That man was the leader of the scattering mob. He didn't stop to wonder why The Shadow's shots had spared him. Coming upon the cloaked fighter, crime's leader made a quick shift as he saw The Shadow wheel the other way. Bloated lips bawled for gunners to "get The Shadow," and, with squinting eyes, the leader turned to see it happen.

It was then that a very surprised crook found he no longer had followers. Even worse, in shifting so that his absent gunners could down The Shadow, the crooked leader had put himself right in the path of The Shadow's changing whirl. Turning to jab a shot of his own, the thug's move ended like his snarl, as a sledging gun reached his skull.

STANDING above the prisoner he had taken, The Shadow listened to the roar of departing cars and the blare of police whistles. Soon, cars with sirens were roaring through this very street, throwing searchlights everywhere, even into the passage where The Shadow lurked. Those lights did not disclose The Shadow or his unconscious prisoner.

The Shadow had removed his cloak and covered his stunned captive with it. Close against the wall, motionless as a statue, The Shadow escaped passing observation, along with the cloak-covered mass that was huddled at his feet.

The running fight—if fight it could be called—had carried far from this brownstone neighborhood. Begun by The Shadow, furthered by his agents, it had developed into a chase so far afield, that police, attracted by the sound of gunfire, were unable to catch up with the pursuers, let alone the pursued.

Returning to seek the source of the trouble, those same police had failed to locate it. The commotion might have started in any one of half a dozen blocks, where brownstone houses frowned reprovingly at the uniformed men who threatened to disturb their lethargy of many decades.

Taking it to be a rivalry between two groups of hoodlums who had fled after a chance meeting, the police went their way. In so doing, they served The Shadow. He doubted that his agents had overtaken any of the routed gunzels; but that did not matter.

The Shadow had claimed one, the most important of the lot, as his own prisoner. Moreover, The Shadow had won the vital issue. He had preserved the quiet of this neighborhood, keeping Kelburn's hideout unsuspected.

What came next depended, in part, upon The Shadow's captive. Noting a stir beneath the black cloak, The Shadow lifted it and flung it across his own shoulders. He focused his tiny flashlight upon the prisoner's face. He saw features that were thick and bloated, yet not exactly ugly. He watched eyes open and squint into the light.

The Shadow whispered a laugh. He recognized his prisoner as an underworld character known as Case Brandle. It wasn't surprising that Case had let his followers in for it, regardless of how tough they might have been. Case wasn't known as an expert in matters of gunnery.

His reputation, as his nickname indicated, lay in his ability at "casing" places where criminals expected trouble. In other parlance, Case was a clever watcher, useful as an outside man when other crooks were planning crime.

Whenever Case assembled a crew, he trained its members in the tactics that he knew so well. This crowd of his tonight were evidently handy men with guns, but they needed a different type of leadership than the sort Case had supplied.

Though he couldn't see The Shadow against the light, Case heard the whispered laugh and winced. Half propped against the wall, he remembered that his crew had no longer been with him when the crisis came. But Case was a canny person at talking his way out of trouble, and he tried it with The Shadow.

"The bulls ain't after me for nothing," Case argued. "They ain't got anything on me. We wasn't intending to use our heaters, Shadow—not unless you started shooting first."

IN his own way, Case was pleading self-defense, and The Shadow listened. Case didn't mention the murderous tactics that he had ordered later; he seemed to think that all was fair in battle with The Shadow. To a degree, Case's implication was a compliment. There was another point, however, that Case was quick to emphasize.

"They say you ain't too tough on guys that come clean," continued Case, "and that's what I'm doing, Shadow. We was only here to see that nobody bothered the joint across the way. That ain't anything much against us."

"It might depend upon who hired you," informed The Shadow, "as well as your reasons for accepting his offer."

Again, Case winced. Then:

"It was Smead Kelburn hired us," Case admitted. "He phoned the joint where I hang out and told me where I'd find a bundle of cash, with more coming if I went through with what he wanted. He wasn't asking much; just that we'd stick here and see that nobody bothered him.

"Nobody except coppers." Case was hasty to add that point. "Kelburn said they had him all wrong, but if they blew in, he'd give himself up. He was afraid of other guys—guys who wanted to pin a bum rap on him. Wanted time to clear himself, but he figured they'd be out to stop him.

"You ought to understand that, Shadow. They say you help guys that are in bad jams. Anyway, I took up the job for Kelburn, the way he wanted it. Kind of let that crew of mine get out of hand, I did, but they're quick boys with their triggers. Too quick!"

The Shadow's laugh carried a note of correction. The trouble with Case's "boys" was just the opposite. They hadn't been quick enough with their guns. Case managed to force a grin, though he didn't go too far with it.

"Have it your way, Shadow," he said. "And if you're handing any breaks to anybody, I'd like to be the guy to get one."

"You will be, Case," assured The Shadow, "if you follow my instructions. You will also have a chance to clean your slate, perhaps very soon. Meanwhile, tell me more about Kelburn."

Case couldn't tell much. He'd only talked to Kelburn over the telephone. He'd never actually met Kelburn, though he had seen him several times. Case explained that part of it.

"He's like an old rat hiding in a hole, Kelburn is," affirmed Case. "A wise old rat. Pokes his nose out every now and then, and if everything is jake, he comes out farther. Or maybe he comes out because things ain't too jake. Kind of hard to tell, because he's so cute.

"I've seen him start along the street, and then do a duck just because he sees a car come by. If one stops, he waits—like he was watching what somebody else was going to do. D'you know, I think he's casing his own joint, when he does that. Maybe it's what gave him the idea to hire me."

The Shadow did not reply. Looking up, Case saw burning eyes fixed upon the brownstone steps across the street. He was sure though, Case was, that those eyes would swing his way if he made a budge, and that a gun muzzle would accompany them. From the way his hip flattened against the wall, Case realized that he no longer had his own revolver.

Sudden worry seized Case Brandle. Maybe The Shadow was taking him too much at his word. Kelburn must have heard the shooting in his hideout. According to Case's own opinion, this would be a time when Kelburn would poke his nose out. It might be, though, that the shooting had made him overly wary. If so, Kelburn would remain hidden, and thereby brand Case's statement as a lie.

Each passing minute made Case worry the more. When he heard another whispered laugh from The Shadow's hidden lips, Case reconciled himself to the worst. He felt that the laugh was marking him a double-crosser, and by all the rules Case had ever heard of, double-crossing The Shadow was like asking for a pass to the morgue. Case's squint was fearful as he again looked toward The Shadow's eyes.

Those eyes were still fixed across the street. The hand that clamped hard on Case's shoulder meant that he was not to stir. Case let his gaze follow The Shadow's and saw the thing that his cloaked captor had observed.

The door beneath the brownstone steps had

stirred. The things that Case had said were being proven. Smead Kelburn was emerging warily from his hideaway, to learn what had happened in the world outside his door!

CHAPTER XIV
THE TRAP REVERSED

AT first, a wide face peered from the space beneath the brownstone steps; broad shoulders followed; finally a stocky figure was entirely in view. Then Case Brandle went jittery again, for Smead Kelburn, quite out of keeping with his usual procedure, was turning back toward the door.

The Shadow understood the reason. Kelburn had found that the door was unlocked. He was fearful of lurkers within his own premises, and would have to take a look before proceeding farther.

The look took Kelburn a few minutes—most disturbing minutes to Case. Then Kelburn was coming out again, and The Shadow's low-toned laugh was accompanied by another warning grip on Case's shoulder.

Up to the sidewalk, yet still sheltered by the brownstone steps, Kelburn looked one direction, then the other. After that, he again did the unexpected.

Lifting himself erect, Kelburn stepped into open sight, something that Case had not seen him do before. Turning toward the next corner, he walked away quite briskly. Case couldn't hold back his thoughts.

"Maybe he's lamming," spoke Case, in a hoarse undertone. "He ain't ready to dodge, like he generally is. He ought to be, though, seeing as he found the door unlocked."

The Shadow did not move. He kept watching Kelburn. Near the corner, the stocky man turned, and Case thought he was gone for keeps. The Shadow considered otherwise.

"You were right, Case," spoke The Shadow coolly. "Kelburn is a clever dodger. He went behind the last steps in the row. Watch, and you will see him working back again."

Case watched, and caught a momentary glimpse of Kelburn; whereupon Case saw matters as The Shadow did. Kelburn was suiting the unlocked door to his own strategy. Calculating that persons might be watching him, he was trying to coax them to the brownstone basement, that he might spot them in his turn.

Then The Shadow was moving forward, drawing Case along with him. They were half across the street before Case realized that Kelburn, with all his cunning, could not see them. The Shadow was an enlarged patch of blackness, nothing more; a shape that could not be identified as a human figure. As for Case, he was invisible, too.

He was on the side away from Kelburn's sight, and The Shadow was covering Case completely. They were bound straight for Kelburn's own steps, while the hunted man was working back from door to door. Kelburn did not see them, and they were due to reach his goal before he did.

The only slip occurred as they reached the steps down to Kelburn's door. There, Case stumbled, quite accidentally, making more noise than was good.

Instead of blaming Case for the misstep, The Shadow turned him toward the door itself, opened the barrier far enough to shove him through, and followed, giving himself a twist that brought the door shut behind him.

Case was half-sprawled on the floor, for The Shadow had given him a quick shove to get him out of the way. A gripping hand brought Case to his feet again, and The Shadow was conducting him to Kelburn's inner lair. Finding that he was still in The Shadow's good graces, Case questioned:

"Do you think Kelburn heard?"

The Shadow nudged for silence. The outer door was creaking slightly, and creeping footsteps followed. Leaving the door of the storeroom open, as he had found it, The Shadow moved Case to an inner corner amid total darkness.

Case felt The Shadow's cloak half about him, as though to furnish needed concealment. Then a low whisper was planting instructions into Case's ear; orders that made Case begin to plead he couldn't follow them.

A gun muzzle pushed the middle of Case's back, and he capitulated; then, as Kelburn reached the door itself, Case felt the cold steel of the gun right in his own hand. He hadn't time to think of what came next, before The Shadow propelled him to a corner by himself.

A sudden stir occurred at the doorway. The door flipped open wider, though it didn't quite strike the wall beside it. A hand pressed a light switch, and there was Kelburn, a gun in his fist, swinging to look for The Shadow.

Across the room, Kelburn saw the black-clad figure that rose suddenly from its corner, shoving a big automatic toward him.

Before Kelburn could even aim, his opponent's finger moved against its gun trigger. The cloaked marksman couldn't afford to give Kelburn a chance in this emergency, yet Kelburn was to live to tell it. The most unaccountable of things occurred.

The Shadow's gun misfired!

SAVAGELY, Kelburn drove forward, swinging his own gun. Probably The Shadow's .45 had jammed, for the cloaked figure was beginning a writhe toward shelter. There would be no shelter for The Shadow.

Kelburn intended to win this resumption of last night's feud. His lips were hardened in their gloat.

The Shadow had reversed the trap on Kelburn, who, in his turn, was reversing it on The Shadow. Permanently, Kelburn hoped!

At that crucial instant, The Shadow reversed the trap again. He planted a big gun squarely against Kelburn's neck; delivered a laugh that the stocky man couldn't help but recognize. Kelburn froze, as though the chill from the gun had permeated him. But it was the laugh that actually iced him.

The laugh meant that The Shadow was behind Kelburn; whereas, he *saw* The Shadow squarely before him! Hearing The Shadow one place, seeing him another, was too much for Kelburn. He let his revolver fall from his stiffened hand; then, before his eyes, a transformation happened.

Scrambling up from the floor, a frantic man flung away an automatic, shook a black cloak from his shoulders and flipped a slouch hat from his head, as he took another wild dive for an opposite corner, where a closet door stood open, offering a refuge.

He wasn't The Shadow any longer, that fellow; in fact, he had never really been The Shadow. He was just Case Brandle.

The Shadow, in person, was turning Kelburn around with the ever-prodding gun. Indeed, Kelburn thought he felt the press of metal on his neck after the gun had left. For The Shadow was turning, stooping, to reclaim his cloak and hat, along with the extra automatic, an empty one, that he had made Case take to help in this deception.

Peering from the closet, Case stared, amazed to see The Shadow, cloaked again, calmly reloading the extra automatic, while Kelburn, faced toward the closet, was standing grimly, his hands raised under the imaginary pressure of an absent gun muzzle.

Scooping up the revolver Kelburn had dropped, The Shadow pocketed it, then ordered Kelburn to turn around, adding that Case could come from the closet.

Two much-subdued men soon found themselves seated, listening to what The Shadow was telling them.

To Kelburn, The Shadow announced that he had come here as a friend, in strict accordance with a promise that he, The Shadow, had given Joan. Last night's interlude with Nevlin could be overlooked. The Shadow wanted Kelburn's true story on the Aldriff deal.

He didn't add that he could decide that Nevlin question on the merits of Kelburn's previous activities, since all were related. Instead, The Shadow took time out to mention Case's new status.

Case had cleaned his slate by risking his life while rigged in The Shadow's garb. The Shadow had been thinking more of Kelburn than Case, while arranging that stunt.

Had Kelburn shot Case in self-defense, the loss would not have been great, considering that Case had willfully tried to kill The Shadow, earlier. However, since Case had come through the ordeal, he could be regarded as worthy to aid The Shadow.

As for Kelburn, he was more than glad to establish his own status. He'd told Joan the truth, he said, when he stated that Dulther, Sigby, Aldriff, all three, were Pharco backers. According to Kelburn, they all had met at Aldriff's more than once, always on nights when the servants were off, though Nevlin had been present.

"They said that if I dealt with Aldriff," declared Kelburn, "they would legally avoid the restrictions about Magnax backing chain stores like Pharco. Later, though, Aldriff became worried about getting needed support from Magnax. He told me to take a trip, while he settled it with Dulther and Sigby.

"Whether he thought they were tricking him, or whether he wanted to trick me, I don't know. I didn't need those documents of his, because I had receipts for all the money that I'd turned over to Magnax, through Aldriff. I wanted to see Aldriff, though, and demand a showdown.

"When I saw Joan there, I waited next door, hoping for a chance to speak to her. Next thing, trouble broke loose, and servants were in the next yard, coming after me. I headed here after I was blocked off from the airport. I wasn't the masked man who entered Aldriff's."

Finishing, Kelburn stared directly at The Shadow. Finding that the burning eyes were friendly, Kelburn declared steadily:

"The masked man was either Dulther or Sigby. His object was to place me in a difficult position. Am I correct?"

"In part," replied The Shadow. "It is also likely that the masked man had another, and more important purpose."

That puzzled Kelburn. Hoping to learn more, he pressed his original statement further.

"Either Dulther or Sigby," repeated Kelburn. "But which was the masked man? How can we learn?

"Quite simply," returned The Shadow. "We must learn which of the two murdered Aldriff. The masked man was the other."

KELBURN'S eyes and mouth popped wide. Case lost his squint and gave an open stare. Coming from anyone other than The Shadow, the reference to Aldriff's death as murder would have been preposterous. But both of these listeners had seen enough of The Shadow's ways to know that his theories would never prove wrong; they were sure, too, that The Shadow never jested in such matters.

"Aldriff... murdered—"

Like mechanical things, Kelburn's lips spoke those slow words. He simply couldn't understand it. He'd read every detail regarding the finding of Aldriff's body in the room of doom, a room that no one could have left before others entered; a room, too, in which every possible hiding place had been thoroughly probed, without delay.

Then, before Kelburn could get around to asking more about it, The Shadow passed on to other matters.

"We may assume that Dulther and Sigby collaborated in the death of Nevlin," declared The Shadow. "They had Nevlin call you through Joan, and then told him to summon the police. They made him believe that you would be trapped, Kelburn, under circumstances pointing to another attempt at crime.

"Thereupon, they murdered Nevlin, getting rid of the one man whose testimony might ruin them, and saving themselves the payment of hush money from the million that Aldriff had placed in their keeping. In killing Nevlin, they made it even worse for you. If the police had found you, they would have accused you of the murder."

Kelburn nodded. He owed more to The Shadow than he had realized last night. Indeed, Kelburn was very much impressed by his own stupidity in not accepting Joan's advice regarding a meeting with this black-clad friend.

"And now," spoke The Shadow, turning his gaze from one man to the other, "we come to a matter that concerns you both. Case thinks you phoned him, Kelburn, and hired him to watch outside here."

"I don't think it any longer," put in Case promptly. "His voice"—Case gestured toward Kelburn—"ain't the one that talked to me. I know that, even though the guy that did talk was making his voice sound different than it was."

"Dulther or Sigby," analyzed The Shadow. "One or the other must have made the deal with Case. It does not matter which one phoned claiming to be you, Kelburn."

"But how did they know that I was here?" inquired Kelburn.

"They must have trailed you last night," replied The Shadow. "I saw a car speed after yours when you fled. They had learned, those two, that I was in the game and might come here. They hired Case in the hope that he would dispose of me."

Inasmuch as Case had tried to do just that, The Shadow's theory held good. Mention of the matter, however, made Case shift uneasily. He relaxed when The Shadow's conversation moved to another phase.

"Whether Case succeeded or not," The Shadow added, "Dulther and Sigby felt sure that a battle hereabouts would lead the police into this basement, Kelburn, and thereby produce your capture by the law. They may try again, so I suggest that you move elsewhere. I shall provide a place for you."

The Shadow spoke as though he had settled all of Kelburn's problems. He was gesturing for his listeners to rise and come along with him, which they did.

When they reached the street, The Shadow flashed a tiny green light that the others did not see. But they observed the taxicab that arrived in sudden fashion.

Motioning Kelburn into Moe's cab, The Shadow turned and handed Case his revolver. Case stared, half amazed, at this display of The Shadow's trust. While Case was slowly pocketing the gun, The Shadow gave him something else.

"You will probably hear again from the man who called himself Kelburn," declared The Shadow. "If you do, simply tell him that I got away. Also tell him that afterward, you found this, right here beside the steps. Something that I must have dropped."

By "this" The Shadow referred to the business card which bore the name of Wilstead & Co., wholesale art dealers—the card that The Shadow had found in Nevlin's pocket.

He stated the truth when he said that he had dropped it on the steps, for the folded card was fluttering from The Shadow's fingers before Case could take it.

Stooping, Case picked up the card and squinted at it; then looked toward the Shadow. Not only was The Shadow gone; he'd taken Kelburn with him, cab and all, while Case was fumbling for the dropped card.

Back from the corner came a strange, trailing laugh, a reminder to Case Brandle that from now on he was working for The Shadow!

CHAPTER XV
THE SHADOW'S BUSINESS

THE manhunt began that very night. By dawn, the police had found the empty stronghold in the cellar of the brownstone house. Talk of a gun fray in that vicinity had caused Commissioner Weston to order a search of all suspicious looking houses, and the boarded-up mansion came under that head.

There were enough clues to prove that Kelburn had stayed there, but none to show where he had gone. Despite its widespread coverage, the search languished the next day; though, by evening, it came much closer to Kelburn than the police supposed.

In fact, at one time Commissioner Weston could

have shaken hands with Smead Kelburn, had the wanted man been foolish enough to reach from the window of a limousine in which he was riding. The car was Cranston's, and during the ride Kelburn had talked to Joan's "other" friend, finding him quite as understanding as The Shadow.

Cranston stepped from the car alone, and Weston was too busy greeting him to notice Kelburn deep in the rear seat, when the limousine pulled away. Cranston was to meet Dulther and Sigby; hearing it, Kelburn had suggested that a pair of guns might convince those partners in crime that their game was up.

The idea hadn't appealed to the lackadaisical Mr. Cranston, and Kelburn wished that he had suggested it to The Shadow instead.

Actually, The Shadow had his own ideas about handling the two conspirators, and it happened that he and Cranston always thought alike. Meeting Dulther and Sigby with Weston, Cranston listened quietly while they talked about the manhunt and expressed the hope that Kelburn would soon be apprehended.

The Shadow would have liked to corner this brace of rogues and give them a power treatment, but he preferred to let them play their cards a while, inasmuch as The Shadow held a trump, in Kelburn, to be used at the right time.

Between them, Dulther and Sigby pictured Kelburn's murder of Nevlin. They could see Nevlin, they said, shaken and voiceless, at the point of Kelburn's gun, while Kelburn towel-wrapped Nevlin's own revolver and used it to kill its owner. From their description, one might have thought that they had actually heard the muffled death shot.

Which they had. With all their cunning, they gave it away, though not sufficiently for Cranston to interrupt and point to them as murderers. Their account was too good, too graphic, to be given by persons who had not seen Nevlin that night at the hotel.

But The Shadow knew that if he accused them, they would simply refer to newspaper reports as the source of their description, and Weston would believe them. It was probable that Dulther and Sigby were actually baiting Weston and his friend Cranston, to make them betray suspicions, if they held them.

Weston held none, and Cranston's immobile visage betrayed nothing. Behind that masklike face, The Shadow was forming his own picture of Nevlin's death. He'd heard two sets of footsteps going out of Nevlin's, before Kelburn's had entered. The later sounds had drawn The Shadow from the other trails, for the creepings had been elusive.

Two sets going out: Dulther's and Sigby's. Men whom Nevlin had admitted without fear or question. One had held the victim helpless, while the other had wrapped Nevlin's gun for the death shot.

It did not matter who had fired the fatal bullet; both were equally guilty. But proving it was another question. With circumstantial evidence badly against Kelburn, the problem was almost insurmountable.

That was why The Shadow had planned a campaign even more incredible: that of proving Aldriff's death a murder. The thing seemed impossible; yet, if accomplished, it would reap its own fruits. For, in Aldriff's case, the very circumstances so heavy against Kelburn would work in his favor. He couldn't have been a murderer and the masked man, too.

Of course, Kelburn had been neither, but that point could wait. The Shadow wanted a starting point from which to guide the law, step by step, in cracking this impossible case, with its perfect crime.

He had already won over Cardona, though Joe did not know it. The Shadow would be ready to crack the case, Dulther and Sigby with it, when he had added a few exhibits of his own to go along with those that Cardona had put away.

WHEN the conference ended, Dulther and Sigby left together in a car driven by Dulther's chauffeur, with Sigby's secretary, a husky chap for such a job, as a third passenger. The chauffeur and the secretary had the look of bodyguards, which meant that the arch conspirators weren't taking chances on a sudden meeting with The Shadow.

They had been without bodyguards, however, the night they murdered Nevlin. The same applied, of course, to their earlier activities; most specifically, their murder of Aldriff and the cover-up which followed it.

How Dulther and Sigby had managed that phenomenal accomplishment was something that The Shadow could answer, when he chose.

He preferred, however, to make Dulther and Sigby answer it, in a way that would leave no doubt. The simplest process was to lure them into attempting another crime, and trapping them in the commission of it. Once known for the crooks they were, by the world as well as The Shadow, Dulther and Sigby wouldn't be able to stand the pressure.

The thing was to provide the bait, and The Shadow believed that he had done it. The pair probably believed that they had cleared their books when they disposed of Nevlin; but they would find out that they hadn't, should one of them phone Case Brandle. When he told them about the Wilstead card, dropped by The Shadow, the two conspirators would have another job on hand.

So far, they hadn't phoned Case. It was likely, though, that they had waited until after their meeting with Weston, to see if anything new cropped up. So The Shadow did some waiting of his own, lounging about the foyer of the Cobalt Club in the guise of Cranston. When he felt that he had waited long enough, he entered a phone booth and called Case Brandle.

It was The Shadow's sinister tone that Case heard across the wire. Case was in the back room of his favorite joint, and his tone was eager when he told The Shadow that he had again heard by telephone from the speaker who called himself Kelburn, but wasn't.

Case had pretended, of course, that he thought the caller was Kelburn, and had mentioned the matter of the card. It had produced results.

"The guy hung up kind of quick," informed Case. "He just said to stick around; maybe he'd have something more for me. What do I tell him if he does?"

"Tell him that your men have scattered," ordered The Shadow, "and that you don't know how soon you can get them together again. If he keeps insisting, tell him you'll go out and try, no matter how long it takes. Once you leave on such business, stay away."

"I get it," acknowledged Case. "They'll think I'm still trying, but they won't want to wait. Whatever they want done, they'll have to do on their own."

Leaving the club, Cranston chose Moe's cab because his limousine had not returned. Becoming The Shadow, he intoned a low laugh as he considered what Dulther and Sigby would be up against when they operated on their own, again.

Case Brandle had understood. It would mean a meeting with The Shadow. Time was when Case had looked forward to such an adventure, but his experience in the brownstone basement had taught him much. Case had run into trouble that wasn't worth the cash he had been paid for it. Such payment five times over wouldn't buy Case for another effort of the sort.

Nor could Dulther and Sigby find another man of Case's caliber. They were rare in Manhattan, at present. The underworld boasted gunzels and cover-up workers, but no combinations of the two, other than those that Case could supply. Besides, Case was one of gangland's elite, belonging to the chosen few who weren't wanted by the police.

Only from such could Dulther and Sigby draw helpers, and The Shadow had checked carefully to make sure that there were none available on call.

WHILE he was mentally reviewing the list, and finding it to his satisfaction, the cab stopped in front of a loft building in the wholesale district.

The ground floor premises bore the name of Wilstead & Co., and the place was still open. Dimly lighted, it showed its collection of art objects, displayed in random fashion.

Most of the stock came under the head of furnishings. Tapestries were hanging from the walls, screens were standing in the corner. On one side of the showroom was a row of full length mirrors, set at various angles, while the opposite wall was fronted by a long counter given over to smaller ornaments and picture frames.

At the rear of the shop was a partitioned corner that served as office. As The Shadow entered, he saw a baldish man coming from the office. The man was Junius Wilstead, proprietor of the business, and he was very small of build. His face, wrinkly in appearance, looked both timid and shrewd.

Evidently Wilstead was a nervous man, at home only in his own business. He knew how to bargain about art goods, but that was his limit. The Shadow had good reason to know; for, earlier today, as Cranston, he had called on Wilstead and had sounded him out well.

Wilstead did not see the shrouded figure, automatic in hand, that emerged from behind a screen and turned toward the counter. He had excellent chances of spying The Shadow, had he looked the proper way, for six cloaked shapes were moving in procession.

The Shadow was in front of the mirrors, and they were reflecting him from various angles, producing the remarkable effect of living shadows on the march.

With a quick movement, The Shadow put his gun away.

When a weird whisper spoke across the counter, Wilstead turned, startled, almost dropping some rare curios that he was taking to the office safe. Obligingly, The Shadow caught the objects before they fell and settled them on the counter, as he made the surprising comment:

"These are insured, of course."

It was so matter-of-fact, that Wilstead managed to find his tongue, even though he couldn't help but stammer.

"Every... everything is insured," Wilstead faltered, in tremolo tone. "All... all the things you see. Against fire-"

"And burglary."

Wilstead nodded at The Shadow's comment, then suddenly winced. But before Wilstead could speak again, The Shadow added:

"I suppose you carry life insurance, too."

Wilstead had turned quite white. He sank clear down to his shoulders, as he settled in a chair behind the counter. Having driven his first points home, The Shadow changed the subject.

"I am interested in Chinese screens," he said. "One screen, in particular—a very tall one, with gold decorations, that you sold about a week ago. I doubt that the purchaser gave his name."

"He... he didn't," stuttered Wilstead. "He... I...

there wasn't any reason to ask him. Cash... special order... shipping, he arranged it—"

"Along with something else."

Wilstead nodded. Weakly, he raised his hand and pointed. Then, to be exact, he added:

"A very special one. Filled—I mean made in Philadelphia. Dimensions very exact. I went to the factory myself, to get quick service. Cash in advance, of course."

Oddly, The Shadow's influence was soothing Wilstead, partly because the cloaked visitant was calmly discussing the subject on which Wilstead thrived. When The Shadow's gloved hands produced a bundle of currency, instead of a gun, Wilstead's fear of burglary ended. "I would like to duplicate that order," stated The Shadow. "You must give it your personal attention, as you did the other. Name the cost."

Wilstead named it and The Shadow counted off the money. Thus having won Wilstead's confidence, he reverted to the insurance theme.

"There may be a burglary here soon," he said. "I am glad that you are insured against such loss. If you would like to cash in on your life insurance, too, I would advise you to stay. Or, perhaps, you might prefer to leave for Philadelphia at once."

WILSTEAD did prefer the latter. Convinced that some real menace was afoot, he became putty in The Shadow's hands. He listened, nodding, to further details, including the fact that someone else would capably handle the business while he was gone.

Very soon, Wilstead was on his way out the front door, carrying a suitcase with him.

Close beside Wilstead was the shrouded friend who merged so well with darkness that the art dealer

Wilstead had excellent chances of spying The Shadow, had he looked the proper way, for six cloaked shapes were moving in procession.

could scarcely see him. Locking the front door, Wilstead looked about and spoke to blackness.

"But who is the man?" queried Wilstead. "Someone will have to take the risk—"

Already, the risk was being accepted. A gloved hand was plucking the keys from Wilstead's fingers. With guiding grip, The Shadow steered the art dealer into Moe's cab, and it started on its trip to Pennsylvania Station.

Staring back through the rear window, Wilstead couldn't even glimpse The Shadow. The black-cloaked master had faded into the night. From the enveloping darkness, Wilstead caught the strains of a parting laugh, wishing him a successful journey. But that tone carried something more.

Usually, The Shadow's laugh spelled doom to men of crime. This time, it signified that he had gone into the wholesale art business. Perhaps the two would prove identical, before The Shadow's work was done!

CHAPTER XVI
FRIENDS OF THE SHADOW

OLD Junius Wilstead stood behind his counter, as was his wont every evening when he waited for late customers. Only he wasn't Wilstead, and he wasn't standing.

He was The Shadow, transformed facially to resemble Wilstead; and he was seated in a chair close to the counter, so that his tall stature was reduced to Wilstead's height.

It was a fact, however, that the man behind the counter was awaiting customers. Two of them, who, by The Shadow's calculations, would arrive tonight.

Just as Weston had given Cardona twenty-four

hours to find Kelburn, so had The Shadow allowed Dulther and Sigby another twenty-four, to find—The Shadow!

During the day, The Shadow had called Case Brandle, to learn that the former crook was gone. Case's absence from his favorite hangout indicated that he had received pressing calls from a pretended Kelburn, and had finally promised to go out and raise a mob.

Since Case wouldn't return, the buck would be passed right back to the pretender, who represented two people: Dulther and Sigby.

Those two who posed as one man, Kelburn, would be worried about a foe who passed as two, The Shadow. Whether they suspected that he was also Lamont Cranston made very little difference. They certainly wouldn't expect him to be Junius Wilstead.

Much though Dulther and Sigby might wish to eradicate The Shadow, Wilstead came first. He was a link that they had overlooked; a link important enough to replace Nevlin, the tool they had used and destroyed.

If Wilstead learned that Nevlin was the man to whom he had sold certain decorations, and revealed what they were, Aldriff's suicide would no longer be the perfect crime for which it passed.

It wouldn't be difficult for two clever men like Dulther and Sigby to handle an easy victim like Wilstead. All they needed to do was arrive near closing time, present themselves as wealthy customers and suggest that they talk business in the office. Their business would be the sort they conducted with Nevlin the last time they went to see him.

In the mild light of the showroom, The Shadow's disguise was perfect. He hadn't overdone the make-up; he preferred to act the part of Wilstead, rather than do a window-dummy imitation. His only problem would be the trip to the office, and he had arranged for that detail.

There was a screen at the end of the counter, beyond it, an antique sofa. A table piled with bric-a-brac was farther on, and another screen partly hid the office door. As Wilstead, The Shadow could travel, crouched, clear to the doorway. He'd have to swing the screen to open the door, and once inside, he could gain his black hat and cloak in a single sweep, for they were hanging just beyond the door.

He'd go in as Wilstead, and while allowing his customers full chance for a wary look, would become The Shadow, fully caparisoned to meet them. Once Dulther and Sigby were trapped, a mere touch of a burglar alarm would summon police. Arrested on these premises, Dulther and Sigby would find it very difficult to explain themselves.

The office, incidentally, was an excellent trap. It had only one window, just large enough for a man to squeeze through but too small for rapid flight. The window was frosted, and it opened into an air shaft; hence there was no likelihood of any outsider looking in through it.

Part of the Wilstead act was to keep glancing toward the street. Old Wilstead always did it when behind the counter, for he had an eye toward customers. The Shadow had just finished one of those glances, when something caught the corner of his eye. He shifted at the counter, then made a casual turn of his head. His first glance was justified.

Across the street were lurkers, and they were edging toward this side. The Shadow saw two men, and doubted that they were Dulther and Sigby; they might be the chauffeur and the secretary, but that was unlikely, too, for it meant that Dulther and Sigby would be letting new accomplices into their confidence.

Knees bent, The Shadow performed a perfect Wilstead waddle behind the counter. Partway to the office, he paused, fingered a picture frame and decided to place it elsewhere. In turning, he obtained a new view of the doorway.

The two men had reached it, and there were others working up behind them. As yet, however, they showed no direct intention of invasion. The Shadow decided to allow more leeway, before making an opposing move.

This time, The Shadow waited too long. There was a quick rattle from the office door. As The Shadow turned in Wilstead style, he was confronted by a gun around the corner of the screen. The Shadow hadn't expected invasion from that quarter; nor did he anticipate this particular invader.

The man with the gun was Case Brandle!

HIS own hands on the counter, to lull the men outside, The Shadow hadn't time to draw an automatic from beneath Wilstead's long-tailed frock coat. It was likewise too late to deal with Case as The Shadow had the other night, because the men from the street were shoving through the front door, drawing their guns, too.

Case's sudden appearance was the signal they awaited, these gunzels who had rejoined their leader.

The Shadow could only play the Wilstead act. He did it by raising his hands in shaky style, as he delivered a very convincing bleat. Case pushed forward, shoving his gun The Shadow's way, and rasped a query:

"All right, Wilstead—where's The Shadow?"

The trembling Wilstead showed a quiver of his chin. He managed to stutter that he'd never heard of anyone called The Shadow. Meanwhile, Case's crew were flanking along the counter, darting looks in other directions in quest of a black-clad foe.

"A tricky guy, The Shadow," spoke Case sneeringly. "Nobody knows who The Shadow is. *You* might even be The Shadow. Just in case you are, I'll tell you why I came here. I had another call from that certain man. He offered me real dough, this time. I wouldn't have taken him up for five times what he gave me before, but he made it ten.

"If you aren't The Shadow, Wilstead, it won't make much difference. You're getting yours just the same. Only, we can risk lugging you away alive, quietlike, which wouldn't do with The Shadow. The funny thing is"—it wasn't sounding funny with the snarl Case gave it—"The Shadow ought to be here, but he ain't. Maybe we'll give you a break, Wilstead, if you tell us how come."

A headshake was the only answer. It indicated ignorance, rather than refusal to reply. Certain that the real Wilstead couldn't stand the heat that he had given, Case resolved upon a final test.

He reached for a light on the counter; one Wilstead used when displaying curios to customers. As he pulled the lamp cord, Case ordered:

"Move over here, Wilstead, so I can make sure. If you ain't Wilstead, it's curtains for you!"

Case was watching keenly as The Shadow came along behind the counter. The knee crouch was a perfect job. His legs out of sight, The Shadow wobbled just as a doddering codger like Wilstead should have.

As he came into the light, he cringed, which was natural enough. But it didn't look like a trick to hide his real identity, for it brought The Shadow's face right into the brilliant light.

It also brought his hands closer to the counter. Thrust forward, The Shadow's made-up face was so clearly shown that it gave trifling evidence of its disguise. But the advantage that he thus lost was gained elsewhere.

The light itself made a dazzle between Case's eyes and The Shadow's left hand. As Case, intent upon his study of the face, let out a gloat of discovery, The Shadow shot his left hand forward.

It took the lamp with a pluck and flung it, not at Case directly but along the counter. The Shadow was near the end of the flanking line, to which Case had shifted.

Every gunner in the row made a sudden duck as the lamp went flying by. It crashed before they could aim, and by then, The Shadow had lengthened to full stature and was wheeling behind the screen at the counter's end, gesturing with his own gun as he disappeared.

GUNNERS were scattering at Case's call. He'd figured the way to beat The Shadow was to scatter first. Crooks heard The Shadow's taunting laugh, but they were the first to fire.

The Shadow made a bad slip, this time, in his choice of shelter. That screen wasn't stout enough to stand the gaff of gunfire. Case's marksmen blasted it in a single volley while they were coming to their feet.

Their gleeful howls would have been short lived, if the screen hadn't toppled under the impact of the riddling slugs. As it fell, it revealed no sign of The Shadow, either as Wilstead or another figure. It was Case who guessed the trick.

Instead of stopping at the screen, The Shadow had dropped and was making at quick crawl past the sofa and the table that made a path to the next screen.

If The Shadow reached the office, he would have a handy pillbox. Case leaped forward to intercept him, yelling for others to follow. Gunners were swinging around past the screen, when it became alive.

On his feet, The Shadow gathered the folds and revolved into the midst of his foemen, whirling as he came. They were scattered right and left, their gunshots going wild.

Using the screen as a battering ram, The Shadow used it to floor an aiming thug; then turned and flung it broadside at a pair near the counter. He'd cleared a path to the outer door, and could have used it for an exit, but for one thing.

The Shadow still was Wilstead!

His stretched proportions gave him better speed, more flexibility, but he lacked the vital garb that he needed for a fadeout. Uncloaked, The Shadow was simply another fighter, in the eyes of half a dozen foemen. Even his laugh couldn't halt them. It sounded as false as Wilstead's face really was.

With his enemies lunging after him, The Shadow stabbed a pair of shots; then, as their guns began to rattle, he was fooling them with the quick reverse shift that he made. The Wilstead disguise helped that ruse somewhat. Mobsters overshot their mark, only to find that The Shadow was darting elsewhere.

Darting into doom, he was letting them cut him off from both the office and the street. A closing semicircle, they had The Shadow, an ordinary human, trapped by the wall across from the counter. So they thought, until—

As The Shadow wheeled, his laugh ringing strident with its mockery, half a dozen fighters sprang into sight with him. Friends of The Shadow, they were aiming at every vital angle. When his gun blazed, so did theirs.

This was too much for Case's tribe. With wild accord, they flung themselves away. Some went over the counter, others toward the office, a few dived for the outer door.

Turning with each shot from his gun, The Shadow was clipping them, and might have cleared the battleground entirely if Case hadn't howled something that rallied his remaining men.

Caught in the very thick of things, Case had sprawled across an antique chair and couldn't continue his flight. From the floor, he saw those fighters who were battling on The Shadow's side.

They were wheeling as The Shadow did, timing their shots to his, though they changed the angle of their fire. The trouble was to find The Shadow. He and his friends were all alike! No wonder they weren't getting the results they should have. Only one gun out of six was doing actual duty.

The Shadow had turned a trap into a vantage spot by choosing a background, instead of a rampart. He had placed himself directly in front of Wilstead's row of full-length mirrors; turned askew, they were reflecting him in half a dozen poses, in each of which the main feature was a gun.

One shot from The Shadow's .45 brought spurts from all the others, and the echoes from the flat fronts of the mirrors were helping with the rapid-fire illusion.

By that perfect ruse, The Shadow had turned the tide of battle. His laugh, drowning out Case's yells, told that this master fighter still could win the fray, though the remnants of the crooked crew were turning back to fire at him again.

Echoing, The Shadow's laugh had the sound of six, proclaiming the astounding truth—that the only friends of The Shadow had been himself!

CHAPTER XVII
THE FATAL FLIGHT

IF ever tricked crooks were ready to gun for vengeance, Case's tribe were that lot. Enough of them were still afoot to give The Shadow trouble; more of it than he could fling their way. He was switching guns, bringing a fresh .45 into play, but he hadn't thinned the opposition quite enough.

Even the men that his quick shots had wounded were forgetting their agony in a surge of hate. Propped on their elbows, ready with their guns, they were as dangerous as their fellows; perhaps more so, considering that the range was close and their propped-fists were steady.

They aimed for The Shadow and let rip as he twisted along the rows of mirrors. The shatter of glass formed an obbligato to The Shadow's strident laugh, but the mirth remained unbroken. Nor did The Shadow cease his gunfire.

A gawky-looking fighter, with his frock coat and wizened disguise, he had escaped the blast of half a dozen guns that had taken him as a point-blank target.

Again, it was Case who recognized the reason, while The Shadow was picking off more foemen.

CLIFF MARSLAND

The mirrors that had spurred The Shadow's offensive had proven themselves a defensive factor, too. Those friends of The Shadow still had played their part.

Case's gunners hadn't been able to tell The Shadow from his own reflections. They'd been shooting at the mirrors, not at him. One chance in six, they had, to clip their only human target, and they'd missed out in their guesses. Indeed, The Shadow hadn't given them a chance at all.

He'd swung toward the mirrors when they fired, and in response, five mirrored images had lunged forward. Not one of his opponents, Case included, had thought that The Shadow would retire. Individually, each had picked a figure that was on the advance.

And now, The Shadow was away. He'd picked a space between the mirrors, and it was still a question which direction he had gone. Case thought it was toward the office and beckoned that direction. Those that could, sprang up to follow him. A mere few, they turned abruptly when Case came bounding toward them.

Their leader had spotted The Shadow near the outer door.

"Get to the mirrors!" howled Case. "We'll turn the trick on him. Get there, and give it!"

They got there, but they didn't give it. As they swung in front of the great glasses, The Shadow's guns were jabbing, and each punch nailed its man. Such precision was uncanny; it wasn't possible that even The Shadow could offset the deceptive factor of the mirrors and score a bull's-eye every try, at a time when a single miss could have been fatal.

In the midst of it, Case saw the reason. The illusion wasn't working any longer. No wonder

The Shadow had wheeled from the background that had served him so well earlier. In their barrage that didn't count, the men with Case had smashed the mirrors with their bullets.

Instead of viewing a dozen figures or more, The Shadow was looking at a mere few, and all were real, none images. Of course he had bagged them promptly, and he'd have dropped Case with his final shot if the leader hadn't fled, flinging broken mirrors as he passed them.

The Shadow was coming after Case, hoping to take him alive. He'd be useful, Case would, as a witness when the showdown came. Case was dodging to the office, and he managed to spill the table with its bric-a-brac squarely in The Shadow's path.

Sidestepping it, The Shadow wasn't quite in time to stop the door when Case slammed it shut and bolted it.

Coolly, The Shadow began to splinter the woodwork with bullets, knowing that Case would have to keep away from the door while shots were coming through.

Police were arriving along the street to see what the shooting was all about. By the time they reached Wilstead's, the office door was shattered.

Case was gone when The Shadow sprang in. Gone, too, were The Shadow's cloak and hat that had been hanging there. The little window was open; it was the route by which Case had come, and he had squeezed out the same way. Across the air shaft was another window, marking his route.

THE SHADOW followed, bent on the strange task of trailing himself, since he knew that Case must have put on the black garments, hoping that they would hide him in darkness along the street.

Emerging into a little alley, The Shadow moved through it, keeping well obscured despite the handicap of the Wilstead attire. He was prepared for trouble when he reached the rear street.

Trouble *was* lurking there. Black-clad trouble in the person of Case Brandle. In a darkened doorway, Case was getting the thrill of posing as The Shadow. The black garb gave him confidence; it was the perfect thing for this sort of work. To ambush The Shadow by being The Shadow was something that Case could brag about.

He edged out from the doorway. There were lights along the street, but they didn't matter. The Shadow would be coming from the alley and couldn't get the slant he needed. A few steps more were safe enough. Case took them, and kept ready with his gun.

Detecting motion in the alley, Case took another sidestep and spotted an outline against the grimy wall. It was The Shadow, still handicapped by Wilstead's guise. Wheeling about, Case aimed his gun straight down the alley.

The Shadow was coming with a lunge. He saw Case in the light, and was driving in to grapple with him before the double-crosser could again reach splotchy darkness. A strange thrust, this—The Shadow springing for a foe who looked so much like himself. Only a quick grapple could put the feud on equal terms.

From across the street, near a corner where a car was parked, only the mouth of the alley was visible. From such a lookout spot, Case Brandle, the masquerader, made a perfect replica of The Shadow. The fact that the impostor had whipped into the open did not betray the masquerade. The Shadow, himself, might have done so while turning to oppose a single foe.

Besides, there was The Shadow's laugh. Its challenging taunt, issued from within the alley, might have come from the cloaked man who had swung to use his gun. The illusion was quite as effective as the mirror business. It fooled two men who were watching from the parked car.

They saw Case as The Shadow, and thought the cloaked fighter was too busy to be wary of their presence: The Shadow, stalking someone in the alley and shifting too far into the light. Two guns came to aim and ripped a simultaneous message, blasting straight toward the battler in black.

Driving low, to come under Case's gun, The Shadow suddenly changed his charge into a drop. Full length, he slid along the alley paving, yards short of his given mark. Strange that The Shadow should have rejected his own attempt to overwhelm a murderous foe; but it was fully explained by the thing that happened to Case Brandle.

The lunge Case made was not of his own choice. Flaying bullets caused it, as they stabbed Case in the back. His gun hand jolted high, Case couldn't have clipped The Shadow even if he had pulled the trigger, which he didn't. For Case's lunge was just the beginning of a sprawl.

As a cloaked figure flattened on the curbing, the echoes of the gun spurts opposite were drowned by the roar of a departing motor. Coming to his feet, The Shadow sprang to the corner of the alley and poked his own gun past the wall which had hitherto hidden him from the assassins across the way.

He was too late to halt them; a mere glimpse of taillights was all he saw, as the murder car clipped the corner opposite, to escape along a cross street.

Case was still alive when The Shadow reached him. The Shadow did not have to hear the names that Case tried to cough. He knew them: Dulther and Sigby. They'd been in the offing, to play their hand if Case failed. They hadn't deemed it necessary to tell their tool of their intention. Thus Case Brandle had taken the dose meant for The Shadow.

AGAIN, Case was The Shadow's prisoner, and this time it would be difficult to hide him, for police would be coming through the very alley that The Shadow had used.

The problem was solved in timely style when a cab whipped into the rear street and stopped short as its occupants saw a grotesque sight in the headlights.

The Shadow was writhing with a prone foeman, who seemed to be contending for ownership of a black cloak and slouch hat. Actually, it was the other way about; The Shadow was reclaiming his own garb, in order that these newcomers would not make the same mistake as the assassins.

For these new arrivals would have spared a black-clad target to wither an uncloaked figure instead. They were two of The Shadow's stoutest agents, Harry Vincent and Cliff Marsland, riding in the cab piloted by Moe Shrevnitz.

Seeing the tangle ahead, the two sprang out of the cab. When they reached The Shadow he was cloaked again, and they recognized Case Brandle on the ground.

The agents lifted the wounded crook into the cab. It was away, The Shadow in it, before police appeared. But there wasn't any use in rushing Case to a hospital, or to The Shadow's own physician, Dr. Rupert Sayre. With dying, incoherent coughs, Case spat out his life before the cab had covered a dozen blocks.

Leaving the disposal of the body to his agents, The Shadow transferred later to his limousine, which was parked in a convenient place. As he rode away in the big car, he not only packed away his cloak and hat; he removed the wig and erased the makeup that had identified him as Junius Wilstead.

Again The Shadow was the immaculate Mr. Cranston, when he stopped at Margo's apartment to meet her guests, the Kelburns. There, Cranston informed Joan and her uncle that he had received a singular message from his unknown friend, The Shadow.

Cranston hadn't much to tell about the fray at Wilstead's and Case's fatal flight. The Shadow, it seemed, had been very sketchy on such details. But there was nothing hazy about the instructions that concerned the Kelburns.

"The Shadow wants you to move again," Cranston told them. "He has chosen the perfect place for you to stay, where the police will never look for you. Aldriff's house on Long Island."

Sudden amazement gradually erased itself from their faces, as Joan and her uncle realized the subtle merit of the plan. Aldriff's mansion had been closed the day after its owner's death. It was indeed the perfect residence for Smead Kelburn. Joan could keep house for him, and the police would never find them.

At least, not until The Shadow so decreed. There was indication of that prospect, when Cranston was riding back to the Cobalt Club, alone. His whispered laugh, The Shadow's, carried a prophetic note.

The tone meant that in this game of strange reverses, The Shadow saw the value of the unexpected and would use it to the full!

CHAPTER XVIII
INVITATION BY PROXY

LAMONT CRANSTON listened idly while Commissioner Weston voiced his theories on crime. It was another evening, and there wasn't much reason for Cranston to be interested in Weston's comments.

Cranston had heard it all before; at present, he was merely sitting by while the commissioner talked for the benefit of two others: Lloyd Dulther and Hubert Sigby.

Indeed, Cranston was scarcely listening to Weston at all. He was more interested in the way Dulther and Sigby talked. Not so much in the things they said, but in the manners of their speech.

So set were their styles that it wasn't surprising that one, or both, had found trouble faking Kelburn's voice when dealing by telephone with Case Brandle.

Dulther's speech was blunt and heavy, much in keeping with his facial appearance. He kept his tone solemn, in order to be deliberate and important.

Sigby's way was as changeable as the registration of his pointed features. He spoke quickly, with a high inflection when he made assertions, a lower tone when he replied to questions. He had a habit of pausing in between, to avoid committing himself.

"So you believe that Joan Kelburn has joined her uncle," said Dulther, at the end of Weston's comments. "Poor girl!" He struck that solemn note of his. "It is not for us to condemn her loyalty."

"It is our task to help her," put in Sigby quickly. "We can do that if you find her, Commissioner." A pause; then Sigby added shrewdly: "When you find her, you will discover Kelburn, too."

Weston nodded. The trouble was the finding of either one. The commissioner was beginning to see the faults of an all-out manhunt. He feared that Kelburn had flown New York entirely, taking Joan with him.

"Of course, it has no bearing on the stock swindle," declared Dulther, in his serious style. "Kelburn's guilt has been fully established, through competent investigation. I am glad to state that the Magnax Corp. will weather the storm caused by the Pharco scandal. Kelburn is no longer a concern of ours."

"In a sense, he still is, Dulther," corrected Sigby quickly. "We'd like to help in bringing him to justice and forcing him to restore the million to the dupes he defrauded."

"Kelburn would never admit having the funds," returned Dulther. "If captured, he will claim that he delivered them to Aldriff."

"I suppose you are right," conceded Sigby, his voice lowered to a reflective pitch. "Yes, you must be right." He waited a moment, then added: "And Aldriff's affairs are so mixed that it might take years to learn the truth. Kelburn would be out of prison by that time."

It was Weston who disagreed on the final point.

"Kelburn will never be out of prison, once there," the commissioner assured. "The duration of his stay depends upon whether he is given a life sentence, or the chair, as penalty for murdering Nevlin."

Cranston noted that Dulther and Sigby were wise enough to not exchange their satisfied glances. Then their faces showed respective interest as Inspector Cardona arrived. It was only Weston who looked annoyed, for he thought Cardona's business had no bearing on the Kelburn matter.

CARDONA'S information concerned a robbery in the wholesale district, maneuvered by a crook named Case Brandle. Cardona had a hunch that The Shadow had routed the raiders, for wounded thugs had talked along that line.

Only Case had escaped the premises, but he had not traveled far. He had been found dead in the back room of his usual hangout. Badly wounded, he had managed to reach that goal before he succumbed.

One curious feature of the case was the disappearance of Junius Wilstead, proprietor of the raided store. He had fled during the excitement; and it was first believed that he had come to harm. But Cardona was bringing word that Wilstead had been heard from, through his attorney.

"He'd been going on a business trip," declared Cardona, "out to Chicago. He was so scared, he said, that he kept right on his way. Managed to find a cab after he'd run a couple of blocks. There's one thing, though, that bothers me.

"When he phoned his lawyer from Chicago, he said he'd have gotten away sooner if the first cab he saw hadn't taken on someone else. But it couldn't have picked up Case Brandle. Wilstead said he saw a man in black, who fell while getting into the cab. The driver had to hoist him through the door."

It answered the description of The Shadow, and Cardona was worried, in consequence. Weston's face seemed troubled, too, though he didn't officially recognize The Shadow's existence. However, the commissioner had other pressing matters.

He turned to Dulther and Sigby, whose faces were repressing their elation at hearing news which made them sure they had settled The Shadow permanently.

"I shall inform each of you, if I hear any report concerning Kelburn's whereabouts," assured Weston. "Good evening, gentlemen, and thank you."

While Weston was reading Cardona's final report on the attempted robbery at Wilstead's, Cranston strolled to the foyer of the Cobalt Club. Wilstead actually was in Chicago; he'd continued there after hearing from The Shadow by telephone, while still in Philadelphia.

Having completed his business in Philadelphia, it was wise that Wilstead should go farther away. In fact, Chicago was merely another stopping point for him. Until The Shadow settled the Aldriff case, he wanted Wilstead out of harm's way, on the chance that Dulther and Sigby might still deem his death necessary.

Judging from their faces, however, they had decided, independently, that Wilstead was harmless, now that The Shadow had been eliminated.

If Wilstead had believed himself connected with the Aldriff matter, he would have sent such word through his lawyer, rather than let a menace still hang over him. Actually, Wilstead didn't know of the connection. He simply knew that he had completed some business for The Shadow.

After lounging a while in the foyer, Cranston made a telephone call. He spoke to Burbank, using The Shadow's tone. Reports were to his liking. One was from Kelburn, at the Aldriff house, stating that The Shadow's agents had come there in a truck, and gone. Others were from agents themselves, on the same subject, and another. Moe's report was the added one.

In his cab, Moe had trailed Dulther and Sigby from the Cobalt Club, and they had gone to their respective apartments. This was the thing that gave The Shadow his chance to name the zero hour. His final plan could only be sprung at a time when Dulther and Sigby were apart.

That time could be now.

With a glance from the phone booth, The Shadow saw Weston and Cardona coming through the foyer. He quickly ordered Burbank to contact Kelburn and give the necessary word.

Then, strolling out as Cranston, The Shadow intercepted Weston near the street door.

THOUGH in a hurry to leave, the commissioner couldn't be too abrupt with Cranston, even though his friend was slow in stating what he had in mind. In fact, Cranston hadn't gotten to the point, when Weston was told that a phone call had just arrived for him.

He strode to a booth, with Cranston and Cardona

following. What Weston thought was a mere routine call proved to be an eye-popper.

After a few words, Weston gulped. Planting a hand over the mouthpiece of the phone, he thrust his head from the booth and told his companions:

"It's Kelburn! He says he wants to talk to us."

A voice was still talking from the receiver. Getting back on the wire, Weston kept responding.

"Yes, Kelburn... Certainly... Of course I shall... Fair enough... What's that?"

Ending with a scowl, Weston turned from the booth.

"He says he wants me to meet him," declared the commissioner, "and I'm to bring along Dulther and Sigby. Kelburn says Inspector Cardona can come, too, but he won't tell me where, unless I give him a fair hearing before attempting to arrest him.

"I told him I would, but he wants somebody else's word for it. Somebody not in an official capacity. Here, Cranston! Take this phone and assure Kelburn that I shall abide by his terms."

Cranston entered the booth and picked up the receiver. Pausing, he turned deliberately to Weston and inquired coolly:

"Will you, Commissioner?"

Weston glared, began to fume. Then, impatiently, he stormed:

"Yes, Cranston! I'll go through with it as Kelburn wants. You have my word for it!"

Cranston told Kelburn that it was all right; received a return statement. Hanging up, he stepped from the booth and stated in his most casual tone:

"Kelburn is out at Aldriff's."

To Weston, this was an incredible surprise, greater than that produced by Kelburn's call. He began to brand the whole thing as a hoax, but both Cranston and Cardona took it as a likely fact. Deciding, at length, that he could lose nothing by going out to Aldriff's, Weston turned toward the door. It was then that Cranston reminded him:

"Those calls to Dulther and Sigby, Commissioner—they were part of the bargain."

Sending Cardona out to summon his official car, Weston went back into a phone booth. He was sure that Dulther and Sigby would agree to come to Aldriff's. So, for that matter, was The Shadow. His question was whether or not they would arrive in keeping with such a promise. It was The Shadow's job to see that they did arrive.

Noting that Weston was calling Dulther first, the calm Mr. Cranston stepped into another booth and dialed Sigby's number. When he spoke, however, his tone was not Cranston's, nor was it the sinister whisper of The Shadow. His words were blunt, heavy, with a note of the solemn.

The Shadow was voicing a perfect imitation of Lloyd Dulther!

He told Sigby about Kelburn's call to Weston, and stated that he had just heard from the commissioner. This was close to fact, for, at that moment, Weston was talking to the real Dulther. Finishing bluntly, The Shadow declared:

"I am going to Aldriff's, Sigby, to see this thing through. I shall also expect to see you there."

"Do you take me for a fool?" demanded Sigby. There was a pause, while Sigby breathed hard; then, in lowered tone: "Suppose I don't come, Dulther. What then?"

"The answer is simple, Sigby." The Shadow voiced Dulther's tone as he would a knell. "I shall tell Commissioner Weston that you murdered Arthur Aldriff!"

A pause; then Sigby gave incoherent utterance. Catching himself, he snapped in vicious style:

"You'll see me there, Dulther!"

Weston was just finishing his call in the other booth. Knowing that the commissioner would phone Sigby next, The Shadow dialed Dulther's number the moment that Weston was through. He had to be quick with it, to get the real Dulther before he called Sigby. But then, Weston was helping out. He was shoving a call through to Sigby's, trying the line at that end.

The Shadow's call clicked home. Dulther's voice came on the wire, and The Shadow chopped across a statement that had all of Sigby's higher pitch:

"I've just heard from the commissioner, Dulther! I've been trying to reach you—"

"You couldn't," interrupted Dulther heavily, "because he was calling me. You're going out to Aldriff's, I suppose."

There was sarcasm in Dulther's heavy boom, but The Shadow decided to let "Sigby" take the statement as though he thought Dulther meant it. He gave a trifling stammer to Sigby's quick tone, as he declared:

"Why, why—yes, I thought it best." A pause came, before The Shadow added: "We ought to see this through, you know."

"*You* see it through," put Dulther bluntly. "Good luck to you, Sigby. I won't be there."

"You *will* be there." Lowering the Sigby tone, The Shadow gave it a decisive ring. "If you aren't—"

"Then what?"

"I'll name you as Aldriff's murderer!"

There was a snarl, as Dulther lost some of his solemn sham. But there was only one answer that he could make to the threat that he took as Sigby's. Angrily Dulther gave it:

"I shall be there, Sigby!"

COMING from his own booth, The Shadow ran into Weston, and in Cranston's casual style informed him that he had just been talking to some friends who expected him elsewhere.

When Weston insisted that he must come to Aldriff's, Cranston reminded the commissioner that Kelburn hadn't extended any invitation. A stickler on the matter of Weston's promise, Cranston had to be equally formal in social matters.

Outside the club, Cranston stepped into his limousine and rode away, while Weston was getting into his official car. Within a few blocks, however, Cranston transferred to a much swifter vehicle, Moe's cab.

Off on a longer ride, Cranston smiled as he recalled the parting statement that Weston had given him, outside the doorway of the club.

"Dulther and Sigby both said they would be there," the commissioner had affirmed. "You'd better come along, Cranston. If you aren't there, you may be missing something."

True enough; Dulther and Sigby would be at Aldriff's, thanks to The Shadow. So, too, would Cranston be there, but not in his present guise.

He would be there as The Shadow, and he would not be missing anything!

CHAPTER XIX
THE PROOF OF MURDER

ALL the way to Aldriff's, Inspector Cardona was wishing that Lamont Cranston had come along. Those significant glances they had exchanged while convincing Weston that Kelburn's call was not a hoax, had made a profound impression on Joe Cardona. Having noted it, Cranston had not found it necessary to express a certain reminder.

Once, Cranston had said that Kelburn, to suit his own ends, might claim that Aldriff's suicide was murder. On that account, Cardona had collected a compact package of exhibits, which he carried in a little suitcase. The bag was in Weston's official car, in keeping of the chauffeur, at Cardona's special request.

So far, Cardona had not mentioned the exhibits to the commissioner. Joe was keeping them until the blowoff came. He wanted to put them right in front of Kelburn, with Weston present to see. Joe hadn't supposed, however, that the chance would come at Aldriff's. That had been too much to expect.

But at Aldriff's it would happen, and Cardona felt it quite too bad that Cranston would not be on hand to witness the triumph which he himself had arranged for Joe to spring.

Commissioner Weston didn't hurry the trip to Long Island, for he wanted to give Dulther and Sigby time to get there. As he rolled in front of the big, dark mansion, a light appeared over the door. Joan Kelburn stepped from the house to greet the police commissioner.

Before they had time to enter, another car appeared. It was Dulther's limousine, and he was riding alone with his chauffeur. He suggested that they wait for Sigby, and a few minutes later, a coupé rolled into the drive. Sigby stepped out, told his secretary to park the car.

No one noticed that Dulther and Sigby were none too cordial. It wasn't surprising that they had come in different cars, for Weston had suggested that they hurry. Nor were nods particularly important, considering that everybody was anxious to meet just one man: Smead Kelburn.

Conducting the group into the house, Joan studied faces and decided all was well. She called upstairs, and after a few tense seconds, Kelburn appeared, carrying a briefcase. His broad face looked firm, and his nod was businesslike. Without a word, he led the way into Aldriff's den and turned on the light.

The room was not materially changed from the evening when Aldriff had died there. Objects like the moose head and the Chinese screen had been replaced. The broken chess table was gone, but the two light chairs were in the nook, set at an angle toward each other.

Requesting first that Cardona frisk him, to see that he did not carry a gun, Kelburn gestured the visitors to seats close by the desk. Perching himself upon the edge of the desk, Kelburn opened his briefcase and produced a collection of documents.

They weren't the papers that had been in Aldriff's dispatch box. Those were in the hands of the authorities who were investigating the Pharco swindle. Kelburn had some duplicate letters to show; but his really important items were receipts and account books signed and certified by Aldriff.

"I want to prove to you," said Kelburn, very firmly, "that I turned over every dollar to Aldriff. But you won't find that he had those funds in his possession. By agreement, he must have given them to Dulther and Sigby, to keep with Magnax assets."

As he spoke, Kelburn looked from Dulther to Sigby, and both returned his gaze in characteristic style. Dulther showed a grieved expression, while Sigby wore a know-it attitude. Kelburn was behaving according to prediction, trying to bolster his totally unproven claim that Dulther and Sigby were behind the million-dollar Pharco swindle.

Then Kelburn sprang his bombshell. Not that Dulther and Sigby hadn't expected it, when they heard that Kelburn wanted to meet them here. Neither would have come, had he felt he could have helped it. Each would have liked to have started a quick flight immediately upon hearing what Kelburn wanted.

They could have pinned those departures to their

mutual fear of Kelburn, after the thing blew over. They were quite sure that Kelburn was trying a bluff, and nothing more. Still, they'd have resorted to the safer course, if The Shadow had not used the ingenious system of transposing Dulther and Sigby, each, to the wrong end of a threatening phone call, reputedly from the other.

"I shall prove that Aldriff's death was murder," assured Kelburn. "That, in itself, will show that these two"—he gestured from Dulther to Sigby—"are responsible. Certainly, I could not have covered myself by killing Aldriff."

KELBURN was going too fast for Cardona. The inspector expected the accused man to play up the masked-man incident, but Kelburn wasn't finding that part necessary.

"When I declare that Aldriff's death was not suicide," added Kelburn pointedly, "I am speaking for a friend of mine who calls himself The Shadow. Every ounce of proof supplied in this case was furnished by him."

The reference to "every ounce" carried a peculiar significance of its own. Kelburn asked to see the photographs taken of the death room. When Cardona produced them, Kelburn compared them with the room as it stood at present.

"The present arrangement is satisfactory," stated Kelburn. "The fireplace, too small of chimney for anyone to use it for entry; the chess nook empty except for those two light chairs; over here, the screen covering the filing cabinet.

"This photograph shows the nook quite innocent, while the fireplace and the space behind the screen were immediately inspected. Yet in this room lurked a murderer, planted while Aldriff and Joan were absent on the sun porch. For that was the only time when he could have entered and waited for the kill."

Laying the photographs aside, Kelburn picked up a diagram that Cardona had made of the death room. Before referring to it, Kelburn stated briefly:

"According to The Shadow, the deed of murder was no more important than the arrival of a masked man later. For a perfect crime, it would have been better if the room had been left unmolested. There must have been some reason why it couldn't be; hence the masked man came.

"The reason was that the murderer was still hiding here, and could only escape through darkness and confusion. The masked man produced both, and the killer fled with him. Of course, both were aided by their accomplice, Nevlin."

The theory was sound enough. Nevlin's way of blowing hot and cold marked him as a likely accomplice. He had boldly yanked the lamp from the desk, producing the necessary darkness. The rapid wrecking of the room pointed to quick assistance on the part of Nevlin. But it still didn't prove the factor of a hidden murderer in a sealed room that had both been viewed and probed as empty.

"You are all wondering about the hiding place," concluded Kelburn, ignoring derisive stares from Dulther and Sigby. "There it is, in plain sight! Indeed, I might say too-plain sight!"

Kelburn's argument had reached the limit of absurdity, for when he pointed, his finger was squarely toward the empty chess nook deep in the wall of the room!

While Weston glowered, Cardona decided to halt the hoax. He opened the suitcase, to bring out its exhibits, and Kelburn gave a quick, approving glance that way. Then, drawing a pencil from his pocket, Kelburn wagged it toward the nook and stated:

"Note the square walls of that space. It looked empty, but it wasn't, the night when Aldriff was murdered. I shall tell you why. At an angle across the nook, from one front corner to the rear, ran an upright mirror, which divided the nook into two triangles. Its reflection made the visible triangle appear as a full-sized square. In the hidden triangle, behind the mirror, the killer stood hidden while the room was searched!"

Using the diagram, Kelburn pointed to the square that represented the nook, and drew a diagonal line from one rear corner to the opposite front. He showed it to Weston, who kept bobbing his head from diagram to nook.

"There were two chairs in that nook," said the commissioner. "The photograph shows them, exactly as you placed them, one on each side of the center. How could the mirror have been there with two chairs in sight?"

"*One* chair," corrected Kelburn. "The Shadow mentioned it, and called special attention to its angle. Set in the open half of the nook, that chair was reflected by the mirror to show its mate turned toward it. Thus the nook appeared to have the two chairs that belonged there, exactly as you see it now.

"Why was the table out of the nook, lying overturned upon the floor? The Shadow knew the answer, Commissioner. It belonged in the very middle of the nook; hence it couldn't have been left in place and allowed the mirror, too."

When Weston began to question how the mirror was planted in the first place, Joan began to pour out her answers. She'd told The Shadow her whole story, and he had analyzed its essential details.

"IT came in with the screen," explained Joan. "The screen was packed flat; they could hardly get it through the door. It was Nevlin who unpacked it, after Aldriff and I went out."

"And set it up alone?"

"The murderer could have helped him," replied Joan. "He must have come in about that time."

"Then the murderer hid behind the mirror—"

"After he killed Aldriff, yes. When the masked man arrived, and the lights went off, he came out."

Weston shook his head.

"It won't do, Miss Kelburn," he said. "You can't explain what happened to the mirror. The murderer certainly couldn't have taken it with him. We searched this room afterward, and in tapping the walls, we actually entered the nook."

"Of course you did!" exclaimed Joan. "The murderer had disposed of the mirror. Look, Commissioner"—the girl pointed in back of Aldriff's body on the photograph. "See that huge empty space? Look at the photos and you'll see what belonged there. A great looking glass in a Florentine frame.

"During the fight that the masked man started, that huge glass was hauled from the wall and flung over by the nook. The masked man did it, aided by Nevlin. When the framed mirror smashed, the killer thrust his mirror out from the alcove and crashed it, too. Nobody except The Shadow realized that there was glass enough for two mirrors—"

"Or that the glass in each would differ," added Kelburn, plucking chunks of silvered glass from Cardona's collection of exhibits. "The Shadow must have inspired you, too, Inspector, when you were making up this collection. See for yourself how these pieces differ."

They did differ, and while Cardona was comparing pieces, Weston began to do the same. Some chunks, those from the Florentine frame, were thick; others, from the invisible mirror that had produced the illusion of an empty chess nook, were thin. They varied, too, in luster, and the painted backings were not alike in shade.

These exhibits were proof of murder, not of suicide. That fact was drilling home to Joe Cardona as he stared at his own reflection in a fragment of glass, then looked toward Weston, to see the commissioner nod.

Others saw that nod and used it as a signal for themselves. Two voices—one blunt and heavy, the other quick and querulous—demanded that everyone else turn around. All did, to find themselves confronted by the partners in murder.

Forgotten in the eagerness to solve the death of Arthur Aldriff, the men who had killed that victim were taking over the scene. Each with a drawn gun, Lloyd Dulther and Hubert Sigby stood masters of the situation.

Masters in the absence of The Shadow!

CHAPTER XX
MURDERERS TWO

THOUGH neither was feeling cordial toward the other, Dulther and Sigby were shrewd enough to know that their old alliance was essential to their safety, once their game was revealed.

In a sense, each was operating on his own, but they had the precision of a perfect team. Once the victims were covered and had their hands raised, Dulther kept them at bay, while Sigby whipped away the screen that hid the filing cabinet, to make sure that no one was hidden there.

Then, with Sigby taking over, Dulther closed the room door and locked it. Sigby was studying the sullen glares of Weston and Cardona; but Dulther preferred to examine the faces of Kelburn and Joan.

Both were glum, for they hadn't expected this climax. They'd gone through with everything The Shadow ordered, and they had not seen him since. He'd left them to drop the curtain on the final act, and they had done it.

"Yes, we were in the deal with Aldriff," spoke Dulther. "He handed us the Pharco million, and we disposed of him. He thought it was going to be a three-way split, himself included, with Kelburn as the only man to take the blame."

"But it couldn't have worked that way," snapped Sigby. "We had Aldriff bluffed into thinking we'd find a way to cover up for him. When he began to worry, it was time for us to quit. We hadn't expected to build the Pharco stock sales much past a million, anyway."

"And now," decided Dulther, "we'll dispose of these fools as we did with Nevlin."

"Hardly the best policy," argued Sigby. "Why not just kill Weston and Cardona. If we take Kelburn and his niece with us, they will be blamed for the deaths of the others."

Dulther's tone became a sneer.

"Take Kelburn and the girl," he scoffed. "Why not just Kelburn? The girl would only be a burden."

"Kelburn wouldn't shoot his own niece," objected Sigby. "Nobody would believe him quite that tough. Even a murderer can show some soft spots."

"Are you showing a soft spot, Sigby?"

At the question, Sigby turned angrily, to meet the leer that Dulther gave him.

"Don't forget, Sigby," Dulther declared, "that less than an hour ago, you phoned me and said that in a pinch you would accuse me of murdering Aldriff. Maybe you've forgotten your sojourn in that nook, the night that Nevlin helped you plant a mirror across it."

"You're the man with the poor memory," snapped Sigby. "It was you who called me and threatened to tell the truth, if I didn't come here.

You knew I'd killed Aldriff, and you were going to declare it. That makes you a double-crosser, Dulther!"

With a savage bellow, Dulther swung at Sigby as though intending to blast him with bullets. With a quick bound, Sigby was around, with his own gun leveled at his partner. The Shadow's telephone ruse was bearing dividends. It was ruining the team of Dulther & Sigby.

It hadn't mattered which one had murdered Aldriff; the psychology was perfect, in each case. Dulther, who had played masked man instead of murderer, had been swept with indignation when he heard Sigby's voice declaring that it would put the blame on him. As for Sigby, he'd regarded it an outrage when Dulther's tone had bluntly promised to speak the actual fact.

The Shadow had foreseen that this would happen. Once divided, the partners of evil were sure to quarrel. They'd laid themselves right open for a quick attack by Weston and Cardona. If ever criminals had put themselves on a spot, Dulther and Sigby had done it.

UNFORTUNATELY, Weston and Cardona were on a spot of their own. They'd stepped behind the desk to look at the slivers of glass, and their interest in those baubles was their undoing. To get at Dulther and Sigby, they had to swing around the desk, and the process took too long.

They weren't even started, when Dulther turned and saw them. At that moment, Kelburn and Joan sprang forward, hoping to give aid.

Both killers were dropping back, each knowing that he would need a little firing range to jab two gunshots home. It was in that moment of peril that intervention came. The sort that no killers, especially these two, could afford to ignore for a single instant.

To Dulther and Sigby, The Shadow's laugh was like a taunt from the grave!

What else could it be than a ghostly gibe, for it reverberated within this very room. How could The Shadow have entered, unseen, and remained hidden while Dulther and Sigby were in control!

In the stress that gripped them, the murderers flung wild gazes everywhere—toward fireplace, past screen, even to the corner that held Aldriff's trophy case.

Everywhere, except the right place, the one they should have thought of first—the murder nook in the deep wall of the room!

Others saw the thing that happened there. It looked as though the fourth dimension had split asunder to loose a strange, weird creature of another sphere. For the nook was empty, except for those flimsy chairs; yet The Shadow was appearing from its core!

Equally remarkable were the gyrations of the nook itself. The little alcove had become alive. It was folding back into itself, while the chairs it contained were doing the amazing feat of blending from two into one.

It wasn't until The Shadow was completely clear that the jackknife motion ended. Then, as the black-cloaked fighter came lunging forward, explanation dawned on Dulther and Sigby.

All the while that Kelburn had been pointing to an empty nook, and explaining how it could have been transformed into an invisible hiding place, he had been extolling the merits of the genuine article. Dulther and Sigby, designers of the illusion, had been deceived by their own device!

Today, The Shadow's agents had come by truck, bringing the purchase that their chief had made through Wilstead—a special mirror, shipped from a Philadelphia factory, a duplicate of the one that Nevlin had ordered when he bought the Chinese screen. A mirror cut to the exact diagonal dimensions of Aldriff's chess nook.

In place, put there by the men who brought it, the mirror had needed only a single chair in front of it to produce the precise mystery that even photographs had failed to expose: that of emptiness that wasn't empty!

Arriving earlier than Weston, The Shadow had posted himself where he could have the final say. He was showing how easily the mirror could be swung. Had he chosen to topple it, the big glass would have broken as the original had done. But The Shadow wasn't breaking mirrors. He was simply here to see that bad luck landed on two men who had.

Bad luck in the shape of leaden slugs. For The Shadow waited only until Dulther and Sigby turned his way, each from a front corner of the room. Whirling, he drew their fire away from the victims over whom they had disputed. But The Shadow, back from the dead, out from empty space, wasn't an easy target while he was on the move.

Dulther and Sigby were easier, fixed in their positions. Dulther's gun hand sagged, as a bullet thwacked the wrist above it. Sigby, a bit shiftier, took a bullet in the opposite shoulder, but the pain made him clap his gun hand across to it. Then, to the tune of The Shadow's taunt, others were upon them, seeking deserved vengeance.

Trying to twist from Weston, Cardona and Kelburn, Dulther and Sigby somehow managed to get the door unlocked. On the fringe of that melee was Joan, frantically hoping that she could find a way to help.

All the while, The Shadow was skirting toward the door, ready to deliver any final stroke that might be needed. He was close by when frantic hands wrested the door inward; he saw the group break apart as the barrier gave. Then two men were shouldering through it.

One man's shoulder struck, and he slipped back with a shriek of pain. The man was Sigby. As he grabbed at his competitor, Dulther gave a ruthless gun thrust. He had the gun in the wrong hand, but that mattered little, for he was close enough to shove the muzzle against Sigby's body. A muffled shot, and Sigby was sliding down against the doorway, while Dulther, leering above him, was taking a back step through.

The Shadow's .45 had been covering both. It shifted to Dulther alone, but it didn't speak. Though mortally wounded, Sigby still could use his uninjured gun hand, and the doorway was propping him, even as he sagged. Blindly, but straight at Dulther's heart, Sigby shoved his gun and tugged the trigger.

As Sigby reached the floor and rolled across the doorway, Dulther caved and landed heavily upon him. Sigby's last coughs were smothered by the bulk that flattened him. Partners in crime had become partners in death!

THEN blackness shrouded those dead forms—blackness like a passing cloud, except that it was solid. Yet, like a cloud, it faded as a cloaked figure stepped across the men of murder and reached the hallway beyond. There, like swirling smoke, the black-clad victor vanished into the gloom beyond.

The Shadow needed no mirrors to come or go from nowhere, when he chose. He had used one simply to show how it had served the murderers who had planned so well that their own trick had fooled them, when The Shadow performed it for their benefit.

Wafted back from outdoors came The Shadow's parting laugh. It seemed to cling within the room of doom, a reminder of the being who had solved the riddle of a perfect crime. Shivery was that mirth that marked The Shadow's triumph over crime!

Only Dulther and Sigby failed to hear it. In this room where they had managed to make Aldriff's murder look like suicide, those murderous two had dealt in suicide of their own. Mutual murder, it might be called, but whatever the proper term, the craft of The Shadow had turned the hands of killers each against the other.

Later, in the calm of Margo's apartment, Joan Kelburn told the story of that strife to Lamont Cranston, the other friend who had so ably aided her. Smead Kelburn was also present, and he supplied Cranston with some other facts, while Joan was answering questions asked by Margo Lane.

"Dulther and Sigby had the cash, all right," assured Kelburn. "Their safe-deposit boxes were stuffed with it. They didn't care what happened to the Magnax Corp.; not while they had half a million apiece.

"They did right by Magnax, though." The thought made Kelburn smile. "It was the best way for them to cover up; that's why. And do you know, with a million dollars' worth of Pharco stock all sold with cash in hand, Magnax can't do better than to get behind the Pharco chain and put it over.

"This may have started as a swindle, though I didn't know it. But I'll sell a million more of the best stock on the market. I still rate my commissions on the last lot, and when I'm finished, Joan and I will be fixed for life."

Joan heard the final comment, but it wasn't the thought of the future that impressed her. She was thinking of the past, and she recalled it vividly. The thing that stirred her recollections was the smile on the lips of Cranston.

Strange, how memories could etch themselves and link together in unaccountable fashion. When Joan Kelburn saw Lamont Cranston smile, she fancied that she heard the laugh of The Shadow!

THE END

INTERLUDE by Will Murray

"It's all done with mirrors."

That's the famous all-purpose explanation of the professional magician and illusionist to explain his baffling illusions. Certainly there is a grain of truth in this, in that many magical devices employ the trickery of mirrors to produce their astonishing effects. Of course, a great many more don't use mirrors at all.

For this clever Shadow volume, we have selected two enthralling novels in which Walter B. Gibson's knowledge of stage magic and illusion play key roles.

Our lead novel, *Room of Doom*, is actually a locked room mystery in the classic sense, as popularized during the Golden Age of mystery fiction by Gibson's fellow Pennsylvanian, John Dickson Carr, who went on to become an Edgar Award winning practitioner of the tricky subgenre.

Under the able editorial guidance of John L. Nanovic, Gibson explored virtually every convention and trope of the mystery-suspense genre. Written in September, 1941 and published in the April 1, 1942 issue of *The Shadow*, *Room of Doom* is not the first sealed room mystery The Shadow ever confronted. Far from it. But it is quite a good story.

Nanovic's preview editorial delved into this key aspect, and his high opinion of it:

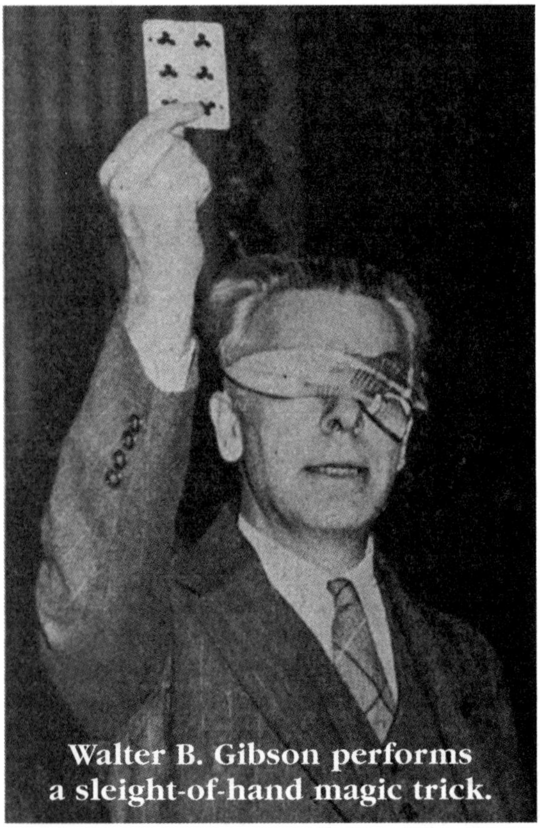

Walter B. Gibson performs a sleight-of-hand magic trick.

> Maxwell Grant has written a novel that is going to be the top-ranking one, without a doubt, of all those that have gone before, and we're giving it to you in the next issue. It's called "Room of Doom," and it will give you everything in the way of chills, excitement, interest, and a clever plot that will have you stumped completely.
>
> We'll give you just a little idea of it. There's a murder in a room; a murder committed in a room in such a way that no one could possibly have done the murder and gotten out of it. That, you might say, is not so unusual; there have been other "sealed room" murders before. True. But in this case, after the murder has been committed, a killer comes around ready to murder to get *into* the room! Not to escape from it; to get into it!
>
> Why?
>
> Well, that's what we started out to tell you—that's what is going to make the story such a hit with every one of our readers. We often tell you that the next novel is going to be better than the last, because we really strive to make each one better than the other. But we don't go overboard too often by claiming as much for a story as we do for this, and whenever we do, you know we come through. So don't miss the next issue.

Nanovic seems to have slightly misunderstood the nature of the locked-room concept. Typically, it involved a body being discovered in a room or space in which the murderer could not have *entered* in the first place. He repeated this in the editorial prefacing the story:

> If you want a good, tough mystery to puzzle you; something that will make you reach for pencil and paper so that you can really figure out the answer—and find out you're wrong after you've figured—you can get it in "Room of Doom," the complete Shadow novel that starts on page 9 of this issue.
>
> You've probably read a lot of so-called "sealed room" mysteries in which a murder occurs under seemingly impossible conditions. No one could have gotten out of the room after the murder.
>
> Well, here's a mystery in which such a murder does occur, and it is mysterious enough; but it is more mysterious when the killer tries murder in order to get *into* the room, after the first murder has been committed!
>
> As we said before, get out your paper and pencil, if you want to have some fun. Or perhaps you might as well give up right away and just read how The Shadow solves this unusual case in his most exciting manner. It's a great novel.

Nanovic's blurbs did not usually reflect humor, but here, after inviting the reader to respond to the challenge of Maxwell Grant's ingenious plot, he essentially tells his audience that they're basically wasting their time!

Rita Hayworth and Everett Sloane in *The Lady from Shanghai*

Well, Walter Gibson had been fooling his readers on a semi-monthly basis for a solid decade at this point. And he would continue to do so to the end of the decade. As a friend and confidant of famous stage magicians such as Harry Houdini, Joseph Dunninger, Harry Blackstone and others, he understood the power of misdirection—even as practiced on the printed page. While he may not have been privvy to all of their secrets, the Man Who Cast The Shadow understood magical apparatus in principle, and had devised tricks of his own.

But the cover is what we would like to focus on now. It is one of George Rozen's best of 1942, indeed one of the top Shadow paintings of the entire decade, and we've reproduced our front cover from George Rozen's original painting.

Rozen clearly had not lost his touch upon his return from his enforced sabbatical in 1941. His approach may have become more action-oriented, but the prolific artist could still produce a knockout Shadow painting that stood up to the best of his 1930s output.

Based upon the scene involving multiple reflecting showroom mirrors, Rozen went the extra dozen miles and gave us an array of striking images of the Dark Avenger. When you compare this to the 10th anniversary *Time Master* cover for which interim artist Graves Gladney painted ten Shadow heads, you can see that Rozen far surpassed him in composition. Adding four more Shadows to the *Room of Doom* cover might have been difficult, but it would have made a more appropriate 10th anniversary cover.

We often throw the spotlight on aspects of The Shadow that foreshadowed Batman and other popular cultural icons. Here, Gibson and Rozen together foreshadowed the iconic scene in Orson Welles' 1947 film noir, *The Lady from Shanghai*, wherein Welles' character and Rita Hayworth are stalked in an amusement park maze of mirrors by villain Everett Sloane. This climactic scene features images of a pistol-wielding Sloane that are strikingly similar to Rozen's dramatic painting.

Although Welles played The Shadow on radio a few years prior to *Room of Doom*'s publication, it's entirely possible that the great radio actor and director continued to pay attention to the Master Avenger's exploits. During the late 1940s, he had explored the possibility of doing a serious feature film based on The Shadow.

Wouldn't it be interesting if the mirror scene from *The Lady in Shanghai* was actually based on this Shadow image? Interesting, but not probable. For the famous scene had originally been conceived for a completely different and unrelated planned film called *Don't Catch Me*.

Decades in the future, the scene was replicated in the 1994 Alec Baldwin *Shadow* film during a confrontation in Shiwan Khan's headquarters, the

Orson Welles and Rita Hayworth in *The Lady from Shanghai*'s hall of mirrors.

Alec Baldwin and John Lone (as Shiwan Khan) in *The Shadow* (1994)

Hotel Monolith. That striking scene was originally planned as much more elaborate than the one that appeared onscreen. Unfortunately for the production, the complex hall of mirrors set constructed on the Universal backlot was destroyed during the January 1994 Northridge, California earthquake. When it was rebuilt, time and budget constraints required that a smaller version be assembled, resulting in a much-reduced spectacle.

Did the filmmakers take their inspiration from Orson Welles or from George Rozen's cover? Probably both, since they certainly researched The Shadow deeply and screenwriter David Koepp, along with director Russell Mulcahy, could hardly have been unaware of Orson Welles and his magical approach the cinema. For Welles performed magic, as did Walter Gibson and later "Maxwell Grant" Bruce Elliott. In later years, the two men resembled one another as they both became more portly, though Walter Gibson was somewhat dismissive of Elliott's claim to be Welles' double.

We jump ahead to the digest era of *The Shadow* magazine for *The Chest of Chu Chan*. Written in April of 1944, this tricky tale first saw print in the September, 1944 issue. Despite the evocative title, this is not one of Walter's memorable Chinatown stories. Editor Babette Rosmond seems to have had an antipathy for those types of yarns. But the story is built around yet another bit of magician's stage apparatus, transferred to criminal use.

Cabinet vanishes were a specialty of Gibson's friend, Harry Houdini. One of his most spectacular performances was the "Vanishing Elephant" illusion, first demonstrated to a rapt audience at New York's Hippodrome in 1918. An ornate cabinet was stationed on the stage and, after the audience was invited to inspect its empty interior, a five-ton elephant was escorted inside. Doors and curtains were duly closed. Twelve strong men rotated the cabinet and it was reopened to show the absence of any pachyderm! Since the cabinet was suspended twelve inches off the floor and no trap door was involved, audiences were astonished.

In *The Chest of Chu Chan*, Walter Gibson contrives, not to make an elephant disappear, but a murdered victim appear—seemingly out of thin air.

In this baffler, one may ask: was it done with mirrors? Well, we're not telling. Read on and find out for yourself! •

Houdini performs his famous "Vanishing Elephant" illusion.

THE CHEST OF CHU CHAN

by Maxwell Grant

Mad murder! And a body in a locked chest pierced by the priceless Burmese katar! Can a mere statue of a beautiful Siamese dancer come to life? A pulsing, dramatic climax gives The Shadow his startling answer.

CHAPTER I

JARED SHEBLEY leaned back in his teakwood chair and toyed with the Burmese katar. His crisp smile, slicing across his parchment face, would have suited an Oriental potentate more than a New York curio collector.

Shebley's surroundings were in keeping with his appearance.

This was his curio room, the pride of his Manhattan penthouse. Its walls were adorned with tall, narrow tapestries, woven mostly in gold and silver, set alternately between the glass-fronted cabinets that housed the rarities comprising

Shebley's collection.

It would have required a sizable pamphlet to describe those items. In fact, such a pamphlet was already in the making; the proof sheets were scattered all over the chess table which Shebley used as a desk. The table itself, a bulky and elaborate affair inlaid with squares of black and white mother-of-pearl, was one of Shebley's chief prizes. It was supposed to be the table on which a Persian prince had been maneuvering his men when he was captured, along with his royal tent, by Hulagu, the Mongolian invader operating under the banner of Genghis Khan.

As with most of Shebley's curios, the authenticity of this number was a matter of some doubt, but not to Shebley. He believed it to be the genuine article, and the only thing that bothered him was what Hulagu had done with the chessmen that belonged with it. Shebley would be very unhappy if some day that ancient chess set showed up in the possession of another eccentric collector.

What bothered Professor Giles Frescott was the way in which Shebley toyed with the Burmese katar.

No weapon more insidious could have been imagined, let alone fashioned, than this royal katar or Oriental thrusting dagger. As he studied it across the chess table, Professor Frescott lost some of the benign expression that usually characterized his broad, elderly features. His eyes narrowed under his thin gray brows, though whether through suspicion or envy, he didn't declare.

With all his genial ways, Frescott mistrusted collectors as a whole, perhaps because he recognized that he, too, had the basic urge to lay his hands upon rare items and hold them. But as curator of the Museum of Antiquities, the noted professor had managed to curb his secret desires.

Shebley noticed Frescott's gaze and broadened his peculiar smile.

"I was about to discuss the chest of Chu Chan," remarked Shebley, dryly, "but I see that you are more interested in the katar of Pagan Min."

Frescott's eyes widened immediately.

"You mean Pagan Min, the Burmese king?"

"Precisely," replied Shebley. "Pagan Min, the son of Tharawaddy, ruler of Burma, until deposed by his brother Mindon Min, who proved to be the only humane king in the entire line of Alompra."

Professor Frescott gave a knowing nod.

"That was the curse of Alompra," he recalled. "Beginning with a warrior chieftain, the dynasty degenerated and finally perished through descendants who were the victims of a homicidal mania."

"A fratricidal mania, too," added Shebley. "One of their greatest pastimes was killing off their brothers—and all their families were large."

Again Frescott nodded.

"I've often wondered about Pagan Min," continued Shebley. "He must have hated his brother Mindon, and why he let him live, I cannot understand. Why, if Mindon had ever come within Pagan's reach—"

With a sudden pause, Shebley studied Frescott's gaze as though trying to guess what lay behind the narrowed eyes. Then, crisply, Shebley asked:

"You are interested, Professor?"

"Very much," assured Frescott in a dispassionate tone. "You appear to be versed in Oriental customs, and anything Oriental intrigues me."

It was so frankly put that Shebley decided his actions would not be misunderstood. Rising from the table, he stepped around it, the twelve inch dagger lying flat across his hands so that Frescott could study it more closely. The professor had seen many katars before, but none like this.

"Unique."

Shebley voiced the word in matter-of-fact tone. It was his favorite expression, for it applied to every item in his well-stocked cases. As a collector, Shebley valued curios only if they were quite unmatched, and he had reason to prize this katar as such.

The silver blade was six inches long, and ran wide from the hilt, tapering to a dull point. Having no sharpened edges, it appeared to be a ceremonial weapon, as was further evidenced by the hilt. In fact, the hilt was the distinctive feature that caused a katar to differ from other styles of daggers.

Instead of a mere handle, the hilt was shaped like a letter H so that the cross-bar could be gripped by the fist, the knuckles resting in the stirrup-shaped space between the cross-bar and the dagger blade. The upper extensions of the hilt were protective wings for the hand and wrist and were composed of gold, highly ornamented.

It was the cross-bar, however, that fascinated Frescott, as Shebley knew it would. Instead of being mere gold as was customary with the finest hand-grips, the center of the bar was a gleaming, blood-red stone set between two cup-shaped holders. As large as a marble and as round, that magnificent gem seemed filled with the blood for which the dagger's blade unquestionably thirsted.

At first glance, Frescott mistook the jewel for a genuine ruby, worth a fortune in itself, but Shebley, catching his visitor's questioning glance, shook his head.

"A Balas ruby!" defined Shebley. "Merely a form of spinel, though this is a fine specimen, which I doubt that anyone could match. It probably came from Tharawaddy's crown, so he could furnish his bloodthirsty son with a weapon befitting a murderous prince."

Opening one button of his vest, Shebley thrust the dagger through the space so that the silver blade projected below and the gold hilt, with its blood-red eye appeared above. There was something rakish in the slant of the weapon which brought a happy chuckle from Shebley.

"This is the way Pagan Min must have worn it," decided Shebley. "More as an ornament than a weapon, judging by its appearance. But Mindon Min must have known its purpose, for if he had let his evil brother come close enough—"

Shebley gave another of his abrupt pauses, though he could well have added—"this would have happened!" Instead, he demonstrated the deed in question. With a stride toward Frescott, as though the latter represented Mindon Min, Shebley gripped the cross-hilt of the katar and whipped the dagger from his improvised belt. Pulling back, his arm drove forward like a piston, stopping halfway in its thrust.

The jab was comfortably short of Frescott, and it was lucky that it was. For with it, Shebley illustrated the automatic action of the deadly katar. Actuated by the pressure of Shebley's knuckles, the silver blade opened into two sections, scissors-fashion. Those splitting halves were like spreading flower petals, but what they disclosed was by no means pretty.

The silver blade, as dull as it was ornamental, was nothing more than a cunningly fitted sheath for a blade of steel concealed within. Needle-pointed, razor-edged, the deadly prong jabbed into sight like a cobra's fang lashing from a widened mouth!

Professor Frescott might have been expecting something of the sort, for he didn't budge a muscle. Shebley's mock thrust could have scared his visitor into immobility, but Frescott's broad face revealed nothing resembling fear. Rather casually, the professor held out his hand, silently requesting the privilege of examining the weapon. Shebley gave a reverse flip that closed the outer blade; then handed over the katar.

"I admire your sangfroid, Professor," Shebley commented. "Other visitors have been more impressed."

"Who for example?"

"Lionel Graff," named Shebley. "Which proves that Graff does not know as much about Oriental antiques as he claims."

"Graff is merely a speculator." There was a tone of contempt from Frescott. "Surely you do not take his word on anything"—the professor was tilting his head to study Shebley's face—"or do you?"

"On speculative propositions, yes," returned Shebley, "because that is Graff's business. There, Professor!" Shebley became suddenly enthusiastic. "You've got the hang of it already!"

Shebley was referring to the katar, which was performing its scissors trick under the persuasion of Frescott's knuckles. With a style that might have been termed professional, the museum curator was causing the hidden blade to show and disappear by movements forward and back that were almost imperceptible.

Then, closing the katar, Frescott took it by the harmless outer blade and held it so he could examine the large Balas ruby that showed a deepening tint in the glow of sunset that was streaming in from Shebley's well-barred window.

"A magnificent specimen," mused Frescott, half aloud, without specifying whether he meant the katar or the gem which ornamented it. "Yes, I believe that I would class it as unique."

Shebley was quick to take advantage of those words. Eager-eyed, he demanded:

"Unique? Like the chest of Chu Chan?"

Momentarily, Frescott's eyes matched the ruby's glitter. Then, relaxing his gaze, he slid the katar among the proof sheets on the chess table and leaned back, folding his hands across his vest. Frescott's laugh was pleasant, but the elderly professor had a habit of covering his real sentiments with opposite tones.

"You invited me here to discuss the chest of Chu Chan," declared Frescott blandly, "so tell me what you already know about it and I shall supply the rest. We may as well come directly to the point instead of trying to conceal it."

A subtle listener might have suspected that Frescott's final sentence referred to the Burmese katar rather than the chest of Chu Chan, but Shebley was not inclined to be subtle. Seating himself, he began to pour the facts that Frescott wanted.

All the while, the ruby handle of the Burmese katar kept deepening its glow in the dying sunset, like the watchful eye of some evil monster awaiting the chance to deliver a fatal thrust!

CHAPTER II

IT was an interesting tale that Jared Shebley told while Giles Frescott listened with half closed eyes.

The chest of Chu Chan had belonged to a Chinese of the same name who resided in Hanoi, capital of Tonkin, in the north of French Indo-China. For many years Chu Chan had lived there undisturbed until the Japanese began to move into Indo-China, taking whatever they wanted, particularly from Chinese nationals.

Chu Chan had managed, however, to keep a few jumps ahead of the wily Japs, where his treasures were concerned.

First, Chu Chan's belongings had been shipped southwest across the Mekong River to Bangkok, the capital of Siam. By the time the Nipponese arrived there, the shipment was on its way to Singapore, where it cleared again for India before the Japs controlled the Malayan Straits.

At last the goods had arrived in America, there to be auctioned to raise funds for the cause of China, in keeping with instructions given by Chu Chan, when last heard from.

"Dariel Talcott bought the antique chest," concluded Shebley. "You must know him, Professor. He owns the Talcott Antique Galleries."

Frescott nodded as though half asleep.

"A very reliable dealer, Talcott."

"So reliable," assured Shebley, "that he wouldn't guarantee that the chest of Chu Chan was unique, as he did with the katar of Pagan Min. Talcott said that I would do well to check its history personally."

"Quite wise of Talcott."

"He has always been more than fair," affirmed Shebley. "For instance, he wouldn't even think of selling me the Bangkok dancer statue."

Frescott's eyes opened.

"What statue was that?"

"One that came with the chest of Chu Chan," explained Shebley. "It was inside the chest, so the two were sold as a lot. Only I doubt that it even belonged to Chu Chan. Probably it was put into the chest to get it away from Siam before the Japs arrived there."

"A logical theory, but why didn't you want the dancer statue?"

"Because Talcott says there are dozens like it in Siam, all life-sized figures in a seated pose. As I said before, Talcott only sells me items that he knows are unique."

Frescott began to nod in understanding fashion, then paused as though puzzled.

"This chest of Chu Chan," he remarked. "It must be quite large to hold so sizable a statue."

"That's right," returned Shebley. "It is a large chest. Built much like a cabinet."

Frescott gave a disparaging shrug.

"Then it isn't unique," he declared. "It may be antique, but not unique." Chuckling at his play on words, the professor added: "There is a difference, Shebley, as you should know."

"Only I don't know." Shebley stroked his chin. "Simon Benisette bought the dancer statue, and now he is interested in the chest. He's a sharp buyer, Benisette."

"But he doesn't specialize in the unique."

"He specializes in anything that promises a profit," argued Shebley. "That's why I'm beginning to believe what Graff said. You see, Graff told me"—Shebley halted, then decided to out with it—"well, he told me that there might be a fortune in the chest of Chu Chan. So I'm of a mind to let Graff bid for me against Benisette."

Though Shebley didn't notice it, Professor Frescott had become suddenly alert. His eyes by their very sharpness, could have been likened to the hidden blade in Shebley's katar, but they, too, were concealed as Frescott promptly closed his eyelids over them like folding sheaths.

Tilting his head back, Frescott gave a mild, though significant chuckle that puzzled Shebley just enough to take him totally off guard.

"Nobody will bid on that chest," laughed Frescott, "at least not at Talcott's Antique Galleries."

"And why not?"

"Because Talcott has already sold it," informed Frescott. "It went to a dealer in Washington."

There was something of savagery in Shebley's gesture as he reached for the telephone. Frescott waved his hand.

"Don't call Talcott," warned Frescott. "You won't have time. You'd better phone the airport for a reservation on the next plane to Washington. You'll just have time to make it."

Taking Frescott's advice, Shebley dialed the airport, but his gaze carried a query which Frescott answered with a question of his own.

"Did you ever hear of Lamont Cranston?"

Shebley nodded.

"I happen to know that Cranston will be taking that plane to Washington," assured Frescott. "Like yourself, he is interested in the chest of Chu Chan."

Shebley had the number. Finding that plane seats were still available, he ordered one. As Shebley hung up, Frescott reached for the telephone.

"May I call the museum?" asked Frescott. "They may be wondering where I am."

"Of course," replied Shebley. "Only I'll have to say good-bye right now, if I want to catch the plane. If you want, you can wait and talk to Graff, because he's due here shortly. But it won't matter. I'll have my servant tell Graff I've gone out of town."

Nodding toward Shebley, Frescott fumbled the dial in what seemed accidental fashion. Repeating the process slowly, the professor took pains to keep from getting his number before Shebley went, which wasn't difficult, because Shebley was already starting from the room, calling for his valet.

With a smile that marked him capable of conniving practices, Frescott completed the connection. Alone in Shebley's curio room, Frescott asked to be connected with his own office in the Museum of Antiquities. There were a few rings from the line; then came a voice that Frescott recognized.

"Hello, Cranston." Frescott's tone was both affable and confidential. "Sorry to keep you waiting, but I have some last minute news. You know Jared Shebley, of course?"

Apparently Lamont Cranston did, and said so. From then on, Professor Frescott was very precise.

"Shebley has heard on what he regards as good authority," stated Frescott, "that the chest of Chu Chan has gone to a Washington dealer. So Shebley is taking the next plane to Washington. You will just about have time to do the same."

The abrupt click of the receiver at the other end told that Cranston wasn't losing a moment in acting on Frescott's advice. With a subdued chuckle, the old professor arose from his chair and rustled the proof sheets on the chess table as he fumbled for his hat that was lying there.

Leaving the dusk-shrouded room, Frescott went out through the hallway; his hat still in hand, he bowed to Shebley's servant as he left. Taking the elevator down to the ground floor, the professor went out to the street.

There was something crablike in Frescott's rapid gait toward the nearest corner. Over his shoulder, the benign-faced man looked back with a conniving smile. Someone was entering the rather modest apartment house that was noteworthy only because of Shebley's lavish penthouse; somebody whose face Frescott recognized.

The arrival, sallow of face and worried, was Lionel Graff, the speculator who had come to convince Jared Shebley that he ought to buy the chest of Chu Chan. Graff would be sadly disappointed when he learned of Shebley's sudden departure, and that fact gladdened Professor Frescott.

If he hadn't been watching Graff, Frescott might have noticed something that happened on the far side of the street. There, a figure stirred from a dusk-fronted building and kept pace with Frescott as he turned the corner. Possibly the professor wouldn't have seen the shape that trailed him, for its manner was decidedly furtive.

Though its height was uncertain, the figure was lithe, if not slender. Gliding from one dusk-patch to another, it gave the effect of being clad in a dark cape. It dwindled into gloom near the corner, thus adding a mysterious aftermath to the canny game that Frescott had played.

In manner, at least, the mystery figure resembled The Shadow, the famous personage who roved Manhattan's streets at dusk in search of crime to conquer. But there were two good reasons why The Shadow could not be hereabouts this evening.

First, The Shadow had been too far from Shebley's apartment house to reach there before Frescott left; again, The Shadow had decided upon another destination. Whether wittingly or otherwise, Professor Frescott had personally tricked The Shadow with a neat but simple ruse.

The Shadow, in the person of Lamont Cranston, had left for Washington on a blind quest. He and Jared Shebley would be watching each other with mutual suspicion concerning an antique Chinese chest which Professor Frescott wanted neither of them to buy!

CHAPTER III

MARGO LANE hurried from the cab as it stopped in front of the Talcott Antique Galleries. With the delay of rush hour traffic, Margo had hardly hoped to arrive before the place closed, but it was still open.

This trip was the result of a call from Lamont Cranston. He'd phoned from the airport, saying he was leaving for Washington and wanted Margo to visit the Galleries for him. Still, the trip didn't seem very important.

All Margo needed to do was learn the name of the Washington dealer who had bought the chest of Chu Chan from Talcott. That learned, she was to call a Washington hotel by long distance and leave word for Cranston. The reason it wasn't very important was because Cranston had blandly said that he would probably have that information by the time he reached the capital. Nevertheless, he wanted Margo to check the New York end.

There was no reason for Margo to keep the cab, so she dismissed it. Entering the lighted doorway of the Antique Galleries, Margo went up a broad flight of stairs to the second floor which constituted the Galleries proper.

The place was really something to take one's breath away, without assistance from the stairs. Though Margo had been to Talcott's before, the Galleries never failed to intrigue her.

You came into a row of rooms that could have been called an indoor esplanade. The whole second floor, from front to back, a distance of nearly half a block, was a succession of wonders. Only in Talcott's could a person gain a proper appreciation of the ingenuity displayed by the human race during centuries past.

Paintings, pottery, statues, musical instruments, tapestries, furniture—the list ran like the spiel of a department store elevator operator. Only Talcott's items differed from any that you would see in a modern department store. The things he sold were products of forgotten imagination and handicraft.

Literally wading through a mass of antiques, Margo reached a niche that Talcott called his office, only to find it empty. Continuing further back, she passed a side stairway and came to the sliding door of the final room, which was the longest of the lot. There Margo saw Dariel Talcott, a tall, stoop-shouldered man with a drab, tired face.

Beside the antique dealer was a burly, bearded man whom Margo remembered as Simon Benisette.

Indeed, once seen, Simon Benisette was nearly impossible to forget.

Benisette's face was so long that it had a horsey look. People must have marked on that resemblance; otherwise Benisette had no excuse for growing the red beard that adorned his equine countenance. His style of beard was badly chosen, however, for he had nurtured the old fashioned kind that spread around from ear to ear, mostly under the chin. If anything, the beard gave him further claim to his nickname of "Horse Face."

More than "Horse Face," the term "friends" was a stretch of the imagination. Technically speaking, Benisette had no friends; merely an assortment of passing acquaintances. Being a man who lived much to himself, Benisette had come to be all for himself, especially when purchasing antiques. He delighted in making "finds" before other buyers discovered them, and the bearded man was doing that right now.

Simon Benisette was inspecting the chest of Chu Chan!

The fact bordered on the incredible, where Margo Lane was concerned. She couldn't imagine how Cranston had managed to let this prize slip, if he really wanted it. Yet this was the chest all right, for Margo had seen pictures of it. Judging from Benisette's manner, he already classed himself as its owner.

Standing nearly six feet high, the chest of Chu Chan looked like an old-fashioned wardrobe cabinet, or more correctly, it looked like the thing that wardrobe cabinets had been patterned after. It was mounted on six bulky legs, which might better have been termed feet, since they were shaped like dragon's claws.

The bottom of the chest was very thick, finely carved and ornamented with brass work. About four feet in width and three in depth, it had a fairly thick top, decorated like the bottom. Brass fittings predominated, particularly where the doors were concerned. When closed, as they were at present, they made the chest a veritable strongbox.

Nodding curtly to Margo as she approached, Benisette paused suddenly to note the girl's expression. Apparently Benisette didn't know that Margo expected the chest to be elsewhere; as a result, he mistook her puzzlement for admiration of the chest itself.

"Your friend Cranston was too late," boomed Benisette, ending with a chuckle muffled deep in his beard. Then, with eyes widening suspiciously, Benisette added: "Unless he sent you here to bid against me, Miss Lane."

"Sorry, but he didn't," returned Margo. "Or maybe I'm not so sorry. If this is the famous chest of Chu Chan, it's better that Lamont didn't buy it."

Benisette's wide eyes glared. His brawny hands moved upward, tightening into fists, as though he resented this slur against the antique that he admired.

Rapidly, Talcott moved into the situation. His bent shoulders loomed between Benisette and Margo, his hands came upward to spread with pleading gesture. His tired face wrinkling with worry, Talcott wheedled:

"Please, please do not dispute about the chest. I'm sure that Miss Lane did not intend to disparage its merits—"

"Not at all," interrupted Margo. Then, tactfully: "I was thinking only of its size. Why, Lamont has cluttered his house with so many curios, you can scarcely move around. I don't mean"—Margo turned hastily to Talcott—"that is, I'm not criticizing these Galleries, just because they're so packed with antiques. But Lamont is a collector—"

"I understand, quite," interposed Talcott, his worried wrinkles fading with his smile. "A dealer like myself is forced to display all his wares."

"That's right," nodded Margo. "As for the chest of Chu Chan"—she turned to Benisette—"I must compliment you on your choice, Mr. Benisette. I only hope that you have room for it."

Begrudgingly, Benisette relaxed. It struck Margo then and there that Red-Beard liked arguments and could become violent in the heat of them. Certainly she could understand why Benisette lacked friends, if a mere quip could rouse his anger. Just when she thought that she had humored Benisette with a winsome smile, his violent mood returned. Under the glare of the man's mad eyes, Margo shrank back, only to realize that his attention was directed beyond her.

A sallow, slinky man had suddenly arrived within Benisette's range of vision. Turning, Margo recognized the newcomer as Lionel Graff. She couldn't exactly blame Benisette for disliking Graff, since the fellow was notorious as an antique buyer, always trying to forestall other bids, often with promises that he later repudiated. Still, the rage that Benisette exhibited was more than this meeting warranted.

"More of your tricky dealing!" stormed Benisette, shoving his hands toward Graff's throat. "I've warned you to stay out of my business, and this time I mean it!"

Considering that Benisette's face had reddened to a point that made his beard look pale, he showed admirable self-control at the last moment. His fingers lost their clutching itch as his hand suddenly drew apart and clamped, not on Graff's neck, but on his shoulders. Then, roughly, Benisette tried to spin Graff about and shove him from the gallery.

Coming around he struck Benisette's hands aside and bounded back against a squatty Buddha that was seated on a taboret against the far wall.

With a snarl, Graff twisted free. Coming around he struck Benisette's hands aside and bounded back against a squatly Buddha that was seated on a taboret against the far wall. Beside the calm faced Buddha was a bowl from which extended an incense ladle. Clutching the latter, Graff started to raise it in a pose of self-defense.

Benisette quieted with a sneer. Brushing his sleeves as though the touch of Graff's hands had contaminated them, Benisette turned to Talcott.

"Excuse my temper," apologized Benisette in his booming way. "I forgot that you were keeping open until Graff arrived. Very well, if he wants to bid, let him."

Graff gave his lips an eager lick. Like Benisette, he spoke only to Talcott.

"How much did Benisette bid for the chest?"

"Five thousand dollars," replied Talcott. "It is a low price, I know, but—"

"Low!" exclaimed Graff. "It's ridiculous! Why, it's absolute robbery!"

Talcott spread his hands pleadingly, as though fearing that Graff's term would enrage Benisette, but the latter had lost his fever pitch. He was standing now with folded arms, a contemptuous curve upon his bearded lips. The flush was gone from Benisette's face, but somehow Margo felt that his color now represented white heat instead of red.

"It's a fair price," began Talcott, addressing Graff, "because after all, Mr. Benisette purchased the Bangkok dancer statue—"

"Which has nothing to do with it," interrupted Graff. "One sale does not govern another. You have said that yourself, Talcott."

Before Talcott could reply, Benisette stepped forward, striding slowly as though in haughty self-restraint. His tone was hard, icy, as he queried:

"Just how much can you offer for the chest, Graff?"

"More than five thousand," retorted Graff. "In fact, I'll double the bid. I'll make it ten thousand dollars—"

"In cash?"

"Yes, in cash!"

"You have it with you?"

"Of course not. Why should I carry so much money?"

"I do." From his coat pocket, Benisette produced a roll too thick to carry in his trousers. "This is the way I clinch my deals, Graff."

Benisette's hand tightened on the money, but there was too much of it to encircle, even though his muscles strained themselves. Ignoring Benisette, Graff turned to Talcott.

"I've just come from Shebley's," declared Graff. "He'll buy that chest. He really wants it."

"You'd better get Shebley's word for it," taunted Benisette. "Why not phone him, Talcott?"

"Shebley isn't home," admitted Graff. "He left town unexpectedly and his servant doesn't know where he went."

Slowly, Talcott shook his head.

"No money, no sale," stated Talcott. "Sorry, Graff, but it's my rule—in your case."

"But by tomorrow—"

"I told Benisette I would close the bids tonight."

"You must give me time!" Graff was very earnest. "It—well, it might be a matter of life and death to me."

Benisette provided another sneer.

"Are your creditors that close on your heels, Graff?"

Margo expected Graff to challenge Benisette's taunt. Instead, Graff nearly wilted. He darted looks across his shoulders as though expecting some of those very creditors to appear. Then, anxiously, Graff pleaded:

"Let me use your phone, Talcott. If I can't reach Shebley, I'll try other people. Maybe they'll believe me when I tell them this deal is worth their while."

"Worth *your* while, you mean," scoffed Benisette. "Like all the deals on which other people lose."

The sudden flush that came to Graff's face was like a reflection of Benisette's earlier mood. Margo wondered, almost fearfully, what reaction it would bring from Benisette, so she turned to look.

If there was hatred in Graff's glare, Benisette certainly returned it in full measure, but with the same control that had become his policy. Round, livid balls, in centers of white, Benisette's eyes had a cold ferocity that said: "Beware!"

Talcott was nodding in Graff's direction. Plucking the sallow man's arm, Talcott gestured him toward the little office. Turning suddenly, Graff started there to make his phone calls, his fists clenched tightly at his sides.

Margo felt ready to collapse with relief. The strain seemed gone all at once, now that Graff was no longer within Benisette's reach. Somehow, Margo felt that she had just witnessed a scene wherein murder had been in the making. Talcott, too, had noticed it, for his shoulders gave a wearied sag. Talcott, too, was very much relieved.

The tension of those past few minutes produced an effect that Margo didn't realize at present. Limp as a rag, the girl was too relieved to think in future terms. That was why Margo didn't recognize that murder-in-the-making wasn't apt to halt until it reached completion.

Margo Lane was standing on the very threshold of coming crime, without realizing it!

CHAPTER IV

THE next ten minutes seemed very uneventful. During that period, Simon Benisette kept muttering to himself as he inspected the interior of the Chinese chest, rubbing the woodwork and nodding his appreciation.

When he began to examine the outside, Benisette admired the brass work and the carving. Then, abruptly, he turned with a smile so genial that Margo stared in total amazement.

"A fine chest," complimented Benisette. "Worth the five thousand dollars, Talcott. And you are right, Miss Lane"—he gave an appreciative bow—"when you say that a place should never become cluttered. My living room is small and this chest will take up considerable space. But I have an idea!"

His smile broadening, Benisette turned to Talcott and gave a gesture toward the open chest.

"I shall keep the dancer statue in it!"

"An excellent idea," said Talcott, with a routine nod. "After all, the statue arrived in the chest."

"Even though it didn't belong there," chuckled Benisette, deeply. Then, wagging a big finger: "You rascal, Talcott! To make a double sale from a single purchase."

"Two sales at half price," reminded Talcott. "You heard what Graff offered."

A hissing tone came from Benisette's lips; his old glare returned, directed toward the office.

"What's keeping Graff?" demanded Benisette. "He can't be talking to anyone who trusts him, because no one does. He is trying to trick me, Talcott—"

"Easy, Mr. Benisette," interposed Talcott. "By the way, do you have that color picture of the dancer statue?"

Benisette nodded without lessening his glare or its direction.

"Why not show it to Miss Lane?" queried Talcott. "I know she'd like to see it."

Bringing an envelope from his inside pocket,

Benisette drew a picture from it. Receiving the photograph, Margo was duly impressed. The statue indeed was very lovely.

From its colors, the statue was composed entirely of ivory and jade. It represented a Siamese dancing girl, seated with crossed legs, her arms folded in front of her with hands stretched straight against her shoulders. The ivory, an old yellow, formed the girl, while the jade, more precious and therefore sparingly used, composed her garments.

Jade girdle, anklets and bracelets formed the costume, while the realism of the figure was obtained by black ivory, probably a vegetable variety, that represented the dancer's hair and eyes. Indeed, if Margo had been shown the picture without knowing what it was, she would have supposed that it was a photograph of a living model.

"How lovely!" exclaimed Margo. "Why from the tint of that old ivory, it must have been aged for years!"

"And so will I be," snapped Benisette, taking back the photograph, "if Graff doesn't stop making those useless phone calls. You've given him long enough, Talcott!"

Snapping his fingers, Talcott called:

"Homer!"

The man who appeared looked like Talcott's echo. Stoop-shouldered, bowing, Homer fitted the term in voice as well as manner.

"It's time to close up," said Talcott. "Get busy right away, Homer."

"Time to close up," echoed Homer. "I'll get busy right away, sir."

"And bar all the windows."

"Bar all the windows."

As Homer went about his duty, Talcott turned toward the office, saying he would hurry Graff. Arms folded, Benisette kept staring at the chest of Chu Chan until suddenly, he wheeled toward Margo, with sharp query:

"Would Graff be phoning Cranston?"

"I don't think he could be," replied Margo. "I'm sure Lamont went out of town, too."

"Then why are you here?"

"Only because—well, because Lamont was interested in the chest."

"You mean he's coming here to bid against me?"

"Well, hardly, since it's so late."

Benisette's eyes narrowed in fierce style.

"Maybe you're the one who is keeping this place open," he declared. "If I thought you were—"

Homer was leaving, having bolted all the metal-shuttered windows that turned this room into the equivalent of a vault. The glare in Benisette's eyes was just too much for Margo to face alone.

"I'll talk to Mr. Talcott," she said, hurriedly. "Maybe he can rush things. Good evening, Mr. Benisette."

Reaching the office, Margo looked back to see Benisette still staring after her. With a flaunt of his folded arms, Mr. Red-Beard turned toward the open chest of Chu Chan, just by way of ignoring the girl's glance.

In the little office, Margo found Graff setting the telephone on its stand with one hand while he mopped his forehead with the other. Talcott was standing by, registering impatience.

"No luck," declared Graff. "If I could only reach Shebley—"

"It's too late," put in Talcott. "We can't keep Benisette waiting any longer."

"But I'm sure Shebley will pay ten thousand! If he'd only left a note for me!"

"You're sure he didn't?"

"I looked around for one, but there wasn't any. Now listen, Talcott—"

Talcott listened, but not to Graff. Instead, he and the others heard an enormous bellow that could only have come from the rear room. It was Benisette, howling the limit of his patience in terms uncomplimentary to Graff.

"Sold for five thousand dollars," announced Talcott. "If you want to buy the chest, talk to its present owner, Simon Benisette."

Considering the trouble to which Talcott had been put, Margo could pardon his rather bitter jest at Graff's expense. Oddly, though, Graff didn't consider it in a light vein.

"Talk to Benisette!" he repeated. "Say, that's really an idea, Talcott."

"I thought you'd appreciate it."

Again, Talcott was ironical, but Graff's mood didn't change.

"Money would talk with Benisette!" he exclaimed. "Just as with anybody else! I'll close the deal with him right now, pending Shebley's future decision."

"Go right ahead." Talcott gestured to the door. "Good luck, Graff."

As Graff went out, Talcott motioned Margo to a chair and took another for himself. While they waited, Talcott talked wearily of the problems of an antique dealer, wishing sincerely that Cranston had decided to buy the Chu Chan chest before Benisette ever saw it.

"I could have sold it to Shebley," added Talcott, "only I couldn't guarantee that it was unique. He wanted to talk it over with old Professor Frescott up at the Museum of Antiquities. I suppose Frescott was honest with him, too."

Margo wasn't listening closely. She was expecting sounds of chaos from the rear room, but apparently Benisette and Graff had curbed themselves sufficiently to hold a quiet conference.

"Of course Graff would say anything," continued Talcott, after a considerable pause. "But that doesn't mean that Shebley would listen—"

Now Margo was listening hard and Talcott paused to watch her. He caught the sound, too, heavy footsteps approaching the door. Both stared as the door opened and in stepped Benisette. The bearded man's face wore its cold look of satisfaction.

"Now I've experienced everything," declared Benisette, with a deep chuckle. "Imagine Graff trying to do business with me! By the way"—he reached into his pocket—"here's your five thousand, Talcott."

"It can wait until tomorrow," said Talcott, "when you send the truck to get it. I'll have the bill of sale made out by then. Whatever profit you make is your own business."

"You mean profit from Graff?" Leaning his head back, Benisette roared a laugh. "Why, I told that rascal I wouldn't sell the chest at any price. Frankly, Talcott"—Benisette lowered his head as well as his tone—"I think that Graff is desperate."

Talcott gave a half-convinced nod.

"His swindles have caught up with him," added Benisette. "If we don't hear from him again, good riddance. If he clears town tonight and never comes back, you'll have me to thank for it. I'll make the rounds of the dealers tomorrow with twice as much as this"—Benisette produced his bankroll—"and more. From the way Graff left, he won't be back to tag me and up my bids with other people's money!"

"If you're in a buying mood," returned Talcott, with a profound bow, "be sure to stop here first."

"I'll stop to pick up the chest, anyway," promised Benisette, "but there's not much else in your stock that interests me."

Talcott took that comment as a matter of course. From his desk, he produced a large, intricate key which he handed to Benisette.

"Here's the key to Chu Chan's chest," stated Talcott. "I'd better give it to you before I forget it. The lock is automatic, the one modern thing about the chest."

Nodding, Benisette left the office and strode down the front stairway. Despite the bearded man's amiable mood, Margo wasn't anxious to follow. She waited while Talcott called for Homer who

What Margo saw—or thought she saw—was the life-sized face of the Siamese dancing girl—

arrived from the side stairway and slid a door shut to close and lock the rear room, when Talcott announced that both visitors had gone. Noting Margo's glance toward the side stairway, Talcott announced that the door below was still open and bowed a courteous good night.

Margo breathed better when she reached the side street. Meeting Benisette had been an ordeal, to say nothing of Graff. Margo only hoped that neither was in the taxicab that she saw parked near the corner, so when she reached it, she paused long enough to look inside.

There, from the glow of the dim streetlamp against the cab window, Margo saw a face and started back, only to laugh when she realized it must be the reflection of her own. Only the mirrored image didn't laugh, and that was when Margo really gasped.

It was a girl's face in the window, but it wasn't Margo's. To her utter amazement, the sort that approached horror, Margo was staring at features that she had seen pictured only a short while before. Lovely features, but not to Margo's distraught mind.

What Margo saw—or thought she saw—was the life-sized face of the Siamese dancing girl who existed only as a statue that belonged to Simon Benisette!

As Margo Lane recoiled, the saffron countenance disappeared. Tripping back across the curb, Margo was caught by the strong arm of a cab driver, who had seen her from a neighboring lunch room and was coming to claim her as a fare.

"Not feeling good, lady?" queried the cabby. "Here, get inside and I'll take you home."

Was the far door closing as the cab driver opened the near one, or was that just another strained thread in the fabric of Margo's imagination?

At least the cab was empty when Margo plumped into the seat. Then the driver was at the wheel, speeding away from this area where curious recollections built themselves into imaginary realities, if such things could be.

Relaxing, Margo Lane decided she'd tell Lamont Cranston all about it when he returned from Washington.

CHAPTER V

LAMONT CRANSTON smiled across the breakfast table.

Seldom did Cranston smile; almost never was he seen at a breakfast table. Today was one of the rare exceptions, because he had hopped in from Washington on an early plane instead of rising at the crack of noon.

"So Benisette is calling for the chest as soon as Talcott opens shop," remarked Cranston. "Was that the understanding, Margo?"

Margo nodded, rather sleepily. Cranston had wakened her with a phone call from LaGuardia Airport, and she'd just about had time to reach the restaurant where he said he would meet her. Having reported what occurred at the Talcott Antique Galleries on the previous evening, Margo was lapsing back to the dream stage.

"Wake up!" spoke Cranston. "You're half asleep, Margo."

It was odd, the way Margo's thoughts unclouded. One moment she was viewing the dark-eyed face of a yellow ivory statue that smiled; the next that image was gone, and she was staring at Lamont across the breakfast table.

There was something very calm in Cranston's countenance. At times, it was like a statue, too. Only it was the other way about: Cranston wasn't a statue that came to life; he was a living man who could become singularly immobile when he chose. At present, his eyes carried a restful gaze as they studied Margo from a face that was vaguely hawk-like.

"Have another cup of coffee," suggested Cranston. "If it doesn't wake you, you'd better go back to bed. Meanwhile tell me anything else of interest."

Margo couldn't think of anything else. She didn't consider the face in the cab window important enough, because Margo was charging that incident to imagination. Her waking dream confused itself with last night and since the face belonged to both, it would be silly to even mention it. Besides, Lamont wasn't interested in the Siamese dancer statue. He wanted to know more about the chest of Chu Chan.

"The deal is closed," assured Margo. "Benisette is paying five thousand dollars for the chest and Talcott has already given him the key. But Benisette will have to send a truck for the chest! It's too big to put in a cab."

"Too big," mused Cranston, "and perhaps too heavy?"

"Very probably," replied Margo. "Nobody tried to lift it while I was there, but it looked like a three-man job."

Cranston's mood was speculative. Margo knew that he was visualizing the mysterious chest of Chu Chan.

"Only five thousand dollars," calculated Cranston, slowly. "If the chest is worth anything, it's worth more than that—perhaps far more."

"Graff offered ten thousand—"

"Of Shebley's money," Cranston's slight smile was reminiscent. "Only Shebley wasn't around to back it up."

"If he had been," opined Margo, "Benisette might have boosted the bid. Why, he had a bank roll of more than fifty thousand dollars and he said that today he'd be carrying double that amount."

"Benisette always deals in cash," nodded Cranston, "but I don't think he'd bid higher on the chest."

"And why not?"

"Because I don't think he knows how much it is really worth."

"How much is that?"

"I don't know." Again Cranston gave a rare smile. "That's why I don't think that Benisette knows."

That statement cleared Margo's mind, so far as Benisette was concerned. Obviously the bearded buyer wanted the chest purely as a desirable antique. In contrast, Graff the speculator probably rated the chest on the basis of some secret value. So Margo put the question:

"Does Graff know?"

"Do you mean does he know what the chest is really worth?" asked Cranston. "I don't think so, although he may. He managed to convince Shebley that the chest was worth plenty, but he wouldn't have told everything if he knew all. It wouldn't be Graff's way."

Having met Graff, Margo agreed with Cranston's verdict. Cranston amplified it a moment later.

"Graff is playing a hunch, a long shot, or both," declared Cranston. "His creditors are so close on his heels it isn't funny. He needs cash or he can't afford to stay around, and that's literal. Being desperate, he'd sell a bill of bad goods to Shebley—or anybody.

"So on the face of it, I'd say that any mystery involving the chest of Chu Chan could be classed as a hoax, pure and simple. Strange things come floating in from the Orient nowadays, but that would be just part of Graff's build up. But I'm considering the opinion of someone more reliable than Graff."

"And who is that?"

Cranston's eyes fixed steadily on Margo as he pronounced the name:

"Professor Giles Frescott, curator of the Museum of Antiquities."

Margo was very much awake and highly intrigued. Swallowing some more black coffee, she nodded that she wanted to hear more.

"The esteemed professor is anything but a practical joker," continued Cranston, "yet it was his subtle strategy that sent Shebley and myself to Washington to play hide-and-seek with each other. I'm back, but for all I know, Shebley is still down there looking for me, hoping I'll lead him to the chest of Chu Chan. Frescott doesn't want either of us to acquire it."

"And why not?"

"Because Shebley knows Graff," explained Cranston, "and therefore Shebley may have learned something. I know the Orient and therefore I may already know something."

"But Benisette knows nothing!"

"Precisely. Therefore Professor Frescott cleared the way for Benisette to buy the chest."

"Couldn't Frescott have made a bid for it himself?"

"And given his hand away?" Cranston shook his head. "Never. A curator of a museum doesn't go bidding around antique galleries. But you can be quite sure that Professor Frescott is somewhere in the offing."

"How far is that offing?"

"That's for you to find out." Rising, Cranston gestured to a cab outside the restaurant window. "Suppose you go down to Talcott's Galleries and be there when he opens shop. Tell him I'll be along a little later; that I'd like at least to see the chest of Chu Chan."

"You're stopping off somewhere?"

"Yes, at the Cobalt Club," replied Cranston. "I want to have a chat with Commissioner Weston. You know, Margo"—the steady eyes took a faraway stare—"there may be something deep behind this chest of Chu Chan. The slightest clue, perhaps in the form of some trifling mystery that has baffled the police, may be a lead to some impending crime."

They were going out of the restaurant during Cranston's speech and Margo was actually in the cab and on her way to Talcott's, before the very thing popped into her mind again.

Some trifling mystery!

Margo herself could have furnished Lamont with such. That business of the statue face, alive and staring from the cab window, was the very sort of lead that would have intrigued Cranston in his present mood. But it was too late to tell him now, so Margo resolved to wait until Cranston arrived at the antique galleries.

The cab pulled up in front of Talcott's Galleries. The place was already open, and Margo saw Homer staring from the doorway. As the cab stopped, Talcott's echo started to duck like a scared rabbit, but when he recognized Margo stepping from the cab, he halted. Hardly had Margo paid the driver before Homer was gripping her by the arm, hurrying her inside the building and up the broad front stairs to the second floor galleries.

"I'm glad you came, Miss Lane!" Homer was breathless, worried. "We've been calling your apartment, but you weren't there."

"I was having breakfast—"

"It's about last night." Homer wasn't interrupting; he was merely continuing his theme after taking time out for a breath. "You're a witness to what happened, like Mr. Talcott and myself. That is, you're a witness to what happened, before it happened."

"Before what happened?"

"Here's Mr. Talcott," panted Homer. "He'll explain everything."

They had passed the side stairway and were at the doorway of the rear room. The door itself was open, and Dariel Talcott, his worried face drooping to its limit, was standing on the threshold. Peering up from between his bowed shoulders, Talcott gave his hands a plaintive spread that ended with a gesture toward the chest of Chu Chan.

"I'll tell you what's happened, Miss Lane!" expressed Talcott, hoarsely. "There's been murder!"

"Murder?" echoed Margo. "You mean here?"

A sudden horror of her own words made Margo stare about in quest of a body she didn't see. Then her eyes were back upon the object of Talcott's gesture, the chest of Chu Chan, with its heavy, brass bound door ominously shut and locked.

"But how," began Margo, "and who—"

"Lionel Graff has been missing since last night," declared Talcott in a solemn tone, "and the last man to see him alive was Simon Benisette when they were standing here beside the chest of Chu Chan!"

CHAPTER VI

THE telephone bell was jangling from Talcott's office, but Margo Lane scarcely heard it. Through her head was ringing a multitude of other thoughts that were lining up in strictly accountable fashion.

There had been fierce rivalry between Graff and Benisette the evening before, rivalry to the pitch of violence. Then Graff, most unwisely as Margo now reviewed it, had gone into the rear room alone to make peace with Benisette.

Staring at Talcott, Margo could tell that he shared her thought.

Together they had waited in the office, expecting another altercation, but there had been none. Later they had seen Benisette go out alone.

Alone.

That single word summed up the suspicion that Margo now shared with Talcott. Margo was picturing that meeting in this rear room as short and swift. A mere hint of sarcasm in Graff's speech and Benisette's anger would surely have unleashed itself again. A fatal blow would have automatically tumbled Graff into the wide open chest of Chu Chan.

The chest that now stood closed and locked with the key in Benisette's possession!

Noting Margo's horrified stare toward the bottom of the chest's locked door, Talcott shook his head.

"The front is morticed," declared Talcott, "and that door is practically airtight. Blood couldn't flow out under it."

Margo was shuddering as Homer returned. The pale-faced assistant had answered the telephone and was reporting to Talcott.

"Somebody else asking about Graff," stated Homer, shakily. "They've been trying to trace him, but he hasn't been heard from since he came here yesterday. This was his last call."

"The phone was ringing when we opened shop," explained Talcott to Margo. "One of Graff's creditors was calling saying be couldn't find him. Then another phoned and another—"

Breaking off abruptly, Talcott turned to Homer.

"You're *sure* you didn't see Graff leave here last night?"

"No, sir," replied Homer. "I was down at the side door. I'd have seen him if he'd gone that way."

"And you'd have seen him, Mr. Talcott," added Margo, "if he'd gone out the front. You were facing the door of the office while we were in there; while you were saying you wished Lamont had bought the chest, remember?"

Remembering, Talcott nodded; then shook his head.

"But Graff didn't go out," he emphasized. "It was Benisette who finally came along. That's why I thought Graff had gone out the side door."

"Benisette said he'd gone out," reminded Margo. "That was when you gave Benisette the key."

Another nod from Talcott. Then:

"When we unlocked this room this morning," said Talcott, "Homer and I noticed that the chest was shut. It didn't occur to us that Benisette had locked it to hide something until we received more calls regarding Graff—"

Again, the telephone was ringing. Homer went to answer it and came back very promptly.

"It's the truckers," the assistant reported. "They are coming for the chest in half an hour."

"That means Benisette will be here first!" exclaimed Talcott. "He's going to move the chest right out, Graff's body going along with it!"

Margo turned toward the office.

"I ought to call Lamont—"

"Not here!" interrupted Talcott. "Use the phone across the street. I'll use my phone to call police headquarters and ask them what to do. You stay here, Homer"—pausing, Talcott studied his assistant's frightened face—"no, that wouldn't do, you'd give yourself entirely away. I'll have to talk to Benisette myself."

Talcott was tightening himself as he spoke, in preparation for the difficult task of chatting casually with a suspected murderer. He was forced to speed the process because of heavy footsteps coming up the front way.

Those footsteps were announcing Benisette!

"Down this way, both of you!" Talcott's whisper was hurried as he started Homer and Margo down the side stairs. "Homer, you find the patrolman on the beat and bring him here, but keep him down below! Miss Lane, after you've called Mr. Cranston, come back up by the front stairs and wait in my office. Understand?"

Homer was starting down the stairs when he received his order. Margo was following as Talcott gave the final word, but she paused so Benisette wouldn't hear her, for his footsteps were coming close. Then, drawn to the side of the stairs, Margo heard Benisette's booming greeting:

"Hello, Talcott! I've brought the cash for the Chu Chan chest. Let's settle up so I can go about my business. The truck will be here anytime."

Margo couldn't quite catch Talcott's reply, for by then she was stealing down the stairs. Hurrying across to the lunchroom, Margo phoned the Cobalt Club only to learn that Cranston had just left. That meant at least that he was on his way here, which was a great relief to Margo. Then, in accordance with Talcott's instructions, Margo came around by the front way, sneaked up to the galleries and into Talcott's office.

Talcott was already there. He gestured for silence as Margo entered and frantically motioned for her to close the door, adding a slow move of his hand that meant to do it quietly. Talcott was holding the phone with his other hand, and as Margo approached on tiptoe, he spoke in a low tone.

"It's alright, Inspector," said Talcott. "Miss Lane just came in, like I told her... What's that? I'll ask her..."

Turning to Margo, Talcott queried:

"Did you reach Mr. Cranston? Inspector Cardona wants to know."

Margo whispered that Cranston had already left the club for the auction galleries, and Talcott relayed that news to Cardona. Then:

"Well, Inspector," undertoned Talcott, "I guess that covers it. Benisette is in the rear room, measuring the chest... Yes, so as to see if it will fit the corner of the living room... No, he didn't mention a word about unlocking it...

"Yes, he paid me the five thousand"—Talcott was tapping his vest pocket as he spoke—"and he asked me for the bill of sale... No, I hadn't made it out, so he said I'd better, right away... Yes, he's in the rear room alone with the chest, but there's nothing he could do... No, there's no other way he could remove the body, except in that chest...

"It's to go to Benisette's apartment... Yes, I'm sure, because he told me to give the bill of sale to the truckers when they arrived... Yes, so they'd know where to take the chest and would know the shipment was really his..."

Pausing, Talcott did some extensive listening, and Margo could see his face change. Apparently Cardona had picked up something from those instructions that hadn't occurred to the art dealer.

"Why, that's so!" exclaimed Talcott. "Maybe Benisette doesn't intend to wait!" He gave an inquiring look at Margo and pointed in the general direction of the front stairs, only to have Margo shake her head. "No, Miss Lane didn't see him go out the front way, but he may have used the side stairs... Yes, I'll have her look... What's that? Oh, yes, if he's still here, we'll try to hold him... What's that?"

Margo didn't hear the final click from Cardona's end of the line. She was stealing out from the office, working her way toward the rear room. Gaining a look past a cluster of heavy chairs, Margo saw in one view that the final gallery was empty. Cardona was right, Benisette had left!

Turning, Margo gave a signifying gesture to Talcott as he poked cautiously from the office. Arriving around some of the intervening antiques, Talcott likewise stared into the empty room. Despairingly, Talcott turned toward the side stairway and muttered unkind things about Homer's failure to return with the neighborhood cop.

"Smart of Benisette to walk right out on us!" expressed Talcott, finally. "He showed his nerve coming here in the first place to learn if we suspected him of murder."

"At least he thinks we didn't," supplied Margo. "What do we do now?"

"Wait for Inspector Cardona," returned Talcott. "The last thing he said was that he'd start here right away. But we can be sure of one thing"—Talcott threw a grim look at the tight-locked chest—"we still hold the evidence!"

That much was certain, too certain to please Margo Lane, who couldn't forbear a shudder as she glanced at the ghastly chest that needed only a tag to mark it as the last resting place of Lionel Graff.

To Margo Lane, this wait was like a deathwatch for a victim whose murderer had come to gloat over an accomplished crime, only to depart in unmolested triumph!

The only hope was that retribution would eventually reach Simon Benisette, man of secret murder. If the law could not deliver it, Margo Lane was confident that The Shadow would!

CHAPTER VII

PEOPLE were arriving at the antique galleries, almost in a group. First, Homer to announce that he'd given up looking for the neighborhood patrolman because he'd seen the truckers coming along the rear street, so he'd steered them to the side door where they were at present.

Next, Lamont Cranston, who strolled in by the front way just as Homer was finishing his report. Before Cranston had time to lift his eyebrows at Margo's story of Graff's disappearance and how it traced back to his last talk with Benisette, a full twelve hours ago, Inspector Cardona put in an appearance.

He was a poker-faced chap, this inspector, and a past master at the art of hunches. From the look—or lack of it—upon his swarthy countenance, it was plain that Joe Cardona had analyzed Talcott's data down to the last iota and had found it thoroughly conclusive.

Nevertheless, Cardona believed in testing theories wherever possible. His procedure in this instance was simple but effective. Motioning Cranston to one end of the Chinese chest, Cardona set his own stocky form at the other. When he found the chest too heavy to heft, he beckoned for Talcott and Homer to help, which they did.

As the chest was tilted and set down again, Margo sensed the sickly but muffled thud of the body it contained. The others noted it; in fact they could almost feel it through the thick woodwork.

Hardly had the chest settled back to level before loud voices echoed up the side stairway.

"Hey—what about that shipment?"

"The guy said the load would be ready when we got here."

"What do we do? Come up or forget it?"

The calls were from the truckmen, and Cardona settled their problem promptly.

"Bring them up," ordered Cardona. "Benisette wants this job shipped to his place, so we'll let him have it."

Talcott blinked, rather puzzled, and Homer copied his employer's manner.

"An excellent suggestion, Inspector," commented Cranston in his calm-toned style. "Benisette might even be watching somewhere in the neighborhood to see that the chest is taken away."

"All the better," affirmed Cardona. "Only thanks for the suggestion. I was going to follow the truck personally, only now I'm leaving it to you."

"In case Benisette should recognize you—"

"That's right, Mr. Cranston. Since you wanted to buy the chest, he won't be scared off if he sees you heading over to his place. In fact, it ought to bring him there all the quicker so he can tell you it's no sale and send you on your way."

Talcott was sending Homer to summon the truckers. As an added precaution, Cardona decided to step out of sight before they arrived, so he asked the way to Talcott's office.

"Rather than lose time," decided the efficient inspector, "I'll phone the commissioner while the chest is going out."

"And I can call Shebley," added Talcott. "He's the man Graff said would want to buy the chest."

"Does he know about the murder?"

"No. I tried to reach him by telephone, but his servant said he was out of town."

"When is he due back?"

"I don't know," replied Talcott. "Maybe I'd better go over to his penthouse. If he's there, I can bring him to Benisette's apartment."

Cardona gave an approving grunt as he disappeared into the office, with Talcott behind him. Then the tramping feet of the truckmen were heard arriving from the side stairway. When Homer showed them the chest and offered to help them with it, they brushed him aside. These three huskies were confident they could handle the burden and they did.

By the time the chest was loaded and the truck was pulling away, Cranston and Margo were in a cab out front. From then on the trail was constant and deftly handled. This was The Shadow's own cab, piloted by a hackie named Moe Shrevnitz who knew how to tag along at well-regulated distances.

As they rode, Margo regretted only that Shrevvy had been busy taking Cranston to the airport the night before. If Shrevvy had been waiting outside the antique galleries, Margo might have had some answer to the mystery of the Siamese face that she had seen in the cab window. If it had been more than imagination, Shrevvy would certainly have known it.

However, that trifling riddle seemed more inconsequential than ever, now that Graff's murder was an issue. True, Graff's death could hardly be termed an unsolved crime, since only Benisette could be responsible, but placing it upon the murderer might be difficult unless more than circumstantial evidence could be found.

All during that ride, Margo kept glancing at Cranston, trying to imbue herself with some of his customary calm. She'd have to be on hand to identify Graff's body, and it wasn't pleasant to anticipate.

When the truck stopped in front of the old-fashioned apartment house where Benisette lived, the cab pulled right behind it. A few moments later, Cranston was shaking hands with a very surprised but benign old gentleman who was standing on the sidewalk.

"This is Professor Frescott," introduced Cranston. "You've heard me mention him, Margo, and not always in complimentary terms. By the way, just what did I say about the professor after I arrived back from Washington this morning?"

"I'm sorry about that, Cranston," put in Frescott, his tone carrying a well-practiced note of sincerity. "I am afraid that Jared Shebley was misinformed about the chest of Chu Chan." With a beaming smile, the professor gestured to the chest itself. "You see? It was here in New York all the while."

"And now it belongs to Simon Benisette," remarked Cranston. "Well, I don't suppose he'd mind our looking at it. Let's go inside, Professor."

They followed the truckers into Benisette's ground floor apartment where the janitor took them to be friends of the occupant and let them remain. While the truckmen were still placing the chest in its assigned corner, Margo found herself staring in almost fearful admiration at the Siamese statue which rested on a taboret on the other side of the room.

The statue was lifelike, strikingly so, until Margo touched the arms and face and found them solid ivory. Even then, the solemn stare of the countenance impressed her, so closely did it resemble the imaginary features that must have been Margo's own reflection in the cab window.

There must have been something of the hypnotic in those black eyes, so powerful that it seemed to have pervaded the carver's art. Margo's own eyes were riveted by the coal black beads and she was believing that even the mere photograph might have stimulated her imagination, when the sound of voices brought her from her trance.

Commissioner Weston had arrived and was questioning his friend Cranston regarding the trip from Talcott's. In a firm but calm tone, Cranston was assuring the commissioner that at no time had the chest of Chu Chan left his sight while riding on the open truck, a fact which Margo could have confirmed had Weston chosen to ask her.

Cranston's word was good enough for Weston, a point which impressed Professor Frescott, whose shrewd eyes were looking from one to the other. That Frescott was both quick and keen was demonstrated when he shot a sudden glance to the door, just as it opened to admit Talcott. The antique dealer blinked his surprise at seeing Frescott, and the professor smiled smugly in return.

It was Cranston who put the query:

"Any word from Shebley?"

"He isn't home yet," replied Talcott. Then, with a mistrustful glance at Frescott, the wan man inquired: "You haven't seen Benisette?"

"I doubt that we shall," put in Commissioner Weston, in the blunt style he always used when taking full authority. "I told Cardona to remain at your place, Talcott, in case Benisette returned there. But I don't propose to give a murderer more leeway on the slim chance that he may return to the scene of his crime.

"We must view Graff's body to establish the fact of murder. Since Benisette has the only key to this Chinese chest, we shall be catering to his whim if we wait longer. Our proper course is to break the lock, which Cranston believes that he can do with a minimum of damage."

Turning to Cranston, the commissioner gave the order: "Proceed!"

Using some tools that he had borrowed from the janitor, Cranston set to work. His process looked deft to all except Margo, who was sure that Lamont could have picked the intricate lock had he chosen to use the tools and skill that belonged to his other self, The Shadow. At that, the job was rapid, judged in ordinary terms. From hammer and chisel, Cranston reverted to pliers and with a final twist the lock plunked to the floor.

Uncannily the double door began to open of its own accord. The sight chilled Margo, until she realized that the body had probably tilted forward and was toppling in inert fashion. Such proved the case, for as the others dropped back behind Cranston's spreading arms, the dead form literally pitched itself from a huddle and struck the floor at a sprawly angle, to roll over on one shoulder.

This was the horrifying occasion for which Margo had been steeling herself during the past hour. She was braver by far than Talcott, the other person who was here to identify Graff, for Talcott was clear behind the group, blinking worried across their shoulders, while Margo was actually stepping forward.

One look at Graff's sallow, narrow face was all that Margo wanted. No matter how distorted those features might be, she'd recognize them, speak the name "Lionel Graff" and be over with this distasteful business. But as the dead face came rolling upward, all reason flung itself from Margo's brain. Despite herself, she recoiled with a wild, unrestrained shriek.

It wasn't the death twist on the victim's features that produced Margo's reaction; it was the face itself. The horror of the utterly incredible was overwhelming in its own right.

The dead man wasn't Lionel Graff, the sallow victim everyone expected. Glaring upward with death-glazed eyes was the bearded face of Simon Benisette, the alleged murderer!

CHAPTER VIII

HERE was mystery to tax The Shadow's brain.

That brain was working rapidly, smoothly,

The dead form literally pitched itself from a huddle and struck the floor at a sprawly angle—

behind the placid countenance of Lamont Cranston.

His keen eyes revealed the fact, eyes that burned with a sudden glow, like those of a connoisseur examining a masterpiece. Though relentless in his efforts against crime, Cranston never discounted the work of an evil craftsman, and he was viewing an unparalleled example of such warped genius.

No one saw that burning gaze, for Cranston was the foremost of the group. If seen, it would have been mistaken for amazing insight, which it wasn't. Cranston's eyes seldom gave way automatically to the gaze that marked him as The Shadow. It was his policy not to mix those personalities.

The simple fact was that Cranston, for once, was the most astonished of all persons who viewed a murderer's handiwork; doubly astonished, being both Cranston and The Shadow. Of this group, only Cranston had not accepted the absolute notion that the body of Lionel Graff was in the chest of Chu Chan. Cranston had been prepared to see anything or anybody roll out of that mystery cabinet—with the sole exception of Simon Benisette.

Then, as quickly as it had arrived, The Shadow's surprise was ended. He was Cranston again, the cool, calm analyst who prodded others into expressing the findings that formulated in The Shadow's hidden brain.

Moving slowly, emphatically toward Benisette's body, Cranston's hand carried all eyes with it until his forefinger stopped, pointing straight toward the dead man's heart. Or in a more literal sense, to the object that already pointed into the victim's heart.

Burning like a Promethean eye was a crimson bulb that jutted from Benisette's red-stained shirtfront. Not blood, but its replica in solid form, a thing that might have crystallized from the final palpitation of the dead man's heart. Catching the gleam of the sunlight from the window, that carmine object glistened as a murderer's token.

It looked like a ruby, huge in comparison to most gems of its sort. Not only did it mark Benisette's heart; the brilliant stone formed the exact center of a singular weapon that had fully demonstrated its insidious possibilities.

It was Professor Frescott who identified the instrument of death. In awed tone he proclaimed:

"The katar of Pagan Min!"

Pressing forward, Dariel Talcott pressed his way between Cranston and Weston to view the weapon in question. Nodding, Talcott licked his dry, quivering lips.

"That's right," he agreed. "It's the very dagger that I sold to Jared Shebley. There is no other like it, or Shebley wouldn't have bought it."

"Unquestionably unique," affirmed Frescott. "A most deadly instrument, that thrusting dagger. I said so yesterday"—blandly, Frescott turned to face his companions—"when I examined it at Shebley's."

Nobody looked at Frescott; they were all studying the katar. One thing was certain; to identify that weapon was as easy as both Talcott and Frescott said. For in delivering death, a katar was forced to reveal its curious mechanism and leave it on full display.

The gleaming Balas ruby naturally attracted most attention, centered in the gold mountings that formed the crossbar of the stirrup handle. The hand-guards projecting upward, were conspicuous to a degree, but more important were the silver segments of the false blade that actually formed a sheath for the deadly spike within the tricky weapon.

Spread wide, those silver sectors lay like wings across Benisette's breast, each forced up to the horizontal, the limit to which they could be raised. That limit, however, was enough for it had allowed the hidden blade to bury itself full length into the victim's body.

With a katar, a killer didn't exactly stab. Rather, he punched the death thrust home, as was obvious in this case. The stony expression of Benisette's face seemed to hold the moment of surprise that must have petrified him at the brief but fatal moment.

Stooping, Commissioner Weston went through the dead man's pockets. As he did, Weston heard Talcott's anxious but prompting tone:

"Look for his money, Commissioner. He had a bundle of it; how much, I have no idea, but he peeled five thousand dollars from it when he paid me for the chest."

There wasn't any trace of the money. The murderer must have taken it. The only thing of consequence that Weston found was the key to the Chinese chest, which fell from Benisette's pocket during the search. Picking up the key, Weston arose and faced Talcott.

"So you thought that Benisette left your galleries after he talked to you this morning?"

Talcott nodded and Margo did the same. In line with Weston's eyes, she thought she ought to add her silent testimony.

"But you didn't see him go out, did you Talcott?"

"Of course not," replied Talcott. "Otherwise, he wouldn't be lying here dead."

"I was thinking in terms of a possible imposture," stated Weston. "People sometimes wear false beards, you know."

"But it must have been Benisette who arrived this morning," argued Talcott, "because we saw him leave last night. So he must certainly have returned."

Again Margo nodded.

"I'm sure it was Benisette who left last night," the girl declared, "and though I only glimpsed him this morning, I heard his voice and recognized it."

"Could anyone else have come into the galleries?" demanded Weston. "This morning, I mean?"

"Quite possibly," replied Talcott, slowly. "But it would have to have happened while Miss Lane and I were in the office. How long were we there, Miss Lane?"

"At least five minutes," decided Margo. "Maybe longer."

"It was while I was talking to Inspector Cardona."

"Maybe he can estimate how long that conversation took."

Talcott nodded, then queried:

"You came in by the front door, didn't you, Miss Lane?"

"Yes, as you requested."

"But did you notice the side door while you were coming by it?"

"Only with a glance."

"Homer wasn't there?"

"No, he'd gone to look for the patrolman."

"Then tell me, Miss Lane," continued Talcott. "In your opinion could—"

"I'll do the questioning!" stormed Weston in impatient interruption. "Here's something for you to answer, Talcott. You say you sold this death dagger to Shebley?"

"Yes, Commissioner."

"Then you thought it was still in his possession?"

"No, sir. I was sure it wasn't."

Talcott's reply set Weston aback.

"Just when did you begin to doubt the fact, Talcott?"

"Only this morning," replied Talcott. "You see I stopped at Shebley's coming over here from my galleries. Shebley always kept the Burmese katar on the table in his curio room. Only it wasn't there this morning."

Weston wheeled on Frescott.

"But you saw it yesterday, Professor," Weston reminded. "What did you do"—sharp suspicion flashed from the commissioner's eyes—"take it with you?"

"Of course not," retorted Frescott. "But I can tell you who could have: Lionel Graff. He was going into Shebley's just after I came out."

Before Weston could make a rejoinder, a tone sharper than his own spoke from the doorway.

"My servant can vouch for that, Commissioner."

The speaker was Jared Shebley, his expression as crisp as ever. With him was Inspector Cardona; behind them a police surgeon. Shebley gestured to the others as he explained his arrival here.

"I just returned home," stated Shebley, "and found the Burmese katar missing. When my servant told me Graff had called last night, I had an idea he must be the thief. So I went to Talcott's and found Inspector Cardona. He told me that Benisette had murdered Graff. So we came over here—"

"And brought the medico," added Cardona. "I see you've opened the chest, Commissioner. Well, suppose we have a look at Graff's body!"

Even on this scene of tragedy, what happened was funny. Apparently Cardona knew what Graff and Benisette looked like, as did Shebley. As they stepped forward to look at Graff's face and saw Benisette's instead, they behaved like a comedy team with their sudden back-step. Then the others present were getting an idea of what their own faces must have looked like when they saw a suspected murderer lying dead instead of a supposed victim.

While Cardona and Shebley gaped astonished, the police surgeon, knowing nothing of the mistaken identity, stooped calmly and withdraw the dagger from Benisette's heart. The surgeon's surprise came when he saw the halves of the silver casing blade click together so snugly that they left no trace of their joining.

As Commissioner Weston reached for the weapon, his hand came just above the dead eyes of Simon Benisette. The bearded man's frozen face wore appropriate puzzlement, as for the first time his sightless gaze was trained upon the mysterious weapon that had slain him. But Benisette's features were gradually setting into a leer, as though he had cause to gloat over the law's inability to crack this impossible crime.

Perhaps that was the factor that caused Lamont Cranston to gaze toward the real origin of the riddle, the chest of Chu Chan. With that gaze, Cranston caught a glimmer.

Only when the chest was open could anyone have detected what Cranston did. Until Benisette's body had sprawled from it, the chest had not been open since last night. Now, Cranston was the first to give it close attention.

Without a word, Cranston stepped around Benisette's body and reached one end of the chest, motioning for someone to take the opposite end. Cardona was the first to respond, and together he and Cranston began to slide it toward the center of the room. Seeing that Cranston wanted the chest to be in the full sunlight, others helped to lift it there.

Poised at a tilt, the chest of Chu Chan revealed its oddity to all viewers. The inside of its back and sides bore the pockmarks of tiny holes, a few dozen of them, that weren't visible externally, because of the carved surface. That these holes were of recent manufacture was evident when Cranston pointed to slight tracings of sawdust in the bottom of the cabinet.

"Air holes!" exclaimed Commissioner Weston. "They must have been drilled last night." He wheeled to Talcott. "Are there any tools in that rear gallery of yours?"

As Talcott nodded, Cardona put in his say-so.

"I'll say there are," affirmed Joe. "I was looking them over, to see if I could find anything that Benisette might have used to slug Graff."

"Good hunting, Inspector." Weston was rather testy. "But that was before you learned that things were the other way around."

Maybe Cardona picked up his next idea from Weston's words. Or possibly it was Cranston who did so and flashed the hunch to Cardona with a glance. At any rate, the ace inspector played it right to the bull's-eye.

"The other way around," agreed Cardona. "That sums it, Commissioner. We've found the wrong man as the victim and that makes the wrong man the killer. I'll tell you who drilled those air holes: Lionel Graff!"

Then, before Weston could quite complete the chain that Cardona dangled mentally before him, the swarthy inspector did it on his own.

"That's how Graff stayed in the chest all night," completed Cardona, "putting himself among the missing. He was waiting for his chance to murder Benisette with that Burmese dagger. And Graff found it!"

There wasn't a single objection to Cardona's finding among the silent listeners. Rather, faces showed their full approval of the theory, making it unanimous.

Even a dead man cast his ballot in the affirmative. Stiffening into the first throes of rigor mortis, the bearded face of Simon Benisette gleamed with happy hatred. In life, Benisette had detested Graff more than any other man.

It had only needed proper evidence to prove that Lionel Graff had murdered Simon Benisette.

That evidence had been uncovered by Lamont Cranston, the man who was The Shadow!

CHAPTER IX

THE hunt was on for Lionel Graff.

Like all quests for a murderer, it began locally and spread itself wide. Unfortunately, finding pictures of Mr. Graff was quite impossible.

Always a slippery character, Graff proved to have been underestimated when the facts began stacking up against him. Everyone knew he'd been in financial water, but no one had guessed how deep.

Creditors galore began pestering the police with details of tricks that Graff had played on them. The stack of promissory notes he'd handed to these dupes was so large it had to be arranged alphabetically. Estimates were putting Graff more than fifty thousand dollars in the red, provided he'd ever intended to pay up.

Among Graff's defaults were bank checks that had bounced so often they hadn't any rubber left. Threatened with legal action, Graff had been right against the wall that evening he'd come to Talcott's to bid on the chest of Chu Chan.

Of course, dealers like Talcott had known enough not to trust Graff, and they had even warned their customers against him. Talcott personally provided some data on the subject when he called at the commissioner's office a few days after Graff's disappearance.

Cranston was there and so was Cardona. On the commissioner's desk were some of the exhibits from the Benisette case; having discussed them with others, Weston wanted to do the same with Talcott. Nevertheless, the commissioner willingly took time out to let the antique dealer recall a few facts concerning Graff.

"All the dealers wondered how long Graff would keep ahead of trouble," informed Talcott. "So did shrewd buyers like Benisette. They could insult Graff, but we couldn't afford to do so. Not while he still had contacts like Shebley."

"Graff had only Shebley," put in Weston, dryly, "and even Shebley was wary of the fellow."

"I found that out," returned Talcott with a nod, "the night that Graff tried to buy the chest. He pulled every string or I might say he used every phone wire, there in my office. Whenever he called a man, he began with a promise to pay a long-standing debt if only they'd help him on one more deal."

"And they all cut him short?"

"Very, very short." Talcott blinked solemnly. "That's when I realized how desperate Graff was. When people began calling me the next morning, I wasn't surprised, because I didn't think he could afford to be around. But when I learned that all trace of him had ended at my place—"

Talcott broke off with a recollective headshake as though to chide himself for his false theories. Rising, Weston clapped the antique dealer on the stooped shoulders.

"You did good work," complimented the commissioner. "You spotted murder, even though you had it in reverse. Now let's go over the exhibits."

The commissioner opened an oblong box to disclose a set of fine finishing tools that Cardona had brought from the rear room of Talcott's Galleries. Among the tools was a special bradawl with a threaded point. Holding the awl beneath a microscope, Weston invited Talcott to have a look.

Among the threads, Talcott could see tiny fragments of wood from the chest of Chu Chan. This was the instrument that had been used to bore the air holes.

"No fingerprints," stated Weston. "Graff was smart enough to wipe the handle. However, he forgot that the boring point might carry evidence. We've taken photographs of all these tools, Talcott, so we'll let you have them back shortly. I'll let you know later when and where to pick them up."

Talcott expressed his thanks with a nod.

"Now," said Weston. "This!"

He picked up the Burmese katar, gave it a knuckle nudge that sprang the outer blade apart and displayed the pointed steel. Talcott recoiled at the action, only to have Weston smile and beckon him close. Letting the silver casing spring shut, Weston used the dagger to point out a set of photographs which showed the katar full size, open and shut.

"We are keeping these, too," said Weston, referring to the photographs. "Shebley can have his precious souvenir again, when we return the various exhibits. So I want you to check the photographs, Talcott, in case we need your testimony."

"They fully represent the katar of Pagan Min," assured Talcott. "I am willing to make an affidavit to that effect."

"Very good. It may save us a lot of trouble later. In the affidavit you can include the dagger's history."

"I know it thoroughly, because I am very particular on such matters. As I told Shebley when I sold him the item, it is positively unique—"

Weston interrupted with a hand wave that meant for Talcott to put such statements in the affidavit.

Taking the gesture for dismissal, Talcott bowed himself to the door; then turned to ask:

"Any traces yet of Graff?"

"None that count," returned Weston, glumly. "The only reports of anyone answering his description came from places too remote for Graff to reach in the time allowed. Cranston is looking at the reports right now"—Weston gestured across the desk—"and he'll show them to you if you wish."

"Never mind," returned Talcott. "There's something else I'd rather know about. What's happened to the chest of Chu Chan?"

"It's still at Benisette's," replied Weston. "We have it under lock and key."

"I mean what's going to happen to it?"

"Haven't you heard?" Weston laughed indulgently. "You'd better get back to business, Talcott. I supposed that every dealer in town would know by this time. Shebley is buying Benisette's entire collection."

"But many of Benisette's items aren't unique."

"Some are, and since his estate will only sell as an entire lot, Shebley is buying everything to get what he wants. We're shipping it all to his place tonight."

With the stare of a bewildered antique dealer, Talcott went out, closing the door behind him. Talcott's departure was so typical of a man who had lost a real opportunity that Weston lost his smile.

"Poor chap," commented Weston. "He'd have probably liked to buy that lot himself."

"Those antique dealers have a tough time," put in Cardona. "They don't only lose a sale but a customer, when some collector picks up a load of junk direct."

Tossing the report sheets on Weston's desk, Cranston gave Cardona a poker-faced stare that rivaled Joe's own.

"I'd hardly call Benisette's collection junk," remarked Cranston. "It contains some nice items."

"My mistake," apologized Cardona. "Not being a collector, it's all junk to me, particularly that chest of Chu Chan. There wouldn't have been a murder if it hadn't been around, because there wasn't anything else at Talcott's big enough for Graff to hide in and stow the body."

"A good point," agreed Cranston. "You said the shipment was going to Shebley's tonight, Commissioner"—Cranston was looking across the desk—"but does that include the chest of Chu Chan?"

"It will have to stay at Benisette's," replied Weston, "until we return the other exhibits. As an exhibit, the chest is the most important of all. We'll take some photographs of it tonight after the rest of Benisette's stuff has been shipped. We'd be glad to have you come along, Cranston."

"I'll be there, Commissioner."

Cranston was going somewhere else, first. That became plain as soon as he left Weston's office. First, he made a quick phone call from a drugstore phone booth, then summoned a cab and sped uptown, to a favorite restaurant, where he met Margo Lane, the person he had phoned. Though it was early, Cranston insisted upon having dinner.

"This soon?" queried Margo. "Why, we'll be finished before dark!"

"That's the best of all reasons," replied Cranston, "because we're going to be busy after dark."

"For how long?"

"We don't know, because it depends on someone else."

"Upon whom, for instance?"

Cranston met Margo's impatient question with a bland gaze; then, calmly, he asked:

"Did you ever hear of a murderer returning to the scene of his crime?"

Intrigued, Margo nodded.

"And where," inquired Cranston, "was Simon Benisette murdered?"

"Why, in Talcott's Auction Galleries—"

Cranston's headshake came in interruption.

"I think we can limit the scene of crime," decided Cranston. "Let's class it in terms of where the body was found."

"In the chest of Chu Chan!"

Margo's exclamation brought Cranston's approving nod. At the same time he passed her the dinner menu, which she eagerly received. As much as Cranston, Margo was anxious to be on their way by dark on the chance that she could share in the unraveling of the mystery.

CHAPTER X

IT was in Shrevvy's cab that Lamont Cranston summed up the riddle of Benisette's death in terms of past and future.

"Benisette was murdered for his money," stated Cranston. "At least that made the proposition profitable, considering that he had at least fifty thousand dollars on him."

"More nearly a hundred thousand," calculated Margo. "Anyway, more than Lionel Graff needed to pay off his debts."

"Which he wouldn't, then, and couldn't now, even if he wanted." Pausing, Cranston pondered; then: "It's an odd trail that Graff left, Margo."

"Odd? How?"

"The police tried to spread the mesh faster than he could travel, but Graff outraced them. Only he couldn't have gone as fast as statistics show. We know when he must have walked out of Talcott's place, here in New York; yet a man answering his description was seen in Chicago only one hour later and in St. Louis four hours after that."

"But Graff couldn't have reached either city so soon!"

"Naturally not. Which proves that Graff either planted a false trail, or else—"

What else, Cranston didn't specify right then. They were getting close to Benisette's place, and Cranston wanted to discuss the chest of Chu Chan.

"There's something important about that chest," assured Cranston, "and the secret was learned by two men."

"The two that wanted it," agreed Margo. "Simon Benisette and Jared Shebley."

"Double zero," scored Cranston. "The two men were Professor Giles Frescott and Lionel Graff."

"But Benisette was buying it—"

"As any collector would. Frescott wanted Benisette to get it, so it would fall into the hands of somebody who knew nothing about its real secret."

The theory was startling, but it had the ring of accuracy. Since Margo's slow nod was visible in the dusk, Cranston proceeded:

"Graff's only bet was to get it into other hands. So he worked on Shebley, telling him the chest of Chu Chan was unique. Once Shebley owned the chest, Graff would have access to it."

"Of course," agreed Margo, "but Frescott blocked the deal."

"Temporarily, yes," declared Cranston, "but Graff became too eager. I have an idea he stimulated Shebley's interest more than we suppose. Since Shebley is buying the entire Benisette collection in order to acquire the chest, we may regard him as a very potent factor."

"Then the secret of the chest, whatever it is, concerns three men."

"Make it four," completed Cranston. "You can count me in on it."

"Shebley is buying the chest," countered Margo. "He is getting it without Graff's help—"

Eyes wide open, Margo paused to exclaim:

"That's why Graff may come to Benisette's tonight! To get at the chest before it goes to Shebley's! Why, it will be Graff's last chance—"

"Say rather his best chance," interposed Cranston. "But we're getting close to Benisette's. I'll be seeing you later, Margo."

As the cab slackened, a curious thing occurred. One door seemed to open of its own accord, the door on Cranston's side. A blot of blackness covered it; then faded. As the door gave a delayed slam, Margo reached beside her and spoke breathlessly:

"Lamont—"

It was useless. Cranston was gone and Margo should have known it. Mysteriously, without Margo even suspecting it, he had blended into that other self of his, The Shadow. His way of sliding into black cloak and slouch hat was so amazing in itself that it seemed more incredible every time it happened.

Somewhere in that dusk, a strange weird figure was on the glide, unseen by even the craftiest eyes.

Somewhere in that dusk, a strange weird figure was on the glide, unseen by even the craftiest eyes. How any ordinary rival would have a chance against The Shadow, Margo couldn't understand. In fact, experience had shown that the average man of crime wilted the moment he met the Nemesis in black.

But The Shadow wasn't dealing with anybody ordinary right now. Lionel Graff rated as the most sensational murderer in a decade or more, while Professor Frescott had already shown his crafty makeup by sending The Shadow, as Cranston, off on a blind trail. As for Jared Shebley, he could be classed as a potent factor because he had bought the chest of Chu Chan.

Skillfully, Shrevvy parked the cab at a spot where no light reached the back seat. This gave Margo a perfect opportunity to watch Benisette's apartment house without being seen. The place was across the street at an angle, and men were bringing out the various antiques to place them in a truck.

Apparently Shebley, the purchaser, was particular, for the work was being done with care. Everything was either wrapped or crated, so it was impossible to identify the various art objects. At least one thing was certain: the chest of Chu Chan wasn't coming out, because nothing of its bulky size put in an appearance. Nor was it to come out, because a uniformed policeman was on duty and Margo remembered that the chest was supposed to stay.

Margo's own purpose here was important. The Shadow expected cross complications; therefore he would need cooperation. If he flashed a signal, it might be Margo's duty to drop from the cab and put in a phone call either to certain agents of The Shadow or the police.

Shrevvy, of course, would drop her near a telephone and be ready on his own to take up any trail The Shadow ordered. These things had worked out before, but Margo didn't expect the same tonight. Whatever happened would involve the chest of Chu Chan, which was still indoors and would remain there.

So Margo felt more than a trifle annoyed when she saw that the truck was almost loaded. It wasn't until the policeman stepped toward the curb that Margo spotted something of consequence. A figure was gliding across the street, keeping to the darkened patches. Thin and black garbed, that shape wouldn't have been noticed by anyone not on the lookout.

Bold of The Shadow, thought Margo, to come so nearly into the open. Perhaps he was doing it just so she would notice and know that he was entering Benisette's. For at the finish, the figure took to the darkness of the wall, paused there, then whisked right through the doorway behind the backs of the men at the truck.

A sudden impulse swept Margo. If The Shadow's action hadn't been a signal, she could at least interpret it as such. Opening the door on her side of the street, Margo leaned toward Shrevvy and spoke briefly:

"Follow the truck. Orders."

Margo was out and waiting in a darkened doorway when Shrevvy, taking her at her word, started after the truck. Then, as soon as the policeman went indoors, Margo crossed to the apartment house, wondering how she was going to get into Benisette's apartment with a cop on duty there.

Hardly had she reached the house before the officer came out. Stepping away from the door, Margo let the cop go past and saw him turn in the direction of a corner drugstore. Of course he'd probably locked the door of Benisette's apartment, but having come this far, Margo decided to try it.

Reaching the door, Margo found herself in luck. The door was unlatched!

Entering, Margo closed the door behind her. The living room was dimly lighted, and strangely different, now that most of Benisette's curios were gone. In the corner, Margo saw the chest of Chu Chan; its lock had been repaired, but the door was wide open, so the Chinese cabinet wasn't ominous. Then, as Margo turned about, she saw that the chest wasn't the only one of Benisette's curios that had been left.

Perched on a piano bench, instead of its accustomed taboret, was the ivory statue of the Siamese dancer!

Sight of that old friend rather startled Margo; then, approaching the image, she laughed. Yellow ivory, jet eyes, and jade trappings made an attractive combination, but they certainly weren't as lifelike as Margo had once imagined.

Siamese dancers should cultivate graceful poses instead of sitting solemnly with artificial faces staring between the spread hands of crossed arms. Whoever had carved this mass of ivory and added its paucity of jade was thinking in terms of sculpture, rather than realism.

Even the black eyes looked dull in this light. Looking right into them, Margo realized that the glimmer of sunlight must have caused her former impression; that, plus her tense feeling when she had been waiting for a body to pop from the closed chest of Chu Chan. Of course, the foolish dream could have helped; but Margo had long since wiped away the silly recollection of this same ivory face peering at her from a cab.

The jet eyes were no longer hypnotic.

Or were they?

Margo must have lost a few moments, at least, in realizing that a sharp click had come from the door of the apartment, which was directly behind her. It couldn't be The Shadow, for he would have entered silently. So Margo made up for the time loss with quick action.

In her coat pocket she had a small automatic that she always carried on dangerous excursions. Pulling the weapon, Margo wheeled around and pointed it straight toward the door. Her back toward the Siamese statue, she saw a man who was closing the door behind him and though he drew one arm across his face, Margo was quick enough to recognize Professor Frescott.

"Hands up, both of them," ordered Margo. Then, deciding to keep Frescott guessing, she added: "And make it quick, whoever you are."

Frescott brought his other arm up, trembling, the action momentarily covering his face still further. Then, before Margo could gain a good look at him, he spoke in a forced voice that didn't sound like his own.

All the professor said was a single word that sounded like a name:

"Ankhea!"

Two twining things like snakes wrapped themselves around Margo's neck so suddenly that her breath choked off as her head went back. Taken from her feet, Margo flung her arms frantically and lost the gun as she tried to fight the strangling clutch.

Like something out of a nightmare, she saw the face of the Siamese statue, alive and active, but with its solemn expression unchanged. Its eyes were staring down into Margo's own, but the face was upside down as Margo saw it.

Maybe the case was the other way about, for Margo certainly was in a whirl when she struck the floor. She had an impression of Frescott pouncing forward to aid the creature that had staged the initial stroke.

Then everything went black, so very black that Margo Lane could not have seen The Shadow, if he had arrived to save her from the plight that she bad brought upon herself!

CHAPTER XI

PATROLMAN CASSIDY, returning from the corner drugstore, stopped short of Benisette's door and stared.

What Cassidy stared at was blackness, too much of it. The blackness formed a cloud that blocked out the light from the back of the hall, which wasn't sensible because the light had been burning when Cassidy left.

Maybe the bulb had burned out. To find out whether or why, Cassidy began ducking his head left and right, only to have the blackness swirl with him. So Cassidy drew his revolver, aimed it at the blackness and halted in astonishment.

He was pointing his gun right at the missing hall light, burning as bright as ever!

It didn't occur to Cassidy that the blackness could have dwindled in crouching fashion. The fadeout had deceived him because the light, again unveiled, had caught his eye. What the patrolman had actually seen was The Shadow, approaching Benisette's apartment from the rear hall, only to retire at Cassidy's return.

All this was in curious contrast to Margo's impression of The Shadow entering by the front door. It was possible that The Shadow could have continued through to the back, though why was a debatable proposition. However, at this present moment, Margo Lane was in a place where the consideration of such problems wouldn't interest her.

Back in the rear gloom of the hallway, The Shadow watched Cassidy try the door of Benisette's apartment only to find it locked. Bringing the key from his pocket the patrolman opened the door and entered. As he did, blackness moved toward him again, sidling past the glow of the hall light in case Cassidy turned to look. But Cassidy didn't turn to look.

Inside Benisette's apartment, Cassidy was staring at a piano bench. He removed his cap to scratch his head, though why a blank bench should have perplexed him was something else again. Cassidy might better have studied the chest of Chu Chan, standing locked in the corner, but he didn't. Indeed, Cassidy was so puzzled that he failed to hear the slight sound of a window sash being lowered into place, somewhere at the rear of the apartment.

The Shadow heard it and was away, out through the back hall. He was on a trail that he had picked up earlier in back of the apartment house; that of Professor Frescott. The Shadow had spotted the benign worthy sneaking in through an alleyway, but in keeping with his plan of learning other people's secrets, he'd let Frescott go ahead.

Now the situation was different. With Frescott departing, it might be policy to follow him elsewhere. So The Shadow reasoned until he reached the back door and pressed it open. The door creaked; not enough for Frescott to hear, for The Shadow could see the professor sneaking along beside a fence; but there was someone closer who caught the sound.

From a trellis beside the doorway, two powerful tendrils emerged like segments of a powerful, living vine, and wrapped themselves around The Shadow's neck with the tightening force of a boa constrictor!

This wasn't the way to treat The Shadow. He proved it by his lunging twist. It was like a jungle combat between a python and a tiger with the verdict going to the latter. Ending his roundabout lurch with a mighty fling, The Shadow crashed his opponent right through the trellis, sending both on a scaling flight that ended with a splintering thud against the fence.

There was an oddity about the flying figure. One moment it was dark, like The Shadow, as if clad in an enveloping cape. Next, it was all a dullish white, a lithe thing twisting in the darkness. It seemed to roll into the folds of the garment it regained and it was gone again with a fading process that almost matched The Shadow's.

Another crash sounded.

Cassidy was responsible. He'd heard the bashing sound from the backyard and had taken the shortest line toward it, right through to the rear of Benisette's apartment. Such a trifle as a window didn't bar Cassidy when he was in a hurry. The burly patrolman smashed right through the pane and showed his head and shoulders, one hand waving a revolver.

The door creaked; not enough for Frescott to hear.

Shots came from Frescott's corner of the fence. Bullets bashed the house wall between Cassidy and The Shadow. In reply, an automatic boomed from the rear porch, whining its leaden messages above the spot where Frescott crouched. There was a wild scramble as the professor darted out through the rear passage, with a small limber shape scudding after him. The Shadow didn't see that figure go, for Cassidy was bothering him.

Strictly a short-range marksman, the patrolman decided to settle the sharpshooter on the back porch, particularly because there was an advantage in aiming along the line of the house wall. It gave Cassidy a chance of ducking back into the window, which was helpful, but The Shadow had a similar advantage and therefore took it. The Shadow simply went back into the door and waited there while the patrolman wasted bullets. But by the time the shooting ended, it was too late to follow Frescott.

His gun empty, Cassidy tilted his head and decided that his adversary might have doubled around through the hallway. So Cassidy took a similar course and rushed frontward through the living room. At the open door of the apartment, he ran squarely into a calm-faced man who paused in apparent surprise.

A few moments later, this gentleman was introducing himself as Lamont Cranston, a friend of the police commissioner. Cassidy gave a knowing nod and pocketed his gun.

"The commissioner said to be expecting you," recalled the patrolman. "I was just calling him down from the drugstore, the line being disconnected here. A bit of some shooting had me busy out back, but I've chased them, I have.

"It's here where I belong; them's the commissioner's orders, so I'm following them. But there's a bit of a mystery bothering me, unless my imagination is at fault. Look over there, Mr. Cranston, and tell me what you see."

Cassidy gestured to the vacant piano bench. After a glance, Cranston shook his head.

"I don't see anything."

"And that's just the trouble, Mr. Cranston. There was a statue sitting there"—Cassidy rubbed his chin—"or did they take it?"

"They must have," returned Cranston, "because the commissioner said that everything was to go except the chest of Chu Chan. Of course, someone could have put the statue in the chest, only the chest is locked."

"It was open, I thought," said Cassidy, staring at the chest. "It's a funny place, this apartment, but maybe it was just the moving men closed the chest. Anyway, we'll leave it until the commissioner gets here."

Cranston lifted his hand for silence. His keen ear caught a sound so feeble that it entirely escaped Cassidy's attention. In fact, the patrolman would never have detected it, for the weak scraping diminished and ceased altogether as Cranston listened. Cranston's order to Cassidy was quick, but calm-toned:

"The key, right away!"

"The key to the apartment?"

"No, to the Chinese chest, if you have it!"

Cassidy had it and produced it. A quick twist of the key in the lock and the double door came open. Out rolled a limp, gasping figure that collapsed in Cranston's arms. It was Margo, her breath gone almost to the suffocation point.

"Get some water," Cranston told Cassidy. "Maybe we can bring her back to life."

Bringing Margo back was easy, now that she had air again. What Cranston wanted was a chance to talk to her alone. Without waiting for Margo's story, Cranston told her what she was to say and the girl nodded, only to let her head fall back in a pretended faint as Cassidy reappeared.

Shortly Commissioner Weston arrived upon the scene with his inevitable companion, Inspector Cardona. Cranston let Cassidy give the first details, then:

"I told Margo to meet me here," declared Cranston, calmly. "She arrived first and somebody flung her into the chest of Chu Chan. They must have skipped out the back way because Cassidy says he heard some shooting."

"They couldn't have been here long," assured Cassidy, "because I was only gone five minutes. But it's my belief they stole the statue, if it was here."

"That Siamese thing?" queried Cardona. "It should have gone to Shebley's with the rest of the goods. I'll phone him and find out."

Weston had finished an inspection of the shattered rear window when Cardona returned.

"Unlatched," stated the commissioner, bluntly. "That's how the thieves got in and stole the statue."

"Only they didn't steal the statue," returned Cardona. "Shebley says he's already unpacked it, and it's on a taboret in his curio room."

Weston threw an accusing glance at Cassidy, who looked quite sheepish. That was sufficient rebuke for the patrolman's lack of memory; Weston softened the impeachment by commending him upon his prompt dispatch of the unsuccessful burglars and further congratulated Cassidy for remaining at his post.

Cardona summoned the photographers to take pictures of the chest, both shut and open; then arranged for the repair of the broken window. Weston decided that the sooner the chest of Chu Chan was shipped to Shebley's, the better, but meanwhile Benisette's apartment would remain under constant guard.

It wasn't until she left with Cranston that Margo told the story of her meeting with Professor Frescott and its singular sequel. Even in the safety of Shrevvy's cab, Margo shuddered as she added:

"The statue had something to do with it, Lamont! Somehow it seems to come alive. I'd charged it to my imagination, but I'm sure I saw that statue's face peering at me from a cab outside of Talcott's Galleries."

Cranston gave a slow nod.

"You say Frescott spoke some word?"

"It sounded like Ankhea," recalled Margo. Then, in awed tone, she queried; "Do you think it could be some strange Oriental charm—a mystic word?"

"More probably it is a name," replied Cranston. "The name of the living statue, to be precise. It was foolish of you to go in there, Margo, but at least you've proven one thing."

"That the murderer didn't return?"

"If you mean Lionel Graff, no," replied Cranston, firmly, "because you proved that Graff didn't murder Simon Benisette."

Amazement swept Margo's face.

"Suspicion of Graff is based on the assumption that he waited overnight in the chest of Chu Chan," stated Cranston, "in order to murder Benisette later. I am now sure that Graff left New York that night and that reports of persons seeing him in the Middle West are correct."

"But why?"

"Simply because Graff couldn't have stayed in the chest overnight. How long were you inside it, Margo?"

"About ten minutes, I suppose. I was blotto at first, but when I woke up I was almost suffocated. Why!" Enlightenment dawned on Margo. "That must mean—"

"That the air holes were drilled in the chest as a

bluff," supplied Cranston, "to make it look as though Graff had stayed there. You tested them for us, Margo, even though you didn't intend to do so. The holes weren't big enough to supply the air that Graff would have needed."

"Then who murdered Benisette? Professor Frescott?"

"He might be," replied Cranston, cryptically, "but he's not the only man who is interested in the chest of Chu Chan."

Cranston ended with that statement, but it was plain that he must have had in mind the name of Jared Shebley.

CHAPTER XII

A STRANGE blue light glowing from the midst of startling blackness.

Such was the token of The Shadow's sanctum, a hidden room in the heart of Manhattan which served as base for the master crime hunter's operations.

On a polished surface beneath the glowing blue were spread documents of every description from newspaper clippings to large scale global maps. As his keen eyes studied the data before him, The Shadow's hand made notations on a pad that lay nearby.

Not merely words, those notations. The Shadow was drawing diagrams, calculating distances, even sketching from memory a life-sized Siamese statue of old ivory adorned with beads of jet and jade.

Perhaps The Shadow would have sketched the chest of Chu Chan and the katar of Pagan Min, had such drawings been necessary. They weren't needed, however, because they were pictured in police photographs lying among The Shadow's other papers.

Commissioner Weston was very cooperative toward The Shadow, without knowing it. Weston had the notion that his friend Cranston really possessed a keen brain, if he'd only use it; hence the commissioner was always stirring his friend to apply his talents to crime investigation.

Cranston encouraged this through an attitude of indifference, the surest way to make Weston persist with something. As a result, the commissioner was constantly loading his friend with crime reports and photographs, which Cranston usually returned later with apologies for having neglected them.

It really annoyed Weston, the way that Cranston ignored things that should have interested him. It never occurred to the commissioner that the data he furnished was invariably "borrowed" by The Shadow while Cranston was supposed to be studying it.

Of course, it was all one and the same, but that was a very special secret. The less that Lamont Cranston appeared to know about a current crime, the more credit The Shadow could take for cracking it.

Not that The Shadow wanted credit.

What The Shadow wanted was results and he was working toward them right now.

The basic problem in The Shadow's survey was still the murder of Simon Benisette. That crime had created plenty of surprise purely because of the original theory that Lionel Graff was the likely victim in the chest of Chu Chan. The theory had sounded plausible enough when put by Dariel Talcott, because Graff had been known to be missing since the night before.

After recovering from the shock of finding Benisette a victim instead of Graff, the law had formed its own theory and a logical one indeed. The business of boring holes in the chest and staying there overnight to murder Benisette was quite in keeping with Graff's character—or lack of it.

Now The Shadow had spiked the law's theory!

The air holes weren't sufficient, as Margo's experience had proven. They were a bluff, a blind; in fact a canard, since they weren't air holes at all. Graff couldn't have stayed in the chest overnight; hence he couldn't have been in Talcott's strong room, since the place offered no object other than the chest as a suitable hiding place.

Reaching to a sheet of paper that bore a list of names, The Shadow drew a line through the one that topped the column: Lionel Graff.

The Shadow was marking Graff off the list of possible murderers.

Now it was true that Graff might have picked up Benisette's trail in the morning, followed him to Talcott's and sneaked in by the side door. There had been time for a murderer to go upstairs, make quick work of Benisette, stow him in the Chinese chest and hurry out again.

Just about time enough, by The Shadow's precise calculation of the time element, based on a comparison of estimates given by Talcott, Margo, and Cardona. But with the doubt in Graff's favor, The Shadow had good reason to eliminate him as a suspect.

Under the blue light were those reports that the New York police had disregarded because they didn't fit with the accepted theory. Those were the reports from Chicago and St. Louis stating that Graff—or someone like him—had been seen there sooner than he could have arrived following Benisette's death.

The Shadow was interpreting those reports soundly.

A handy airplane schedule proved that Graff could have gone from Chicago to St. Louis fast enough to be seen in both cities as reported. Tracing back, The Shadow considered it obvious that Graff had skipped for Chicago the night before, after leaving Talcott's Auction Galleries as Benisette himself had declared, which was another point in Graff's favor.

Why, then, hadn't Graff been seen since St. Louis?

The answer was lying among The Shadow's exhibits in the form of a newspaper clipping from that city. Marked with the hour as well as the day it had been printed, the clipping proved that the newspaper had been on sale shortly after Graff was last seen.

This clipping told of Benisette's death and named Graff as the murderer. Already wanted by the law for fraudulent activities, Graff had done the logical thing for a man of his ilk in his position; that was, he'd ducked from sight.

The hunt was still on, which pleased The Shadow; therefore he hadn't announced his findings. Graff's apprehension was necessary in order to obtain his valuable testimony and The Shadow knew that police throughout the country would be more ardent in hunting down a murderer than a less spectacular criminal.

What The Shadow wanted to learn from Graff were any facts that the missing man might know about the mysterious chest of Chu Chan, which still loomed as a potential motive for murder. Benisette's money had been stolen, but that was a natural consequence. The murderer wouldn't have left it even if he hadn't wanted it, because his oversight would have pointed to another motive.

His pencil poised, The Shadow paused.

In this strange case, The Shadow wasn't rushing to conclusions. He wanted to check every item doubly and even then, he'd be ready to accept revision. Once more, he traced over the floor plan of the Talcott Art Galleries and made sure that the time element would have allowed a man to murder, enter, and leave just within the brief span.

As he checked that tally, The Shadow laughed.

The laugh, in that curtained sanctum, carried a strange, significant shudder. The walls had a habit of tossing back the mirth in the form of sinister mockery. Withal it gave the impression of omniscience on the part of The Shadow.

Anyone hearing that laugh would be convinced that The Shadow knew all. But no one could have heard it; therefore not one of The Shadow's findings could have reached either of the two men whose names he now tapped with the pencil:

Giles Frescott

Jared Shebley.

Though Frescott pretended that the chest didn't interest him, he had deliberately plotted to keep Shebley from buying it on Graff's advice. Frescott knew that Shebley might have learned some secret regarding the chest from Graff, who rated as a very fancy snooper.

Letting the chest go to Benisette, the man who knew nothing, was a smart move on Frescott's part. In fact, he had shown his hand by his daring trip to Benisette's apartment the last night the chest had remained there. Obviously Frescott had intended all along to get at the chest when it reached Benisette, who had purchased it in total ignorance.

Even under the difficulties which later arose, Benisette's apartment had proved a much easier place to enter than Shebley's ironclad penthouse. Nevertheless, the chest of Chu Chan was going to Shebley's after all, which may have been the reason The Shadow's pencil passed the name of Frescott and paused above that of Shebley.

Again The Shadow toned a laugh, this time a reflective taunt that shivered back in echoing whispers.

There was good reason not to cross off either of those names. One man's guilt would of course prove the other's innocence, but with Graff's elimination, suspicion rested equally between Giles Frescott and Jared Shebley.

The chest of Chu Chan rated only as an objective so far as either of those men might be concerned. There was an item more important in their lives—and in the death of Simon Benisette.

That item was the Burmese dagger, the unique katar that had once belonged to Pagan Min. Except for Graff, no longer a factor in The Shadow's language, only two men had been favored with an opportunity to carry that insidious weapon from the penthouse curio room and use it as an instrument of murder.

One man had been a lingering visitor, Giles Frescott; the other was the dagger's owner, Jared Shebley!

CHAPTER XIII

"WELL, Cranston! How unexpected!"

Giles Frescott looked over the top of his reading glasses and beamed as only he could. He was a happy sort, this elderly professor, particularly in his chosen surroundings.

As on a previous afternoon, Lamont Cranston had dropped by at the Museum of Antiquities hoping to find the curator there. This time Cranston was in luck, for Frescott was in his office.

"I was thinking about you, Cranston," continued Frescott, cheerily. Then, as his face clouded: "I'm afraid though that the thought was sponsored by my reflections on the unfortunate business of Graff and Benisette."

"To put it more briefly," suggested Cranston in a

casual tone, "you might call it the business of the Chinese chest."

Frescott gave his head a solemn shake.

"I doubt that the chest of Chu Chan was really involved."

"Except as a convenient coffin," reminded Cranston. "You were somewhat responsible for that, Professor. If either Shebley or I had bought the chest of Chu Chan, Benisette wouldn't have come home in it."

Frescott shrugged away the impeachment.

"It was all a mistake," he claimed. "I mentioned an idle rumor to Shebley and he took it literally. When he started off to Washington, I assumed that my remark must have confirmed something he already knew. So, of course, I phoned you at once to tell you where Shebley had gone."

"Of course," Cranston nodded. "You were very prompt, Professor. You must have called me right from Shebley's, just after he left."

A sharp flash came to Frescott's frequently keen eyes. Did he suspect the deeper impeachment that Cranston's comment could have carried?

Nothing in Cranston's calm demeanor could have verified any such suspicion, but the remark stood. It meant, in substance, that Cranston knew that Frescott could have picked up the Burmese thrusting dagger between the time of Shebley's departure and Graff's arrival in the penthouse.

It would have been obvious rather than smart for Frescott to harp back to Graff, the man already branded as a murderer. If Cranston thought that he was being subtle, Frescott could be the same.

"At least you arrived back early from Washington," recalled Frescott. "I mean early the next morning. I wonder if Shebley did the same?"

A cunning touch, this, an intimation that Shebley could have stopped back at his apartment and picked up the Burmese dagger if Graff had not taken it the night before. What Frescott was doing was accepting the possible elimination of Graff as murderer only to throw suspicion on Shebley as the most likely alternate.

It was as if Frescott had guessed the very findings made by The Shadow in his sanctum, the hidden place wherein he had switched back to his guise of Cranston only a short while ago. Perhaps Frescott was actually connecting Cranston with a mysterious cloaked figure that had appeared at Benisette's while the professor himself was trying to examine the chest of Chu Chan.

As Cranston, The Shadow's best policy was to divert the theme from the question of the Burmese dagger. So in Cranston's style he followed another track.

"Why Shebley wanted the chest of Chu Chan is the real question" was Cranston's verdict, "but now that he owns it, he ought to know something about its origin."

"I could tell him that," asserted Frescott. "The chest of Chu Chan dates from the eighth century. It belonged to Komyo-Kogo, widow of Shomo-Temmo, an emperor of the T'ang Dynasty."

Cranston was fortunately well-acquainted with Chinese history.

"Komyo-Kogo was quite a patron of the arts," defined Cranston. "In a sense, she was too good a patron, for she employed artisans to revive the crafts of previous dynasties. It is therefore often difficult to tell whether certain Chinese art objects belong to the T'ang or an earlier period."

Slow, approving nods formed Frescott's accompaniment to Cranston's dissertation.

"That is why I am only mildly interested in Chinese antiquities," stated Frescott. "It is too difficult to identify them as such. Something copied from an original of an earlier century is simply a reproduction, even after the passage of further centuries."

"There was a time when they could have been distinguished, Professor."

"You mean at the time the reproductions were made? Of course, but how can we hope to probe into that distant past?"

"By examining all records relating to the period of Komyo-Kogo. An empress who patronized the arts would logically have catalogued her possessions."

Frescott shook his head.

"Such things were done," he admitted, "but often at the expense of previous records. For instance"—he rose from his desk and stepped to a cabinet in a corner—"I can show you some samples of ancient palimpsests, parchments which have been used several times, the earlier writings always being erased."

"I am referring to more permanent records," declared Cranston in his even tone. "The art of engraving upon metal had been developed in China by the time of Komyo-Kogo."

Frescott lifted his eyes as though hearing this information for the first time.

"Imagine what a discovery it would be," added Cranston. "A catalogue from the past, establishing the precise period in which many rarities were created. Why, such a record would be of tremendous value—"

"To a collector, yes," put in Frescott, quickly, "since it would enable him to corner the market on actual antiquities." Slowing his tone, the professor added: "But not to the curator of a museum."

"Why not?" insisted Cranston "You specialize in antiquities, don't you, Professor? You have already expressed your dislike for reproductions—"

"Only when they are misrepresented," interrupted Frescott. "Come, Cranston"—the professor strode briskly toward the door—"and I shall show you exactly what my sentiments are. We shall visit the Babylonian crypt."

Frescott led the way along a corridor and down a flight of hollow-sounding stairs. As he followed, Cranston probed the Chinese question with a few more comments.

"At least something is known about Chu Chan," reminded Cranston. "During all the years he lived in Hanoi, he was recognized as an authority on ancient Chinese art."

Frescott didn't even nod.

"They even say that Chu Chan had intended to establish a museum," continued Cranston. "First he was negotiating with the Chinese government; then with the French in Indo-China. In turn, both were interested in Chu Chan's collection, on his terms."

Still no comment from Frescott.

"Of course, Chu Chan wouldn't trust the Japanese," added Cranston, "because nobody of intelligence would. Whatever Chu Chan valued most would be the thing that he would least desire to have the Japanese acquire."

This time Frescott made response, but not regarding Chu Chan. Halting in front of a large metal door, he raised the metal bar that formed its latch and drew the door wide open.

"The Babylonian crypt," stated Frescott. "You may enter first, Mr. Cranston."

Entering, Cranston kept an eye on Frescott, who immediately followed. Turning on a light, Frescott revealed rows of large clay tablets, standing on shelves around a brick-walled room. The tablets looked like flat trays standing upright, and all of them bore Babylonian inscriptions.

At the inner wall of the crypt was a special shelf bearing a set of tablets that looked darker than the rest.

"The original set," explained Frescott. "Genuine sun-baked clay from Naishapur. As for the rest"—he swept his hand around the crypt—"they are merely replicas, manufactured at my order. Do you begin to understand, Mr. Cranston?"

Cranston nodded.

"These reproductions will go to other museums," continued Frescott, "so that students can study the actual Babylonian inscriptions. But there will never be any doubt that they are merely imitations. I am a stickler on such matters, Mr. Cranston"—the professor smiled pleasantly—"and that is why I prefer the antiquities of Babylon to those of China. There is no mistaking them."

Professor Frescott added a flourish to his gesture, and the wave of his hand took in the open doorway. Then, with a glance at his wristwatch, Frescott exclaimed:

Cranston was a few feet short of the door when it clanged shut.

"My word! I shall miss my appointment! I must leave at once, Mr. Cranston, but you are welcome to remain and study these Babylonian tablets at leisure. You will find smaller ones in boxes under the shelves."

With a nod, Cranston accepted the invitation, as a matter of policy. But he strolled along with Frescott as the professor went to the door of the crypt. Nor did Cranston turn back into the brick-walled room until he heard Frescott's rapid footsteps clanging upward on the spiral stairway.

It was then that something stirred from the corridor side, something that had silently approached and taken its position behind the open door, to look through the crack and catch that final trifling gesture given by Professor Frescott.

The gesture had been a signal, a command that could now be put into execution.

Suddenly sensing danger, Cranston turned about, too late. Before he could reach the metal door, it was swinging shut under the driving weight of a figure from beyond it. Though his strides toward the door were swift, Cranston was a few feet short of the door when it clanged shut.

Outside, the barring latch dropped automatically, trapping Lamont Cranston within the Babylonian crypt!

The dim corridor revealed only a vague figure outside the crypt door, a slender form attired in a dark gray cape. Then, stepping away, this helper who had come at Frescott's summons, turned into the light, revealing a face that was a counterpart of a certain Siamese statue.

The Shadow's trapper was Ankhea, the girl who was aiding Professor Frescott in his quest for the chest of Chu Chan!

CHAPTER XIV

COMMISSIONER WESTON was seated in his favorite haunt, the grillroom of the Cobalt Club, when an attendant entered to announce Professor Giles Frescott. Though he hadn't expected this visitor, Weston said that he would see him, so the professor was shown into the commissioner's presence.

What Frescott had brought was a bundle of bulletins, pamphlets, and other data on Chinese and Malaysian art. Frescott felt that these would be helpful to the commissioner in determining the motive behind Graff's murder of Benisette.

Weston showed Frescott the courtesy of thumbing through some of the pamphlets and even used a table knife to open a few of the many uncut pages. But the idea of reading them bored him and the commissioner must have shown it, for Frescott suddenly said:

"It was Cranston who recommended that you read these. He mentioned it up at the museum—"

"So that's it!" interrupted Weston. "Cranston's excuse for not going through those crime reports will be that I haven't read these. When was Cranston up there, Professor?"

"He was at the museum when I left."

"Didn't he say that he was supposed to meet me here?"

"Not that I remember." Frescott gave an absent-minded gaze. "As I recall it, Cranston was chiefly interested in deciphering the clay tablets in the Babylonian crypt."

Weston gave a contemptuous snort; then, picking up Frescott's package of pamphlets, the commissioner gestured for the professor to follow him upstairs. Reaching the desk near the foyer door, Weston placed the package beside two others, calling Frescott's attention to the fact.

"Here are Talcott's finishing tools." Weston rattled the oblong package that contained the items named. "And this"—he lifted another bundle that was oddly shaped and heavy for its size—"it's Shebley's precious katar. I shall put your package with them, Professor. In case you need it, you can call for it."

"That won't be for a few days," returned Frescott. "I want to give you time to read the pamphlets."

"I've already said I'm leaving that to Cranston," reminded Weston. "By the way, what is the phone number at the museum in case I want to reach him?"

Frescott gave the number and added a slight laugh.

"There's no extension to the crypt," he explained. "No phone cord would go through the airtight door. By the way, Commissioner"—in absent-minded style, Frescott changed the subject—"has the chest of Chu Chan gone to Shebley's?"

"It went there this afternoon," replied Weston. "Shebley is stopping here later for the Burmese katar. It's odd, though"—Weston's own tone was reflective—"that Cranston should forget that I expected him here."

Weston was walking toward a phone booth, as though intending to call the museum anyway. Following along, Frescott indulged in one of his nicest chuckles.

"I hope Cranston didn't forget to hook the door of the crypt," he commented. "It swings shut very easily and locks automatically. Well, good night, Commissioner. I must be going home."

In the phone booth, Weston started to call the museum, intending to have one of the attendants go to the crypt and summon Cranston. It struck him that it would be better to have Frescott give the order, but when Weston looked around, the professor was gone. Then Frescott's words about "going home" suddenly jarred Weston's recollection.

If Frescott was going home, the museum was probably closed, except for a night watchman who wouldn't be answering phone calls. Remembering suddenly that Frescott lived miles out on Long Island, Weston realized that it would take an hour or more to overtake him, now that he had left.

Over Weston swept the greater realization that right now Cranston might actually be locked in the airtight crypt, in need of immediate rescue. The phone bell was ringing but producing no result from the museum. Weston slammed the receiver and hopped from the booth.

On the way out of the Cobalt Club, the commissioner ran into Inspector Cardona, who was just arriving there. Grabbing Cardona's arm, Weston hurried him to a big official car, intending to explain matters on the way to the museum.

There was another person who was wondering about the missing Mr. Cranston; namely, Margo Lane. At that moment, Margo was at Talcott's Antique Galleries, hoping for a few words with the proprietor. Busy with customers, Talcott left suddenly to answer a phone call, and Margo followed him to the office.

Naturally, Margo wasn't impolite enough to dash after Talcott, so he was well into his conversation when she opened the office door. There was something very dubious about Talcott's tone.

"I can't see why you called me," Talcott was saying. "Well, yes, I'm the one person who might believe you... Only what would others say if you accused Frescott?"

There was a pause; then:

"I see," said Talcott. "Yes, Frescott did have an equal opportunity to steal the dagger... Of course, if you get down to fine points, Shebley—"

Noting Margo's arrival, Talcott cut off abruptly. He gave the girl a quick glance; then spoke into the telephone:

"Call me later. I'm busy right now."

There was a touch of indignation in Talcott's tired manner as he turned toward Margo. Meeting an issue fairly was one of Margo's specialties, which she promptly demonstrated.

"Sorry, Mr. Talcott," said Margo. "I didn't mean to interrupt. But since I did overhear, just what would happen if Shebley did get down to fine points?"

Talcott blinked in the questioning manner of an owl.

"Shebley? Fine points?"

"That's what you were telling him," replied Margo, "right after he must have said something about Professor Frescott stealing the Burmese dagger."

Talcott tightened his lips as thought trying to withhold something; then he relaxed with a sheepish smile.

"Why, yes," he admitted. "It was sort of a half-way accusation."

"But what gave Shebley the idea?" queried Margo, wondering secretly if Cranston's theory had spread around. "I thought it was thoroughly established that Graff murdered Benisette."

"It was," acknowledged Talcott, "but you can't satisfy Shebley with anything. He's always full of crackpot notions. I should know, because I've had him for a customer."

Picking up the telephone, Talcott dialed a number and soon was speaking to the Cobalt Club. Asking for Weston, Talcott learned that the commissioner had left in a great hurry without saying when he would be back. Resting his chin in his hand, Talcott stared at the wall, then turned to Margo.

"I can't talk to Shebley," declared Talcott, in a tired tone, "but you might, Miss Lane."

"About what—and why?"

"About this Frescott business," replied Talcott, "because your friend Mr. Cranston was deceived in the same way that Shebley was."

"You mean by that trip to Washington?"

"That's right. I think that's what is bothering Shebley. You see Shebley trusted Graff more or less; in fact, mostly more."

"And he trusted Frescott mostly less?"

"That's the way it stands right now. But Shebley will expect me to agree with him on everything, because he's one of my best customers. I wouldn't mind talking to him, but I think somebody else ought to break the ice."

"Meaning me?"

"Exactly, Miss Lane."

Margo thought it over; then realizing that if urgent business had called Weston from the Cobalt Club, it would have taken Cranston, too, the girl decided in favor of Talcott's plan.

"How soon should I talk to Shebley?" asked Margo. "And where?"

"Right away," replied Talcott. "Over at his place." Stepping to the door, Talcott looked out into the galleries and returned with a pleased nod. "The customers have gone," he added, "so I'll have Homer lock up the place. If there are any calls, I'll tell him not to answer them. We'll let Shebley wait until we get there."

The plan pleased Margo Lane immensely. It struck her that she was just the person to sound out Shebley's sentiments on the Frescott question. Certainly there was much to gain and nothing to lose.

Margo Lane had the wrong idea of nothing. She was going to find that out!

CHAPTER XV

IT was a twenty-minute ride to Shebley's from Talcott's, in a direction directly away from the Cobalt Club. In fact, the Antique Galleries were just about midway between the two places, so Margo was putting herself a good forty minutes from where Cranston was supposed to be.

If she'd guessed that Lamont had been foolish enough to get locked in a crypt at the Museum of Antiquities, Margo could have added further minutes to her estimate of distance. But Margo was too busy hatching plans with Talcott to think in terms of the ridiculous.

The plan worked out very simply. When they reached Shebley's, Margo was to go up to the penthouse while Talcott waited in the lobby. After ten minutes, Talcott would either come up or call up, so Margo could schedule her chat accordingly.

The cab happened to be Shrevvy's, so Margo talked loudly enough for the driver to overhear and Talcott's tone was about the same. So, when they alighted from the cab in front of Shebley's, Margo was quite sure that word of her expedition would be relayed to Cranston if he could be reached.

There was nothing pretentious about the lobby in the apartment house where Shebley lived. There was no office, no direct phone to the various apartments, simply a pay booth in a corner of the lobby. The elevator was the automatic type, so Margo entered it and pressed the button marked "Penthouse."

After the end of a rattly ride, Margo opened the door and stepped into premises that flabbergasted her.

The shabby appearance of the apartment house in general didn't apply to the penthouse. The place was magnificently furnished with soft-tufted rugs that led into a sumptuous living room. Though only eight stories up, the windows of the penthouse afforded a fine view toward the river, or would have except for the settling dusk.

From another window, Margo saw a terrace, part of the penthouse setup and realized that Shebley had chosen his location well. This was just the sort of place to live free from worry; or so Margo would have believed if she hadn't seen Shebley.

The man with the tight-drawn face sprang from a living room chair the moment that Margo entered. His hand went to the pocket of the dressing gown that he was wearing; then relaxed. In the indirect light of the handsome living room, Shebley let his lips break into a smile which he probably thought was equally handsome, but Margo didn't agree.

Shebley looked scared, so scared that he was ugly. His peculiar mood threw its effect on Margo, who began to get jittery, too. Then, when Shebley lowered his dry voice to a soothing tone, Margo began to feel that his whole manner was a sham. Maybe he thought it fun to frighten visitors; but at least he was courteous enough to offer an excuse.

"So it's you, Miss Lane," spoke Shebley. "I thought I was imagining things again, like the elevator coming up here and stopping all by itself."

Pretty thin, thought Margo. If Shebley wanted to have her keep the shivers, talk of bats batting windows would be a better type of horror stuff.

"Maybe the elevator was just acting up," suggested Margo. "They do, you know."

"Do they?" Shebley seemed quite pleased. "I'll have to ask Claude about it. He's my man, Claude, but this is his night off. Very reliable, Claude."

Margo already knew of Claude's reliability. The police had grilled him like a hamburger when checking on the theft of the Burmese dagger. Claude's word would stand on about anything. Margo felt herself wishing that Claude and not Shebley had been here to receive her.

"I ought to be getting down to the Cobalt Club," remarked Shebley. "I'm supposed to pick up that Burmese curio of mine, the item with the Balas ruby in the handle." Shebley seemed anxious not to refer to the katar as the weapon that it was. "But I couldn't go out, not unless Claude was here. On account of the chest of Chu Chan, you know."

Margo faked a puzzled look.

"Too many people are interested in that chest," explained Shebley, with another of his wide-split smiles. "I suppose you'd like to see it; otherwise you wouldn't be here. Well, you're quite welcome, Miss Lane, since Cranston is a friend of yours.

"I'd trust Cranston any time." Shebley seemed straining to put sincerity in his tone. "He's the one man that I'm glad is interested in the chest." Shebley paused and nodded. "Really."

"Really?"

It was neat, that word, the way Margo put it. Just about Shebley's tone and style, but with a slight upward inflection. If Shebley caught the sarcasm, he didn't show it. Instead, he bowed Margo into the famous curio room.

Just across the threshold, Margo started back abruptly. It wasn't sight of the chest of Chu Chan that jolted her, even though she'd spent unpleasant moments in the thing. What produced the real shivers was Margo's view of the Burmese dancer statue, seated on its taboret.

"Lifelike, isn't it?" queried Shebley. Going over to the statue, he tapped its arms. "Real ivory and a better item than I realized, even though it isn't unique." Fingering the eyes, he added: "These are fine specimens of jet, while the jade"—he stepped back to appraise the statue—"is an excellent shade of apple green, which marks it as the best."

Margo was studying the room itself. She noticed that the windows were metal-framed, firmly clamped from the inside. In addition to the strong door that they had entered, there was another, equally formidable, in a rear corner of the room.

"Speaking of jade," added Shebley, as though Margo were really interested, "I can show you something quite unique. Out here, Miss Lane."

Shebley led the way out through the living room. They reached the dining room, and there Margo saw a set of dinner gongs that really intrigued her. Hanging like pendants of different sizes, the sounding bells were carved in the shape of fishes, and each was made of hollow jade.

Taking a small hammer with a solid head of jade, Shebley began to tap the sounding stones. The chimes were clear and well-toned, as musical as any that Margo had ever heard. Like Shebley, Margo became fascinated, and neither noticed what took place within the living room.

From a corner near the elevator entry, a figure stepped from behind a flimsy lattice screen that was transparent but not enough so to reveal the form that had been standing against the darkened background. It was a shape clad in a dark gray cape, so dark that it was almost black.

Slippered feet moved rapidly through the door to the curio room, and several seconds later, the caped figure returned, bearing a burden as large as itself. From the cape peered a face that resembled the statue's own, as Ankhea carried the image to the corner where she had hidden.

Gonging away at the fish bells, Shebley was having so much fun that Margo gave him a genuine smile. Right then was when they lost their one real opportunity to spot Ankhea, for when she had planted the statue behind the screen, her hardest task was finished.

Half-crouched, Ankhea blended with the wall's dark background and also cut off view of the statue. She waited until Margo laughingly suggested that Shebley try another tune. Then, in a single move, Ankhea became a living version of the dancer statue.

Simply stepping from her slippers, the Siamese girl let the cape slide from her own shoulders and fall inside out upon the statue, completely submerging it. The effect was magical, giving the illusion that the statue had bobbed up to life in a kaleidoscopic leap.

She was something from a dream, this creature of delicate ivory turned human, as she stole soft-footed across the tufted floor. Jade beads quivered like the tendrils of a wind-swayed vine with every undulation of her willowy form. Her black eyes, sparkling as no jet could, were fixed upon the far side of the living room, watching to see that neither Shebley nor Margo turned her way.

Only Ankhea's lips were tense and they were compressed simply to hide their ruddiness, the only touch of color which did not correspond with the delicately yellowed hue of the statue that this exotic maiden represented. Ankhea's arms were lightly crossed so that each hand pressed the opposite wrist, but not because she was conscious of any insufficiency in her jade attire.

The girl's only concern was that chance that her wrist bangles might jangle. She handled the anklet situation by the unique process of gliding her feet with every step, so that she seemed to literally flow along the tufted rug. Then, reaching the door of the curio room, the ocher-tinted vision was gone, a few mere moments before Shebley tired of the tune that he was beating on the fish gongs.

"Suppose I lock the curio room," said Shebley to Margo. "I'll feel safer if it isn't on my mind. Then we can chat until Cranston arrives. I don't suppose he will be long."

It wouldn't be Cranston; it would be Talcott, but the time element wouldn't be long. In fact, Talcott was very nearly due, according to the schedule that Margo had arranged with him. So Margo followed Shebley to the curio room, watched him stare into every corner to make sure that no one could be hiding in this chamber of treasures.

Reaching the doorway, Shebley turned to look again and let his eyes rest upon the seated statue that gazed solemnly between the hands of its crossed and upraised arms.

"It's beautiful," breathed Shebley in a tone of complete admiration. "Too bad it isn't unique."

With that, Shebley closed the door and locked it, not realizing that his curio room had indeed gained a unique treasure in the person of Ankhea, the living counterpart of a statue from Siam!

CHAPTER XVI

ANKHEA was at work again. In the darkness of the curio room, she had discarded her statue pose and was using those slim, deft hands of hers to unbar the windows that opened on two exposures. One window was above a sheer wall which Ankhea observed when she leaned outward. That was why she opened the other, which suited her purpose better, since it was almost within reach of the fire tower.

Next, the roving creature of imitation ivory stopped at the door in the deep corner of the room. There, Ankhea drew the bolt, thus opening another route into the curio room. Finally she went to the main door, the one by which Shebley had left, and tried to unlock it. Here, Ankhea failed, because the door had no inside bolt as an attachment to the lock.

With three routes open, Ankhea was satisfied that she had done enough, particularly as Professor

Frescott would hardly choose the orthodox way of entry through the main door. So Ankhea glided back across the room and paused in listening attitude.

First, Ankhea thought she heard sounds from the direction of the fire tower, but before she could thrust her head and shoulders from the adjacent window, another noise attracted her. This sound came from the rear door, the one that Ankhea had unbolted. Turning that direction, Ankhea gave a low, soft whisper as the door opened.

The signal was answered. In his crablike style, Professor Frescott entered and closed the door behind him. At Ankhea's beckon, he approached the chest of Chu Chan, which was standing wide open. There, Frescott lost no time.

With a narrow-beamed flashlight, the agile professor studied the thick bottom of the chest. He ran his fingers from one brass ornamentation to another; then reached to his coat lapel and drew out some ordinary pins, which he carefully inserted in tiny holes that he had discovered at the front corners of the chest, only because he had been looking for them.

Handing the flashlight to Ankhea, Frescott spread his arms and placed a thumb against each pinhead. He pressed, and there was a sharp click, deep within the bottom of the chest. Then, with Ankhea supplying the light, Frescott slid something straight out from the bottom of the chest.

Only briefly did the light reveal a dull brown glisten from flat objects packed within the cache. Then the light was off, with Ankhea whispering warningly. The mystery girl was turned toward the window near the fire tower, listening as before.

Whatever Ankhea might have heard was drowned by a peculiar clang that came from the chest itself. Frescott was having trouble with whatever he had found, and Ankhea's rapid efforts to help him in the dark only bungled matters more. A sound jarred the stillness of the room, a sound like the sharp clang of cymbals. It was muffled, repeated, then muffled again. After that, Frescott and Ankhea caught the hang of it and managed operations with less noise.

By then, Ankhea had forgotten the question of the fire tower, except for an occasional glance toward the window that opened near it. What Ankhea overlooked entirely was the other window that opened above a sheer wall.

Ankhea's eyes never paused when they passed by that window. The glance she gained of solid blackness was sufficient so she thought. What Ankhea didn't notice was that the blackness shifted.

Strangely, that mass of gloom had taken the shape of a human head and shoulders, a figure clad in slouch hat and cloak!

If either Ankhea or Frescott had noted that weird shape, it would have suppressed any notion they might have had concerning a dual identity of Lamont Cranston and The Shadow. For between them, these connivers had planted the enterprising but inquisitive Mr. Cranston in the Babylonian crypt, which he couldn't possibly leave until his friend the police commissioner arrived to release him.

By Frescott's calculation, the commissioner was just now reaching the museum. The Shadow couldn't possibly be here at Shebley's penthouse.

Or could he?

Out in the living room, Margo Lane was asking herself that same question when she saw Shebley give a worried stare in the direction of the curio room. Immediately, Margo glanced toward the elevator, hoping that Talcott would arrive if Cranston didn't.

For Shebley had unquestionably detected some sound from the curio room, a clang which Margo too had caught but was hoping it stood for the elevator.

"Did you hear that, Miss Lane?"

Trying to look unconcerned, Margo shook her head at Shebley's question.

"It came from the curio room," asserted Shebley. "Someone has entered there!"

Thinking in terms of The Shadow, Margo tried to allay Shebley's suspicions.

"But how could anyone be in there?" queried Margo. "And why?"

"Because of the chest of Chu Chan."

"It was empty," insisted Margo. "You made sure of that yourself when you looked around the room. The chest was wide open, so nobody could have been hiding in it."

"You asked *why* would anyone enter," argued Shebley, "and I told you because of the chest of Chu Chan."

"But who even knows that it's here?"

"Anybody could guess. Look at this." Shebley rustled a newspaper that was lying on the table beside him. "Here under auction news, it states that I have just bought the entire collection that belonged to Benisette."

The item was so small that Margo could scarcely read it in the light. With a shrug, she inquired:

"But who would notice this?"

"Everybody," returned Shebley. "That is, everybody interested in the chest of Chu Chan."

Rising, Shebley beckoned for Margo to follow him. On the way around the living room, Shebley turned off all the lights, darkening the entire penthouse except for the glow of the city that showed through the windows. Margo heard a jingle as Shebley produced some keys; when he stopped at the door of the curio room, she could hear him inserting one in the lock. His other hand deep in his pocket, Shebley opened the door.

At that moment, Margo heard a clang, which she

thought came from the elevator door. If such, it was the thing that totally destroyed Shebley's efforts toward silence. But the answering clash, much like an echo, wasn't from the elevator's direction.

The jarring slam of metal against metal came from within the curio room itself, right from a spot close by the open chest of Chu Chan!

Before Margo could even gasp, Lionel Shebley surged into the room, to be met by a stooped man who unlimbered up from his huddle in a fashion that Margo Lane distinctly remembered from an encounter of her own.

In that momentous instant, Margo Lane would have sworn that Shebley's antagonist was Professor Giles Frescott!

There was a flash of steel in a rising hand; then a battering sound of metal meeting metal. A gun stabbed, but its fiery tongue thrust upward, proving that it had missed its mark. Then, as Margo heard a clatter from a window, blotting blackness took human shape, came surging inward to smother the two battlers.

Then came Margo's turn for trouble.

In answer to the spontaneous shriek that Margo couldn't quite suppress, the figure of a living statue, jangling jade and sinuous ivory, came literally from nowhere to clutch Margo Lane in its serpentine embrace!

CHAPTER XVII

IT was The Shadow who lunged in from the window that Ankhea had overlooked. In visiting this curio room where the unique ruled, The Shadow had naturally chosen a unique route. Yet it wasn't love of the spectacular that had urged him to scale the sheer wall in preference to some easier mode.

Simple logic indicated that if any route to Shebley's curio room would lie open, it would be the most difficult one. So The Shadow had come up the hard way, hoping to find it easy. Thanks to Ankhea's methodical preparations it was.

Easy entry didn't mean easy victory.

Hurling himself into the conflict between Shebley and Frescott, The Shadow had the element of surprise in his favor. But those two fighters had been surprised enough, by their own meeting. They were in a mood to battle with anything within reach, and The Shadow belonged in that category.

A gun, swinging downward in the dark, glanced against The Shadow's head before he could throw up a warding arm. Reeling, dodging as he went, The Shadow drove head first into what seemed a wall of metal that lifted to meet him.

Whether they liked it or not, Shebley and Frescott were ganging up against a mutual foe in The Shadow. However, that had nothing to do with their private fight, so The Shadow had another break in his favor. Rallying from his first strokes of bad luck, he was in the fray again, battling groggily, but with purpose.

All The Shadow needed was one foeman less. If he could settle either Shebley or Frescott—and The Shadow was willing to accept one's aid against the other—the handling of a single enemy would be easy. But neither Shebley nor Frescott was willing to give up. Both fought with a fury that carried The Shadow in their whirl.

The three were milling toward the deepest corner of the room. Shebley didn't care, because he thought he was trapping his antagonists; but Frescott carried the fray in that direction purposely. As the mass spun around, Frescott managed to yank open the door that Ankhea had unlatched; then, swinging hard and wide with the flat burdens that he carried, he literally bludgeoned Shebley into The Shadow's arms.

Next, Frescott was through the door and out into the garden, huddled low as he tried to find some spot of security. It wasn't a case of hiding his face; what doubled him was the weight of the metal objects that he had taken from the chest of Chu Chan. Frescott wanted to keep those trophies at all cost.

The clatter of an opening door, the quick-toned signal in a foreign tongue, gave Frescott the chance he wanted. It was Ankhea who called him and opened a doorway in through the penthouse; having quickly taken Margo out of combat, the Siamese girl was back helping Frescott again.

But she wasn't the same Ankhea.

During the interval, Ankhea had regained her dark gray cape; though she was as sinuous as ever, she was no longer visible. As Frescott turned in her direction, she helped him with his burden and the two disappeared into the darkness of the penthouse, slamming the door behind them.

Shoved forward by The Shadow, Shebley heard the door slam and hesitated as he turned about. Then, apparently assuming that the fugitives had locked the barrier behind them, Shebley swung further around and went back through the curio room, hoping to cut off Frescott and Ankhea before they reached the elevator.

The Shadow took the shorter route, through the door by which the others had gone. It wasn't locked, but The Shadow needed more than a few seconds to get to it and open it. Moreover, he wasn't familiar with the penthouse, and a blind trail took him into the kitchenette. By the time The Shadow was again on the right route, the fugitives had reached the elevator.

The Shadow saw the door of the elevator clang shut just as Shebley flung himself against it. There was a rumble, indicating that the car was going down, while Shebley clawed with both hands, as though hoping to tear the door of the shaft apart. Knowing how useless that would be, The Shadow chose the fire tower instead, on the chance that he might reach the street before the fugitives gained too good a lead.

As the door of the fire tower slammed shut behind The Shadow, Shebley turned and gave a puzzled stare. Then, with a shrug, he walked unsteadily into the living room and sat down in a large chair. Reaching for a lamp cord, Shebley tugged it and gave a look of amazement.

Margo Lane was just recovering what wits she still had. All she could remember was that something had whirled her into the living room to fling her against the corner screen. Her hands to her throat, Margo was wondering why the creature hadn't choked her while it had the chance, for its arms had certainly gripped her neck tightly enough.

Then, half to her feet, Margo gasped a half shriek and shied away from what she thought was the enemy of a short while ago. What Margo saw was the Siamese dancer statue, toppling from its corner as though it intended to clutch her again. This time, the statue simply landed face down; for it was really the ivory statue, deprived of the cape that Ankhea had so briefly lent it.

Blinking at the statue, Shebley turned for another look at Margo, then came to his feet, his fists half clenched. A man was stepping forward to catch Margo by the shoulders, and Shebley thought for the moment that this was his old rival, Frescott. Then, as Margo gave a thankful gasp, Shebley saw that he had been deceived by the man's stooped shoulders.

The man was Dariel Talcott and he was quite calm. Selling antiques was a business that worried him, but away from his customers he was a man of steady nerve.

"It's all right, Miss Lane," soothed Talcott. "Whoever was here has gone. Now tell us what happened."

All Margo could do was point to the statue and shake her head, meaning that the ivory image must have grabbed her, though she still couldn't believe it.

"Hello, Talcott." Shebley kept his feet by gripping the arms of the chair behind him. "I think I can tell you what it was all about. Somebody was in the curio room."

"So I heard," returned Talcott, with a nod. "But who was it—and how did he get there?"

"I'd say it was Frescott," declared Shebley, "but I couldn't take oath on it. How he got in there—well, that's what we'll have to learn."

"Which way did he go?"

"I don't know," admitted Shebley. "The elevator door slammed shut, but so did the door to the fire tower."

Slowly, Talcott stroked his long chin.

"I came up in the elevator," he said, "and some people rushed past me in the dark. Then I heard Miss Lane calling from over by the screen, so I came to help her."

"I'm glad I was able to call," put in Margo. "I thought I was completely out until a moment ago. I only wish you'd arrived sooner, Mr. Talcott."

"I should have," admitted Talcott. Then, turning to Shebley: "I told Miss Lane I'd be up shortly to talk to you."

"It was about that telephone call," put in Margo. "I didn't have time to mention it, Mr. Shebley."

Rubbing his head, Shebley gave a dazed stare.

"What telephone call?"

Before either Talcott or Margo could explain, a clang came from the elevator and they both turned in new alarm while Shebley pawed in the pocket of his dressing gown only to find he didn't have a gun. Then sight of familiar faces caused them to relax.

Two men had arrived: Commissioner Weston and Inspector Cardona.

After listening to Shebley's brief description of what had happened, Weston turned to the curio room, and Cardona promptly followed. The others went along to learn what the law would make of the singular invasion and its consequences. Hardly had Cardona entered the door and looked around, before he shrugged and announced:

"It was an inside job, all right, Commissioner."

"Apparently," agreed Weston, dryly, "considering that all the doors and windows were open. But who handled it?"

Cardona thumbed across the room.

"Somebody must have been hiding in the Chinese chest."

"But the chest was wide open," objected Shebley, stepping forward. "Miss Lane can testify to that."

"It's shut now," argued Cardona, "and for all we know, somebody might still be inside it. Do you have the key, Shebley?"

Nodding, Shebley supplied the key. He stared at the chest, puzzled, while Cardona unlocked it.

"I can't remember that chest slamming shut," declared Shebley, slowly. "What's more, I can't understand who would want to hide in it."

"Graff might," reminded Cardona. "He did once before."

Margo could have objected to that statement, but she didn't. If Cardona still wanted to think of Graff in terms of murder, he was welcome to do so. From Cranston's analysis of the case, Graff was out of it altogether.

So Margo Lane thought, and she was wrong as usual. That was proven very dramatically.

As Cardona opened the door of the Chu Chan chest, a figure came toppling from it and struck the floor in the same inert fashion that had characterized Benisette's tumble. There wasn't a doubt that this man was also dead; nobody had to stare at his face to know it.

They stared for a different reason.

The police were looking for a murderer and they had found him. The victim from the chest was Lionel Graff!

It wasn't the drawn expression of Graff's face that caused viewers to draw back in actual horror, nor the fact that death had brought a tawny pallor to his sallow face.

What literally stunned the persons who drew back was the death weapon that projected from Graff's heart. As with Benisette, a blood-red gem, topping the spread sections of a silver sheath, formed an emblem upon the dead man's shirt.

Like Simon Benisette, his supposed victim, Lionel Graff, had been stabbed with the Burmese katar that had once belonged to Pagan Min!

CHAPTER XVIII

THE commissioner's big car pulled up in front of the Cobalt Club and Dariel Talcott stepped out. When Margo Lane started to follow, Talcott gestured her back to the seat and said soothingly:

"Wait right here, Miss Lane, and don't worry. If Mr. Cranston is inside, I'll bring him out. Remember, the commissioner said not to get excited."

"But if Lamont was locked in that vault," began Margo, "what can have happened to him if he isn't there now?"

Talcott wasn't around to reply. He was starting into the club, so all that Margo could do was wait until he returned. At least that was all she could do for a few minutes.

At the end of that time Talcott hadn't returned, so Margo sprang from the car despite the chauffeur's protest and hurried into the club herself. There she found Talcott standing at the desk, quite alone and very placid.

"Why don't you ring the bell?" demanded Margo, pointing at the desk. "I know the club is short-handed; they used to always have a man on duty. But you can always ring for an attendant—"

"I did," interposed Talcott, with one of his tired smiles. "The fellow is looking for Cranston right now. By the way, Miss Lane"—Talcott tilted an oblong package that he was holding—"Here are my tools, the ones that the commissioner no longer needs as evidence."

Margo nodded without looking at the box. She was wondering where Lamont could be.

"And there is Frescott's package on the shelf," continued Talcott. "The one with all the pamphlets that the commissioner mentioned. But there is no other package."

"There couldn't be," rejoined Margo, "not with the Burmese dagger showing up at Shebley's. Do they know who called here for it?"

"I haven't asked," said Talcott, "but I suppose anyone could have taken it; that is, anyone who had time to get to Shebley's penthouse afterward." Looking around the lobby, Talcott added: "I'm still wondering what happened to Cranston."

That final remark worried Margo for a new reason. If Lamont hadn't been in the museum crypt where Weston didn't find him, he might have been anywhere. Therefore Cranston's actions, like those of both Shebley and Frescott, were still unaccounted for.

Talcott might even be thinking that Cranston had stopped for the Burmese dagger and used it to knife Graff!

Another look at Talcott allayed Margo's qualms. The man seemed honestly worried over Cranston's prolonged absence, and Talcott's honesty certainly stood unquestioned. He at least was one person who couldn't have acquired the Burmese dagger, because he had been with Margo since the time when Weston had last seen it. The only interval had been the quarter-hour of Margo's sojourn in the penthouse, and Talcott couldn't have reached the Cobalt Club in that time, let alone returned.

All of which brought back the question: Where was Lamont Cranston?

Just as Margo felt ready to shout that question for all the world to hear, a calm voice spoke beside her:

"Hello, Margo. Have you been waiting here all evening?"

It was Lamont, as unperturbed as ever. He had strolled in through the door while Margo was staring everywhere else. In a torrent of words, Margo began to tell Lamont how glad she was to see him; then, realizing more explanations were needed, she detailed the story of what had happened at the penthouse, with Talcott adding a few supporting facts.

When Margo came to the discovery of Graff's body and the fact that Pagan Min's katar had again been identified as the murder weapon, Cranston's eyes showed a momentary glimmer, which he promptly restrained.

Here was a riddle that formed a real challenge to The Shadow, particularly since it had occurred on the scene where he had been.

Yet there was something reflective in Cranston's stare. In the darkness of the curio room, amid the excitement of a three way battle, even The Shadow couldn't have learned whether the chest of Chu Chan was open or shut. Hence it was difficult to determine whether murder had preceded or followed The Shadow's actual arrival.

The best plan was to view the scene again. Pausing only to pick Frescott's bundle of pamphlets from the shelf, Cranston turned toward the door of the Cobalt Club and said:

"Since the commissioner's car is outside, why should we wait?"

They reached Shebley's to find a huddle in the living room, with Shebley the center of it. Weston and Cardona were both working on one grand idea, for which they would probably each claim credit later. At least Shebley wouldn't want credit, for he was getting the worst of it.

The idea was that Jared Shebley, and no one else, had murdered Lionel Graff.

"But I tell you I didn't!" Shebley reiterated his plea when he saw that newcomers had arrived. "Why should I have murdered Graff?"

"For the same reason you murdered Benisette," jabbed Cardona. "Because he was after the chest of Chu Chan."

"But I didn't murder Benisette—"

"Who else had a better chancc?"

"Talcott for one!" Frantically, Shebley pointed an accusing finger at the first man in sight. "Don't forget, Benisette was packed in that chest while it was still in Talcott's place!"

"And he was stabbed with your katar," reminded Weston. "The only one like it in the world. It belonged to a murderous king originally, and maybe that legend went to your head, Shebley."

"But somebody could have stolen the dagger—"

"Not Graff," put in Weston. "We were wrong about classing him as the killer."

Shebley's trapped expression turned to another furious look, again directed at Talcott, who promptly countered:

"Don't try to blame me, Shebley. I only sold you the dagger; I didn't steal it. I didn't even come here the day the dagger was stolen. I stopped by the next morning, but that was after Benisette had been stabbed with the weapon."

"And today," added Margo, emphatically, "I was with Talcott when the dagger was still at the Cobalt Club. We came directly here and Talcott waited downstairs."

"For only fifteen minutes," reminded Talcott. "It would have taken me half an hour to go and get the katar."

Good points, these, but Weston didn't like to see the quiz falling into the hands of amateurs. Accepting the sound facts, the commissioner followed them through by storming at Shebley:

"The dagger was yours. I told you where I had left it for you, Shebley. You were supposed to pick it up"—Weston's tone was very terse—"and you did."

"I haven't been out of this penthouse all day!" argued Shebley. "Miss Lane will tell you I was here when she arrived."

"So you were," agreed Margo, "but where were you when you made that phone call to Talcott?"

Shebley stared; then demanded:

"What phone call?"

Margo looked at Talcott, who spread his hands in the fashion that he used with unreasonable customers at his antique galleries. Then:

"Miss Lane was present when you phoned me," stated Talcott. "There's no use denying it, Shebley."

"You said something about Professor Frescott," Margo told Shebley, "because Talcott repeated it without knowing that I was there."

Shebley's face was becoming purple, which explained why he was speechless.

"And then"—Margo was recalling the conversation exactly—"Talcott said: 'If you get down to fine points, Shebley'—and that's where I came in."

"So I hung up," added Talcott simply.

His voice back, Shebley became sarcastic.

"It must have been two other people," he sneered. "But since you mention Frescott, what about him? He could have taken the katar from here and he could have picked it up at the Cobalt Club tonight."

"Only he didn't" was Weston's verdict. "I'll tell you why, Shebley. You say you encountered someone in the curio room, don't you?"

Lips tight, Shebley nodded.

"And we found someone in the curio room," added Weston. "We found Lionel Graff."

"All tucked away in the Chinese chest," defined Cardona. "Where only you could have put him, Shebley."

That was enough. The law had found a man who could be properly charged with double murder. Handcuffs clicked on Shebley's wrists when Cardona applied them; still fuming, the suspect was led from his luxurious penthouse. Since the police had taken over, the others were invited to remain.

Lamont Cranston accepted the invitation. He wanted to have another look at the chest of Chu Chan, the mysterious source of all this trouble.

CHAPTER XIX

TWO days in jail hadn't weakened Jared Shebley in the least, but that was a thing to be expected. In his position, his best plan was to deny everything, whether he was innocent or guilty. Of course, meanwhile the police were supposed to be piling up evidence on both counts, only they weren't.

Lamont Cranston stated so, rather smilingly, when he called on Dariel Talcott. The chat took place in the rear room of the Talcott Antique Galleries, the spot where crime had technically begun. Margo Lane was there, too, though she couldn't see why this discussion was important.

However, it soon became so.

"The commissioner actually asked me what to do next," concluded Cranston. "So I told him."

"And what was that?" queried Talcott.

"I told him to release Shebley," replied Cranston. "In fact, I even suggested that all charges be dropped—on one proviso."

"Which is?"

"That Shebley should voluntarily join us in a visit to the Museum of Antiquities, which I think he will. Shebley would certainly like to see certain of his prized curios."

It was Margo who exclaimed:

"You mean they've been shipped to the museum?"

"A few have," explained Cranston. "The chest of Chu Chan, the katar of Pagan Min, and the Siamese dancer statue. They're all important exhibits."

Talcott shook his head.

"I don't see why the statue is."

"Because it was found outside the curio room," stated Cranston, with only the slightest side glance at Margo. "How it arrived there is something of a mystery, unless Shebley purposely flung it there, just to add another puzzle."

"But tell me," queried Talcott. "What good will it do to take Shebley to the museum?"

"Plenty," replied Cranston. "Professor Frescott happens to know a great many things about Oriental art, things that Shebley doesn't. If we get the two of them talking together, something may develop."

"You said 'we.'" This came from Margo. "I think you are the only person who could start a chat between those two, Lamont."

"I'm relying on Talcott." Cranston gave a polite bow. "He knows art, too. By the way, Talcott, some of Frescott's pamphlets would interest you. He has one that is very rare, in fact unique."

"That should interest Shebley," returned Talcott, dryly, "unless he has lost his collector's urge."

"This one is on Burma," specified Cranston, "and it tells all about our old friend Pagan Min. Unfortunately, I didn't read it; some of the pages were uncut, so I didn't open them. Frescott says that I can borrow it again, but now that he's interested, he intends to read it first."

Glancing at his watch, Cranston noted that it was nearly time for the appointment. He didn't have to suggest that Talcott come along. The art dealer said that he would follow as soon as he could; it was too early now to close up shop, but after a few phone calls, he'd be able to let Homer take over for the rest of the day.

All the way to the museum, Margo was wondering about Frescott. It had occurred to her more and more that the professor was getting off very lightly. All counts considered, he was a more likely suspect than Shebley. When the squat museum came in sight, Margo suddenly blurted her opinions.

"What about Frescott?" she demanded. "Why don't you out with it, Lamont, and say he did those murders?"

"Why, Margo!" Cranston's tone carried genuine rebuke. "I never say that anyone ever murdered anybody."

"Well, in Shebley's case—"

"The opinion was Weston's—or perhaps Cardona's. Each is now blaming it on the other, though at first they had it the other way about."

"But Frescott entered Benisette's apartment," began Margo, "and he may have come to Shebley's penthouse."

"Not necessarily for murder," argued Cranston. "We must learn his motive, and how far it may have carried him. I think we may uncover something very soon."

Weston, Cardona, Shebley were all in Frescott's office. As soon as Cranston appeared, Shebley came over to shake hands earnestly, at the same time sidling a look of denunciation at Frescott. Beaming from behind his desk, the benign professor purposely misinterpreted Shebley's glare.

"Don't worry about your curios." Frescott gave a sweeping gesture. "The museum does not want them. They will be returned when—and if—you are where you can receive them, Shebley."

The chest of Chu Chan was in one corner of the room, the Siamese statue in another. On the desk lay the Burmese katar as a final exhibit. But Shebley wasn't thinking of his curios, except possibly the dagger. From the increase in his glare, he might have been contemplating using that weapon on Frescott.

"It's likely to be your turn!" stormed Shebley. "I mean it, Frescott, when I say you'd do anything to acquire what you want."

"But I want none of these," repeated Frescott. "My interest lies in Babylonian antiquities, such as these ancient tablets." He pointed to a row of the clay plaques that were standing against the wall behind him. "I brought them here especially for Cranston to see."

Cranston bowed his acknowledgment and with it continued a glance toward the door. Talcott was entering, having hurried along as soon as he could. Since everyone in any way concerned with the case was present, Cranston was ready to open his attack on Frescott.

"The Babylonian tablets," repeated Cranston.

"Nice of you, Frescott, not to send me down to the crypt again in order to see them. I spent an unpleasant time there."

Frescott raised his eyebrows, as though puzzled. Moving his chair closer, Cranston found the chest of Chu Chan in the way and started to move it. Cardona stepped over to help him, but it wasn't necessary. Using his knee, Cranston just managed to lift the chest alone.

An odd flicker came to Frescott's eyes, but he said nothing.

"Maybe I too need an alibi in this case," remarked Cranston. "So, Professor, if you will admit you locked me in the crypt, it might help."

The flicker gained the proportions of a glare.

"After all," added Cranston, "if I was in the crypt, I couldn't have gone to Shebley's as you did—or could I?"

Frescott came to his feet, slamming a big fist on the desk.

"If you were locked in the crypt, it was a mistake!" he roared. "Anyway, I stopped to see the commissioner and gave him the hint that you might be there—"

"So I would survive?"

"Of course not," retorted Frescott. "There was enough air in that crypt to last you all night!"

"Just as there was enough air in the Chinese chest," suggested Cranston, "to last Margo when you put her there."

"The chest had air holes."

Frescott caught himself. It wasn't that he knew the inadequacy of the air holes; if he had, he probably wouldn't have mentioned them. Frescott was chewing at his tongue because he had gone far enough off guard to be tricked into admitting that he was responsible for Margo's plight that night at Benisette's.

"We supposed the air holes supplied Graff overnight," said Frescott, suddenly, "if that's what you mean. Anyway, Cranston"—smartly, the professor was trying to parry—"if you were locked in that crypt, how could you get out?"

"The way I did get out," replied Cranston. "With a razor blade. It's the best of wedges, Professor, to get at a latch through a crack that's hair-thin. That latch works very smoothly, by the way—"

"With a razor blade!" interrupted Frescott impatiently. "You don't expect us to believe that!"

"Why not? You expected the commissioner to believe he was coming here to rescue me, when your actual purpose was to keep him from going to Shebley's."

"What's that, Cranston?" Weston was on his feet. "You mean Frescott was playing a double game?"

Cranston nodded.

"A double game," he replied, "with these."

Hands moving from the lapels of his coat, Cranston produced a pair of black pins. Eyeing them, Weston snorted.

"What's this, Cranston, a joke?"

"No more than the razor blade was. Professor Frescott uses even simpler equipment than I do. I found these on the floor in Shebley's curio room. I finally figured their purpose."

Turning to the chest of Chu Chan, Cranston asked Cardona to move it closer, which the inspector did.

"It took three men to lift that chest when there was a body in it," recalled Cranston. "With the body gone, two men could lift it. Now only one can, which means that it has lost more weight."

Probing along the brass mountings, Cranston found the pinholes in the bottom corners of the chest. It was already dawning on others that the loss of weight could only have come from the thick bottom; hence Cranston's discovery was logical. In went the pins; muffled clicks sounded.

The bottom of the chest slid out like a drawer. The hidden compartment was empty, but it revealed crossbraces and little pegs, which had obviously been put there to hold something tightly in place.

"From the size of those spaces," observed Cranston, "I would say that this secret drawer contained engraved plates of the T'ang period, unquestionably of bronze, which would allow for the missing weight."

Turning toward Frescott, Cranston demanded:

"Where are those plates, Professor?"

"You can search this whole museum," retorted Frescott, "and you won't find them, because there are none."

"You're sure? Suppose I begin right here."

Cranston was stepping past the desk. With a roar like a bull, Frescott sprang to stop him. When Cranston shoved the professor back in his chair, Frescott grabbed for a desk drawer and pawed among his pamphlets, shouting:

"I warn you, Cranston—"

The warning wasn't needed. Cranston was quicker; his own hand, driving past Frescott's, found the gun before the professor could. To the amazement of all, it was Cranston who was glaring now, and murderously. Half rolling from his chair, Frescott looked frantically about for refuge; trapped, with Cranston bearing down on him, the professor grabbed one of the Babylonian tablets and twisted it in front of him.

On hands and knees, with nothing but a shield of baked clay to protect him, Frescott looked so pitiful and helpless that everyone expected Cranston to laugh and toss away the revolver.

Instead, Lamont Cranston aimed toward the heart of the cowering professor, tightened the gun trigger mercilessly, and fired!

CHAPTER XX

AS the bullet smashed the hardened clay, Frescott sagged back toward the wall, flinging his hands upward. There was no time for Cranston to fire another shot; half a dozen hands were gripping him. However, another shot wasn't needed.

Instead of a body thudding the floor, something was clanging there. Frescott wasn't hurt; all that had perished was a clay tablet, one of the fine dark colored type, but the loss wasn't important. The clay tablet was merely a replica, darkened to pass as one of the priceless originals.

A special replica that Frescott had baked very recently, for it contained another object, almost the same size, the bronze plate that was clanging; on the floor. Engraved with Chinese characters, that plate was one of the very sort that Cranston had pictured as the secret contents of the chest of Chu Chan!

Seeing it, Shebley kicked another of the clay tablets and it broke as the first had. Out of it came another of the Chinese plaques. Then Weston and Cardona were breaking the Babylonian fakes apart to discover more Chinese genuines.

From beside the desk, Cranston spoke pleasantly.

"You gave it away, Professor," he said. "Even in fright, you wouldn't have used a clay shield, not a man of your keen caliber. I fired because I knew that the bronze interior would deflect the bullet."

Coming to his feet, Frescott stood with bowed head. Then, with a slow nod, he decided to state his case.

"Chu Chan sent those engravings," declared Frescott. "You analyzed it correctly the other day, Cranston. All along, I was afraid that you would, you with your keen knowledge of Chinese art. Yes, the plates are a catalog of the treasures of the Empress Komyo-Kogo. Chu Chan was trying to buy up the true works of ancient art and bring them back to China.

"He sent me the plates when he feared he could no longer keep them. Their very existence was unknown and should remain so. In the hands of unscrupulous dealers or collectors, this information would enable them to buy up many little-valued items at low prices; then reveal their true worth and reap huge profit.

"Graff knew something of the secret and was trying to make a deal with Shebley. That's why I wanted Benisette to get the plates. He knew nothing, so I was sure I could obtain the precious plates later. So I went to Benisette's first; then to Shebley's—"

Halting, Frescott raised his head and faced all eyes squarely. He had told his purpose; the plates stood as his proof. Apparently he saw no reason to declare more.

Shebley stepped forward, his hand extended.

"My apologies, Professor," declared Shebley. "If I had known about the plates, I would have given them to you. Surely I could—and would—have removed them as soon as the chest reached my curio room. But Graff told me nothing; he only hinted that the chest had some special value in itself."

A strange laugh suddenly chilled the room. It literally could have been described as mirth from nowhere, for when persons turned, they saw no one who might have uttered it. True, everyone looked in a different direction, which proved that all ears had been deceived.

The laugh of The Shadow, brief but sinister, a whisper that rose to a sharp crescendo, then cut off to let echoes carry its shuddery taunt; such was the tone that was gone before it could be traced!

Even Lamont Cranston was looking around with a puzzled expression. He turned as he felt Weston grip his arm.

"The Shadow's laugh!" voiced the commissioner, hoarsely. "What could it mean, Cranston?"

"Only that we must still find a murderer," replied Cranston, in a slow, even tone. His eyes were upon those handshakers, Shebley and Frescott. "Yes, that would be it. Someone did murder Benisette and Graff."

His arms folded, Cranston let his eyes wander all around the room, passing the people and studying such items as the Chinese chest and the Siamese statue. Then, his gaze ending on the desk, Cranston gave a look of real surprise.

"It's gone, Commissioner!"

"What's gone?" demanded Weston. "If you mean The Shadow, he wasn't even in here!"

"I mean the Burmese dagger." Cranston was staring at the blank desktop. "In all this confusion, someone must have taken it. Yes"—Cranston's eyes studied faces, now—"someone—anyone of you—could have taken that deadly instrument. I would suggest that everyone be searched, Commissioner. Only on the murderer will you find the katar of Pagan Min!"

It was cold, hard logic; a murderer seeing his game go wrong as facts came out, would certainly be the man to snatch away the most important piece of evidence against him. No one had left this office; therefore, Cranston's proposal of a search was proper.

"We can eliminate Margo," remarked Cranston, casually, "since we know she must be innocent. Let us proceed with the others, Commissioner."

Cranston raised one hand slightly and gestured in the direction of Shebley and Frescott. Weston stepped over to search Frescott, while Cardona took Shebley. Both men raised their arms willingly, and it seemed that the search would not be difficult, since a weapon so large as a one-foot katar would not be easy to conceal.

As though to complete a purely technical procedure, Lamont Cranston stepped around the desk, past the statue, and toward the door, to reach the last man: Dariel Talcott.

Then it happened:

With a move that he must have practiced long, Talcott whipped his hand beneath his coat, brought out a silver bladed knife and thrust it, by its stirrup handle, straight for Cranston's heart!

To reach its mark, the dagger would have to pass those folded arms. That it could slither through was proven, when the silver blade clicked apart under the jab of Talcott's skilled knuckles, unsheathing the vicious steel thrusting blade within.

Cranston's hand was quicker. Tucked under his coat, it already gripped the counter-weapon. Out came a flash, a click of spreading silver, and the bared blade of another katar met Talcott's with a cross slash!

A master duel began.

No one dared to intervene. One weapon alone could vie with a katar, and that was another katar. Thrust after thrust proved that ordinary stabs or slashes would be too slow against steel-pointed punching like this. Now the reason for the hand-guards became apparent. These weapons were meant for duels as well as for assassination.

Only the guards were stopping the furious jabs in as fast a fray as could be witnessed; but the blood that was occasionally marring the duel came from Talcott. Cranston's blade was getting its point past his rival's protected wrist and scoring valuable hits.

Twisting as they parried in their ever-thrusting style, the duelists were covering considerable ground. Talcott's free hand slid behind him; unnoticed by the watchers, it gripped a chair. His next move was to swing, around past the corner of the desk, and with the twirl, Talcott sent the chair skidding straight for Cranston.

The whirl that Cranston gave made Talcott look clumsy. Cranston hadn't been deceived; he was ready for the chair when it came. Spinning twice about, he was away and in again, while the chair was clattering onward to bash against the Chinese chest across the room. And with the finish of his double pivot, Cranston was giving a piston stroke to his katar, intending to lay the point against Talcott's unguarded body.

Cranston's pointed punch stopped short.

No longer was it needed. The part of Frescott's story that hadn't been told revealed itself voluntarily. The Siamese statue came to life. Unfolding, hands of living ivory swooped down and caught Talcott's neck, while a lithe figure added its weight to the fling that followed.

There was skilled power in that form of Ankhea. Jade beads rippled in tune with straining muscles, as the girl's whole body seemed to press its force into the strangling tension of her fingers.

The katar clanked from Talcott's hand as he writhed to the floor; then, as Cranston, stooping, placed the point of his own dagger right where it belonged, Ankhea relaxed and drew away. Choking, Talcott couldn't even gasp for the mercy that Cranston gave, now that the murderer was helpless.

Prompt with the handcuffs, Cardona clamped them on Talcott and drew the slumped man to his feet, while Frescott politely introduced Ankhea, the ivory girl in jade.

"She came along with the chest," explained Frescott. "It was Chu Chan's idea to send a guardian. In the chest he sent a matched statue, hoping the two would be kept together if they reached the wrong hands. That was so Ankhea would be able to take the statue's place if needed—which she was."

Even Margo could forgive Ankhea when the black eyed Siamese girl smiled. After all, their two encounters had been along Ankhea's line of duty. What Ankhea needed now was some American attire and Margo would be only too glad to help her choose. Needing her jade no longer, Ankhea might swap some in return for more capacious clothes.

Cranston's voice roused Margo from commercial ideas. Calmly, Cranston was explaining the mystery of the Burmese katars and how they concerned Talcott.

"It was obvious that there must have been two such daggers," stated Cranston. "Frescott wouldn't have killed Benisette because he wanted him to have the chest. Shebley didn't know the secret of the chest, so he had no reason for murder.

"Money was the motive. Frescott wasn't after it, Shebley had enough of it. Graff wanted it and so did Talcott. Graff's death left only Talcott, and there the obvious declared itself. Since Talcott couldn't have picked up the katar before each murder, I knew there must have been an extra.

"Note this clue: After each murder, Talcott had his opportunity. He had to pick up a katar *after* the crime in order to make it appear that someone had stolen the weapon *before*. We had only one man's word that the death weapon was unique. That man happened to be Talcott."

It fitted perfectly. Talcott's visit to Shebley's after Benisette was already being shipped to his apartment; his later trip to the Cobalt Club to pick up his own package and the one that Shebley hadn't—after Graff's body had been found.

"I knew that one katar could counteract another," added Cranston, "so when I checked on the history of Pagan Min, I realized that his brother and successor, Mindon Min, probably survived him by keeping himself equally armed. Their father, King Tharawaddy, was just the sort to provide each princeling with a royal weapon and let them find their own way in life—or death."

Cranston had picked up the katars. He was holding one in each hand, studying their identical features, even to the magnificence of the matched Balas rubies.

"Pagan Min"—Cranston weighed one dagger—"and Mindon Min." He looked straight at Talcott, who was huddled above his handcuffs. "I bluffed you today, Talcott, with the talk of Frescott's Burmese pamphlet. I wanted to see if my theory would work out—and it did.

"You came here armed as usual with your extra dagger, thinking you might have to murder Frescott and blame it on Shebley, all over the hundred thousand dollars you stole from Benisette. I was the person who picked up the dagger that was lying on Frescott's desk. I suggested that everyone be searched, knowing that when the mate was found on you, the dilemma would be perfect.

"You could neither admit that you had snatched the dagger from the desk, nor that the one in your possession was a duplicate. That was just the situation to swell the murderer in you and make you show your hand.

"And by the way, Talcott?"—Cranston called this through the door as Cardona was leading the murderer out—"your job on the air holes clinches the case. You wanted to prove crime against Graff, but you branded yourself. Not just because Graff couldn't have stayed in the chest overnight.

"Someone else could have sneaked up in the morning, killed Benisette in your rear room, and packed him away. There would still have been time for such a murderer to sneak out again, but not to drill the dozens of air holes that were too tiny to be useful. You were the only man who could have found such time, Graff, there on your own premises."

Later, when they were riding away from the museum, a question struck home to Margo Lane.

"The night I went to the penthouse," exclaimed Margo. "Why did Shebley say he didn't phone Talcott?"

"Because he didn't," replied Cranston. "The man who did phone was Graff; he thought that Talcott might help him out."

"But Graff said he was Shebley—"

"No, he didn't. He mentioned Shebley and then Talcott said: 'If you get down to fine points, Shebley—"and he stopped there because he saw you."

"Why, that's so!" expressed Margo. "Just before that, Talcott mentioned Frescott. He was starting to compare Shebley's case."

"What Talcott was going to say," stated Cranston, "was this: 'If you get down to fine points, Shebley could have used the dagger himself."

"Then Talcott murdered Graff to cover up?"

"Yes. He expected Graff to come to Shebley's and he did, up the fire tower and in the other window that Ankhea left open. Coming up by the elevator, Talcott saw his chance and used it. With Shebley tangling with Frescott, Talcott saw that Graff's death would point to one or the other."

There was a note of finality in Cranston's tone, but it didn't quite complete the theme. Margo and Shrevvy were chilled by a strange laugh that rose suddenly within the cab. A laugh that came from Cranston's lips, unseen in the dusk. The same mirth that had stirred within the museum, back to which it now floated from the departing cab. Louder, longer, more strident than before, it must have reached Professor Frescott and Ankhea.

Though weird, the tone was heartening to those who deserved The Shadow's confidence. As the laugh faded, its echoes clung, as though night itself was cherishing The Shadow's triumph over crime!

THE END

SPOTLIGHT ON GEORGE TUSKA

After a three-issue absence, the adventures of Iron Munro returned in *Shadow Comics* #11 with a new artist, George Tuska (1916-2009).

Hoping for a career in illustation, Tuska attended the National Academy of Design art school before beginning his professional career at the Eisner & Iger comics shop. "I worked alongside Bob Powell, Lou Fine, and Mike Sekowsky. Later the studio expanded, with Charles Sultan, John Celardo, Nick Cardy, and Toni Blum joining in. I worked on 'Shark Brodie,' 'Spike Marlin,' and other strips."

During his initial time with Eisner, Tuska created the "Cosmic Carson" and "Zanzibar the Magician" features for Fox and drew "Käanga" for Fiction House and "Uncle Sam" and "Kid Dixon" for Quality. "I was together mostly with Eisner. We would talk about stories. There wasn't much writing for artists then. He told me, 'Hit this guy and throw a bomb at this guy.' And I said, 'Fine. I can do that.' I wrote all the story down. And I drew everything, backgrounds, the layouts, drawing, complete. But I didn't do the lettering and inking.... I would write the story first and from there drew one panel, two panels, three panels."

George Tuska

After Eisner left to produce his syndicated *Spirit* Sunday newspaper supplement, George grew disenchanted with working directly for Jerry Iger.

"I soon left the Eisner & Iger studio to go work for Harry Chesler's shop. Chesler was currently handling some comics for Fawcett Publications, who couldn't keep up with the production of their successful and expanding comics line. It was at this time I drew several early issues of *Captain Marvel Adventures*, as well as some other comic strips." While employed at the Chesler shop, Tuska drew comics features for a variety of publishers including "Iron Munro" and "The Hooded Wasp" for Street & Smith and "Lady Satan," "Black Dwarf" and "Major Victory" for Chesler's Dynamic Comics imprint.

The first seven installments of "Iron Munro" were adapted from John W. Campbell's 1934 pulp serial, *The Mightiest Machine*, with the first two episodes scripted by Otto Binder and the remainder by Theodore Sturgeon, working from synopses provided by Campbell himself. However, Tuska's installments featured radically different storylines owing more to the *Flash Gordon* Sunday feature (illustrated by Alex Raymond from scripts by former *Argosy* editor Don Moore) than to the original Aarn Munro stories, suggesting that Campbell and Sturgeon were no longer involved with the comic book adaptations.

Like many stories from the Golden Age of Comics, Tuska's art in this issue's "Iron Munro" reprint contains numerous swipes from Raymond's *Flash Gordon* and Hal Foster's *Prince Valiant* Sunday strips. Since both story and artwork appear to have been heavily inspired by *Flash Gordon*, it's not unlikely that the scriptwriting could also have been taken over by Tuska, since he had already established himself as both artist and writer.

Moving on from the Chesler shop, Tuska briefly rejoined Will Eisner in his new Tudor City studio. "I helped him with 'Uncle Sam' and other things. Once in a while, I would help him with *The Spirit*." He next worked for Fiction House and, after World War II military service, became a major contributor to Lev Gleason's *Crime Does Not Pay*, while also drawing the "Black Terror" and "Phantom Detective" for Ned Pine's Nedor line and freelancing for Ace, Avon, Prize, St. John, Timely and Ziff-Davis.

With the retrenchment of the comic book industry following the introduction of the Comics Code, Tuska moved on to newspaper strips, writing and drawing *Scorchy Smith* from 1954-59 and succeeding Murphy Anderson on *Buck Rogers* from 1959-67. Following a decade at Marvel Comics that included a long run on *Iron Man*, George Tuska moved to DC Comics where he penciled the *World's Greatest Super-Heroes* newspaper strip from 1978-1982. —Anthony Tollin

A 1960 *Buck Rogers* daily strip illustrated by George Tuska

A 75th anniversary illustrated classic from Volume 1, Number 11 of *Shadow Comics*

illustrated by George Tuska and featuring characters created by John W. Campbell

A 75th anniversary illustrated classic from Volume 1, Number 11 of *Shadow Comics*

illustrated by George Tuska and featuring characters created by John W. Campbell

'TIS THE CIVILIZATION OF CHARON, SOON TO RISE AND DESTROY THE OUTER WORLD.
THAT'S A GOOD IDEA, BUT I DON'T THINK IT'LL WORK!
IRON IS LED UNDER A MASSIVE ARCHWAY IN THE COURTYARD LEADING TO THE QUEEN'S CASTLE...
IN THE PALACE BEFORE THE QUEEN
WHO IS THIS IMPUDENT FOOL WHO DOES NOT BOW DOWN IN THE PRESENCE OF QUEEN TUA?
I'M IRON MUNRO, FROM THE OUTER WORLD.
YOUR DOOM IS SEALED. ALL STRANGERS WHO ENTER THE CITY OF CHARON MUST DIE IN THE ROYAL TOURNAMENT.
AWAY WITH HIM, GUARDS, WHILE I DRESS FOR THE GAMES!
TOO BAD THE HANDSOME ONE MUST DIE, O GRACIOUS ONE!
QUIET, INSOLENT ONE...LEST YOU TOO SHALL FACE DEATH!
WITH THE ENTRANCE OF QUEEN TUA, THE ROYAL TOURNAMENT OF CHARON IS READY TO START...
ALL RIGHT, SURFACE MAN, THE GREEN LION AWAITS YOU!
A DOOR IS OPENED, AND IRON IS FORCED INTO THE ARENA...
WHEW! THIS BABY'S GOING TO BE PLENTY TOUGH!
AS HE TURNS, IRON SEES THE MIGHTIEST KILLER OF CHARON CHARGING TOWARD HIM.

illustrated by George Tuska and featuring characters created by John W. Campbell

A 75th anniversary illustrated classic from Volume 1, Number 11 of *Shadow Comics*